Murder at Harmony Farm

Murder at Harmony Farm

A Molly Raines Story

MERLE McCANN

TV

Twisted Vine

Murder at Harmony Farm
First Edition
Copyright © 2023 by Merle McCann

Cover Design and Interior Format: Debora Lewis
Cover photos courtesy of Shutterstock.com

ISBN: 9798850745110

Printed in the United States of America
Twisted Vine, an imprint of Pumpkin Patch Publishing

Signed copies of The Parmeter File can be ordered at
merlemccann7@gmail.com

This book is lovingly dedicated to the memory of Ruth Baker Field, wise and excellent writer, teacher, gracious mentor, and generous friend.

To the LaCroix family without whom I would know very little about the beautiful Arabian horses as shared in this story.

- 1 -

On Wednesday morning, an Aggravated Assault case with multiple head injuries was assigned to Homicide Detective Molly Raines of the Phoenix Police Department's Homicide Unit. In less than an hour, Molly parked her official car in the marked police space outside St. James' Hospital Emergency Department entrance and walked inside. Dressed for fall, she was surprised by the chilly air-conditioning that caused a shiver to ripple down her spine. People who are new to the desert assume every day is warm and sunny, but long-time residents know there is a winter, and they are accustomed to the changes in seasonal temperatures.

Security guard Ralph Sweeny, recently retired from Phoenix PD, gave Molly a smile, waved, and hustled towards her.

"Molly! How ya doin'?" He extended his hand, and she shook it. "Gosh, you look good. I suppose you're here for the Agg Assault on a Jane Doe that may go sour. Word is she has quite a battle ahead for survival."

Molly nodded. "That's probably why I was assigned the case."

He smiled. "It's my understanding she was brought in yesterday morning around 8:30. Let me make a phone call." He hurried to the information desk, spoke to the clerk then picked up the desk phone. Minutes later he rejoined Molly.

"Your Jane Doe's here all right. In Mathews Neurological Institute's ICU up on five. C'mon, I'll walk ya to the elevators."

"Thanks, Ralph, I appreciate your help."

"Nothin' you wouldn't do for me. The head of Security is a guy named Bill Eastman. He'll take you up. I'll see ya later." He turned and headed back to his post.

Ralph had hardly left her side when the elevator doors opened, and a large man stepped out and smiled at her. "I'm Bill Eastman. You must be Detective Molly Raines."

"I am."

"Ralph speaks highly of you, Detective."

"Please, call me Molly. Ralph is missed at Phoenix PD. I trained with him on patrol before he was promoted upstairs."

"How long have you been a detective?" Bill punched the up button and the elevator doors opened.

"Going on ten years."

They stepped out on five and Bill pointed to the double doors on their right as he pushed the large square button on the wall. The wide doors opened and a young man in scrubs approached them. "Oh, hello, Bill. How can I help you?"

Bill introduced Molly to the nurse and explained their mission. Bill asked, "Can you tell us which nurse has been assigned to care for your Jane Doe?"

"That would be Andrea. I'll take you to her."

The brightly lit, and large four-sided nurses' station hummed with activity.

"Did somebody call my name?" One of the five nurses stepped away from her computer and approached Molly and Bill. "I'm Andrea. I thought I heard you ask for me. Is there something I can do for you?"

Bill nodded. "Yes. This is Detective Raines. She's looking into your Jane Doe." Molly showed the nurse her badge and ID.

Andrea studied Molly's photo and smiled. "Pleased to meet you, Detective." She reached for a pad and ballpoint pen. "I'm writing a note for Dr. Lange, Jane's attending doctor. He'll want your name and badge number. Will you spell it for me?"

Before Molly answered, Bill turned to her. "I'm going to leave you in Andrea's capable hands."

"Thank you, Bill, I appreciate your help." Molly turned back to Andrea, spelled her full name, and recited her badge number. "Do you have time to answer some questions, by any chance?"

"We never have enough time around here, but I'll try."

"I'm investigating the attack on the young woman who was brought here by Fire Department ambulance yesterday, mid-morning—probably your patient, Jane Doe. She had no identification when the Phoenix officers arrived on scene. Has anyone called or come around asking for her?

"No, she's had no visitors I'm aware of. If somebody had come to see her, it would show on her chart. No one has called. And no inquiring messages have been left."

"Any chance I can talk with her?"

"I'm afraid not. She's in an induced coma due to brain swelling. Her injuries are extensive."

Molly relaxed her stance as she studied Andrea's expression. How could the woman remain so calm in the face of the tragedy and heartbreak she dealt with daily? For all the years Molly had worked as a detective and a patrol officer, she was still affected by the unimaginable cruelty she witnessed. "Can you tell me how she's doing?"

Andrea shook her head. "It's too early. Whoever attacked her did a lot of damage—broken ribs, clavicle, and her zygomatic bone is cracked. That's her cheekbone. She also suffered a serious skull fracture. I doubt you'll be able to talk with her for days, maybe weeks."

"Did the EMTs provide any information?" Molly asked.

"The usual. They brought her into Emergency and told the ER docs what they knew about her and her condition at that moment. All we can do is wait for someone to come looking for her and tell us who she is. Disappointing, I know, but it's all we can do. She was dressed in business attire. It suggests she's probably a professional. Somebody is bound to miss her soon and start asking questions."

Molly gave a small shake of her head. "It's not much to go on, but I'll work on it. I'll have a Crime Scene Tech come by and fingerprint her. If she's in the system we'll find out who she is. I alerted our Missing Persons Bureau, requesting they let me know if someone files a report looking for a woman fitting the description patrol gave me. If I discover who she is, I'll let you know immediately."

Andrea's face softened, looking relieved. "That's great. Thank you. We're hoping a family member will show up soon. She wasn't wearing any kind of medical alert, so have to work with extreme caution. Possible medical allergies are always a concern. It slows everything down."

Molly handed her a business card. "I understand. Please let your team know I was here. I'll be checking back frequently. Is there somewhere I should sign in? I don't want to create a problem for the staff.

"Just ask for me when a staff member greets you at the doors."

"If a family member or any visitor shows up, please call me, day or night."

"Of course." Andrea glanced at Molly's sidearm and turned away. "Be safe out there."

Molly gave her a wave. "Thanks."

As Molly stepped into the elevator, Andrea's last words revolved in her thoughts. Was anybody truly safe these days when the world seems to have gone so fricken' crazy?

- 2 -

The following morning, Molly arrived at the downtown Phoenix Police headquarters earlier than usual. Jane Doe continued to weigh on her mind. While sorting through messages, her desk phone rang. Although she knew it was premature, Molly hoped it would pertain to the unidentified female victim and be good news. She picked up before the second ring.

"Detective Raines, this is Clara in Missing Persons. We took a call last night from a Lois Thompson, who is searching for her friend, Jillian Bronson. Nickname, Jill.

"The description she gave of Miss Bronson was similar to the injured woman's description on Patrol's report. Bronson married a man named Randy Winslow but kept her maiden name. Grab a pen and I'll give you Lois Thompson's phone number."

Molly jotted the number on a post-it. "Anything else?"

"Yep. Thompson said her friend, Jill didn't show up for their weekly get-together. Apparently, they enjoy a glass of wine together after work every Wednesday, something they've been doing for about eight months. *Like clockwork* was the term she used. She said Jill wouldn't miss it without calling—and she didn't call this time. Thompson rang Jill's phone several times from the neighborhood bar and that evening from home. Also first thing in the morning. Never did get an answer. She tried to reach Jill at her place of employment but was told she hadn't arrived.

"Ms. Thompson was adamant it wasn't like Jill not to show up. She said Jill was too responsible. Thompson waited until the end of the workday, checked with Jill's employer once more then called us after she put her kids to bed. I could tell the woman was on the verge of tears. Terribly worried."

"I see." Molly contemplated everything Clara told her. "Did Lois Thompson say who Jill's employer was?"

"Not by name. Said Jill is a CPA and works for a small firm. She couldn't recall the employer's name. However, one thing I can tell you, it was a reliable call. I get a lot of these calls and I've been on the job a long time. I believe I can tell when the caller is trustworthy. Lois Thompson sounded equally as responsible as the missing friend she described. I'll be very surprised if her call is a crank."

"Thanks, Clara. At least I have a name and phone number—a place to start." Molly hung up and returned to her messages. One in particular drew her attention. The caller's name was Virginia Dexter and the note read, *I just learned of the attack in the Granite Hills Park and there is something I thought you should know. There's a man who sits in his truck every morning watching people walk into the park.*

Molly returned the call, hoping the woman could provide some additional information. Instead, she got her voice mail. Molly left a message for Virginia to call back as soon as possible.

After thirty minutes of waiting, Molly's impatience brought her to her feet. She paced the aisle to the last cubicle, turned and strode back to her desk. She read the woman's name and number again and considered redialing on the chance she'd pick up. Instead, she walked over to her partner's workstation.

Kelly McMahon was a seasoned detective, open minded, smart, ethical, and determined to always find the guilty party. He was a raven-haired Irish *superhero* with a big heart, blue eyes to die for—a softy who couldn't say *no*. He had replaced Detective Lawrence Hudson, as her partner.

Having worked together for five years, Molly and Kelly understood each other like siblings. She never doubted his judgment, skills or amazing sixth sense. He'd taken her under his wing when Molly was assigned to homicide, and they'd worked together ever since.

As she approached his larger-than-average cube, Kelly's eyes greeted her as though he'd expected her. "Hey Molly, what's up? You look like Mercury is retrograding." She chuckled at his astrology reference. He was basically a disbeliever of the art form, but a few cases back, she'd come close to convincing him to keep an open mind.

"Just checking on you." She raised her hand with the phone message pinched between her finger and thumb and gave it a rattle. "Isn't this the week you go on vacation?"

"Yep, leave tomorrow. My ole buddy in Vail, Colorado tells me they're getting good snow. They no longer need help with the man-made stuff. My brother and I are going to ski every day, chase women, drink like fish, and act like teenagers." He laughed. "Now, tell me about your case."

Molly shook her head in mock disgust then laughed. "It's good to be you." She rolled her eyes. "Doin' your Peter Pan thing, right?" He laughed.

She cleared her throat. "I was assigned this case yesterday—a woman attacked in Granite Hills Park—the park just south of the university. I got a call from Missing Persons. They may have come up with the victim's name. I also received a call from a very interesting witness. Not a witness exactly, more like a tipster. You know, someone with info regarding a possible witness. I thought—"

Molly's cell phone rang. Caller ID indicated it was Virginia Dexter. Molly raised her index finger to pause Kelly and hurried back to her desk. "This is Detective Molly Raines. Can I help you?"

"Detective, my name is Virginia Dexter and I'm calling about the woman attacked in Granite Hills Park. I didn't see it happen, but I noticed there was a guy watching the people walking in and out of the park from his truck. He was parked at the end of the block, a distance away from Granite Hills's south entrance.

"I usually cut through the park to go to work. I'm a researcher at the University. He's there every day. Sometimes when I come out of the park on the north side, he's parked at the end of that street. Like he's looking for someone special... or spying on somebody. It creeps me out. Some days when I leave work, I see him there at that time, too. Thought you should at least know about him."

"You were right to call. Thank you, Virginia. Can you tell me the type of truck he drives?"

"I think it's a newish Ford F-150—kind of a maroon-red color with fancy chrome wheels. Really a nice-looking truck."

"Did you notice his license plate?"

"I'm sorry I didn't. I'm kind of afraid to get too close. I walk from the opposite direction, and he's always parked at the far end of the block. I've never seen the plate on the back bumper, but I can try to get it for you if you'd like."

"No, no. That won't be necessary. We wouldn't want you to do anything that might draw his attention to you. Leave that to me. Could you identify him if you saw him in person, or in photographs with other men?"

"No, I've never seen his face."

"That's okay. Letting me know about him has been a great help."

"When I learned about that lady who was attacked, it really scared me. I hope you catch the guy right away. What he did is horrible. How is the woman doing?"

"Because it's an ongoing investigation I can't share much with you until we make an arrest. I can tell you she is still in the hospital."

- 3 -

Early Friday morning, Molly walked from a nearby parking lot to the south entry into Granite Hills Park located on West Campbell Avenue. She took a few steps into the park and decided to wait on the path leading to and around the swimming pool complex. She hoped to find someone cutting through the park who saw what happened on Tuesday.

From where she stood, the intersections of Campbell and North 31st to the east and North 35th to the west were clearly visible. There was no truck parked at either corner, but if a maroon- red, Ford F-150 pickup *was* parked at one of the locations, she would be able to see it.

Also, the spot where she stood allowed her the possibility of encountering an employee who worked at the pool's service building located east of the walkway approximately fifty feet from the south entrance. According to the patrol officers, the victim had been ambushed behind the building on the east side, not far from the large, sprawling natural area.

An older woman ambled Molly's way. Molly greeted her with a small smile, introduced herself then showed her ID. "I'm investigating the attack on a woman near the pool building three mornings ago. She was cutting through the park on her way to work. It was about this same time. Can you tell me if you saw anything unusual when you walked through the park last Tuesday?"

"I'm sorry. I don't come here often. Today I have a dentist appointment near Camelback and thirty-fifth. Parking my car next to the dentist's building is always impossible at this time in the morning, so I parked in that lot over there on thirty-first." She turned and pointed. "Besides, I can use the walk."

Molly's eyes followed the woman's hand. Now, a few feet from the corner, the sun glinted off the top of a shiny maroon-red, Ford F-150. Molly thanked the woman for her time. She turned and headed for the corner and the man she hoped would be there.

She didn't hurry. Dressed in civvies, she blended in with the other pedestrians who were starting their day. She didn't want to attract the truck driver's attention... before she made her way around the front of the truck and tapped on his window.

The young man's forehead pinched in a frown as he rolled down the window. "Can I help you?"

Molly smiled easily. "I hope so." She introduced herself and showed her ID. "I'm investigating an incident that occurred in the park a few days ago. People tell me they often see you here. May I see your license and registration for the truck please?"

He stared at her as if he were momentarily confused then reached for his wallet. He handed over his license and leaned across the seat to the glove compartment. The hem of his shirt rose above his belt. No sign of a weapon. He flipped open the wide, rectangular door and reached inside. "What kind of an incident? In the park?" He straightened up and handed her his documentation. "Was someone hurt?"

Molly studied his license and compared the picture to the handsome driver of the truck. "I see by your license and registration your name is Randy Winslow."

"Yes, ma'am, that's right." He cocked his head. "Have I done something wrong?"

Molly ignored his question. "Do you wait here every morning like this?"

"Anything wrong with that?"

Her voice became stern. "Probably not. Who are you waiting for?"

His frown deepened. He gnawed at the corner of his lip. "I suspect that's none of your business."

She raised her chin. "It became my business when a young woman was attacked and beaten badly Tuesday morning not far from here. Do you know anything about that?"

Randy's face lost its color. "No, ma'am. Can you tell me her name?"

"No, I can't. I'm hoping you can tell me—since you sit here every morning. I figure you're following somebody. Who might that be?"

He gripped the steering wheel so firmly his knuckles turned white. "I watch my ex-wife walk to work. I want to know she arrives safely. I worry about her. This neighborhood doesn't have the best reputation. She refuses to pick up the phone when she sees my number, but once, when she finally did, she insisted she was okay, said it wasn't a long walk, and nobody bothers her."

"Does she know you're keeping an eye on her?"

"No. If she did, she'd be all over my ass."

"But you didn't agree when she said no one would bother her?"

"Hell, no." He turned away and stared out the passenger's side window toward the park. He appeared agitated when he turned back to Molly. "Can you tell me the name of the woman who was attacked?"

Molly studied him for a moment. "Why don't you tell me your wife's name and I'll tell you if you have anything to worry about."

He hesitated. "Her name's Jill Bronson. She kept her maiden name when we got married."

"How long since you last spoke with her?"

"That call I mentioned was about five weeks ago."

"When did you last see her?"

"Tuesday morning when she walked into the park. I never saw her come out and cross the street to go into the campus. I thought maybe I just missed her, until I didn't see her at all the next morning. I wish I could convince her not to cut through the park."

"You're sure Tuesday was the last time you saw her?"

"Hell yes, I'm sure. I haven't seen her since then and I'm effin' worried—I can't think what to do about it." His hand shook when he raised it and rubbed it along his jaw. "She would never ditch work. She's never been irresponsible... ever." Fear showed in his eyes when he glanced at Molly. He dropped his voice. "Believe me, I know irresponsibility. That would be my middle name." He lowered his voice. "It's why I'm now her *ex*."

Molly glanced down at his license in her hand. "Wait here." She jogged to the nearby parking lot where she'd parked her detective's car, slid into the driver's seat, and ran a background check on the computer for Randy Winslow and his license number. He had no criminal record, no driving violations, not even a parking citation. More than that, something about him, his body language, his manner of speaking, and his facial expressions all rang true in Molly's estimation.

She headed back to Winslow's truck, pleased he had waited for her to return. Pleased but not surprised. He definitely didn't seem to be the type to run off, leaving his license and registration in her hands. She assumed he'd calmed down when he gave her a crooked smile as she again walked around the front of his idling truck. He dropped his side window when she stepped close, and cold air from inside washed over her warm face.

Molly handed him his documents. She noted the anxious look on his face and softly said, "I'm sorry, Mr. Winslow." His faced turned ghostly pale. "It does appear it could be your ex-wife who was attacked."

Winslow's eyes watered. He placed folded arms on top of the steering wheel and rested his forehead upon them. "Goddamnit." Slowly, he raised his face and glared at Molly. "I was afraid something would happen to her." He looked away. "Why wouldn't she listen to me? Why wouldn't she believe me about this neighborhood? And this park?" He rubbed his face with both palms. "She was always too trusting." He gazed at Molly. "How bad is it? Is she alive? Please, tell me. I have to know she'll be okay. Please."

Molly draped a hand over the window ledge. "To my knowledge she's still alive, but I have no information regarding her current condition." She studied him for a moment as she reviewed what he had said. He'd made a good impression on her. At this point in time, she didn't see him as a suspect. She perceived him as someone who might be able to identify the victim if the hospital would allow him access to her.

"Would you be willing to go with me to the hospital to identify the woman? If, in fact, she is your ex-wife?"

"Of course. I'll do whatever you want to help catch the sonofabitch who did this."

He glanced at his watch. "I can go now. I'll call my boss—let him know I'll be late." He ran a shaky hand through his light brown hair.

She shook her head. "How about tomorrow morning? Could you meet me at St. James' Emergency Room entrance at nine?" Molly handed him her card. "

"Saturday? No problem."

"Will you bring me a picture of your wife—and a copy of your marriage license?"

"Of course. Do you think you can catch the rotten bastard who hurt her?"

"I'm gonna try. I'll use all resources at my disposal. Give me your phone number. I may want to contact you. Otherwise, meet me in the morning." She tapped the number he dictated into her phone.

Molly evaluated her impression of Winslow as she headed to her car, the words he chose when he spoke of his wife, his body language. What had happened to his marriage? Did he still live at the address displayed on his driver's license. She wondered if he'd show up at the hospital. She bet he would. He seemed like a good guy, but who knows? It's easy to be fooled by first impressions.

- 4 -

Molly parked her car in one of the designated police spots and hurried to join Randy Winslow, waiting near the ER doors. His striped dress shirt appeared freshly ironed, as did his chino slacks, judging by their sharp creases. He looked relieved to see Molly, although she expected him to be apprehensive about seeing his ex-wife, if in fact Jane Doe was Jill Bronson.

Randy gave her a worried smile. "Hey, Detective, how ya doing?" He extended his hand. "Here's the photo you asked me to bring. I have our marriage license, too."

"Thanks." Molly reached for the picture and studied the dog-eared photo. Jill Bronson's face was turned toward the camera, smiling at someone in the distance. She wore a pair of cutoff jeans and a pink hoody. Her blonde hair was pulled into a ponytail and fed through the back of a red Diamondback's cap. Her dark eyes radiated from a stunningly beautiful face, suggesting an image of someone in love. Molly glanced up at Randy. "She's gorgeous." That was all Molly said, although she wondered how Randy would react when he saw the damage to that lovely face.

They walked side-by-side entering the waiting area. Molly again spotted retired Detective Ralph Sweeny across the room and waved to him. He waved back and hustled over to greet them. "Hi, Molly. Nice to see you again. Can I be of help?"

She introduced him to Randy, indicating Randy had come to possibly identify the Jane Doe recently admitted. "Do we need an escort to go up to ICU?"

"I'll give a call to check." Sweeny strode to the information desk and helped himself to the inhouse phone. He returned, pointing to the bank of elevators. "Go on up to five. I spoke with Head of Security, and he said he'd notify them you're on your way."

The elevator doors opened, and a different male nurse, standing at the entrance to ICU, greeted Molly and Randy. "You must be Detective Raines. I was alerted by security to expect you. I understand you may be able to identify our Jane Doe."

"Call me Molly. This is Randy Winslow. Is Andrea on duty today?"

"I'm sorry. She's not. She mentioned yesterday you might be coming by. Jane Doe's doctor is Dr. Lange. He's due here in about forty-five minutes. He's the only one who can give you permission to go into her room. I can't. You're welcome to wait, perhaps get a cup of coffee. We have a good cafeteria downstairs."

Molly turned to Randy. "Let's do that."

The nurse gave them a wave and turned for the wide double doors. "I'll watch for you to return. Press that large button and I'll meet you here."

They carried their cups to a table, distant from the other customers. Sitting across from Randy, Molly stirred two cream packets into her coffee. "Did you see Jill go into the park the morning of the attack?"

"Yes." Randy's face took on a wistful expression. "She looked pretty. I'd never seen the dress she wore. My sister would call it an elegant summer print. She wore new, white high heel sandals, the kind with straps. Her purse was white also. Jill always said purses must match your shoes." He squirmed slightly as he explained. She wore a pale green blazer over her dress.

Molly smiled, curious about his comments. "How did you know her shoes and bag were new?"

"I'd never seen either of them... before I left. Same with her dress." He hunched in an embarrassed shrug. "I know, I said that before." He gestured with his hand. "She must be doing well in her new job. The dress and blazer looked expensive." He slouched against the back of his chair and crossed his arms. "I've been watching out for her for months. Hard not to know her wardrobe."

"You sound like it's unusual... her expensive clothes."

"Yep. She's had to live close to the bone the last couple years... since we split."

"How long has it been?"

"One year, six months and twenty-seven days."

Molly stared at him. What could have been so bad he'd walk out on Jill when his devotion was this obvious? Unless he was the world's greatest actor?

"Was Jill carrying anything when you saw her Tuesday morning?"

"Yes, she carries a nice briefcase, and an expensive purse of course."

"Anything else?"

"No. That's Jill, just the basics."

"How old were you when you and Jill married?"

"I had turned thirty; she was twenty-six."

"Did you fight a lot?"

"Nope. We hardly ever disagreed. When I screwed up, she'd tell me so... without yelling. It never went anywhere because she was usually right. I was okay with that... admitting I was wrong."

"Earlier you said her finances changed dramatically. Like how?"

"When I walked out, I was so sure I was never comin' back, I signed my interest in the house over to her and sent her support checks for a few months. Figured she'd need help for a while. But Jill returned them all. After the fifth one came back, I quit sending them. She sold the house and her car to pay expenses, rented a small apartment and enrolled at Grand Canyon University. Jill had always wanted to finish her degree; and I'll be damned, she did it in a single year. She worked part time waitressing in a coffee shop in the neighborhood. I assumed her income wasn't enough to be buying new clothes."

Randy paused as a nurse passed their table. "A few months before she got her accounting degree, one of her girlfriends told me she'd already been hired by a firm in Phoenix. Near the end of last year, I heard she passed the CPA exam—all four parts." He rubbed his hand along his whiskered jaw then glanced away. "Jill was always smart." He paused, nodding as if reassuring himself. "She's gonna be just fine if she heals up okay." He lowered his head, staring into his coffee mug.

Molly wondered once again why his marriage failed. The guy looked miserable. He glanced up at Molly with a bewildered look. "She has definitely moved on from me." He chuckled softly. "Ya know? I haven't the slightest idea what I'll be doin' tomorrow or next year. Whereas Jill—even though she's had to scrape by—has picked up her CPA and scored a good payin' job." He gestured with both hands. "It's like she's managed to hike her way across the McDowell Mountains, and I'm still standin' on Scottsdale Road starin' up at Pinnacle

Peak, not known' which way to go. I really am as foolish as she told me I was."

"When was your divorce finalized?"

"It's not. Got a couple more weeks to go. I kept hopin' something would happen to delay it and she'd change her mind, but I never dreamed it would be anything as terrible as this." He wiped his eyes.

Molly stared at him, still pondering his use of the word *foolish*. "I don't get it. Why did you leave her?"

"Cause I'm a stupid ass. After seven years of marriage, I thought I wanted my freedom. Dumbest thing I ever did. Turns out, *freedom's* just another word for loneliness."

The sentiment wasn't lost on Molly. She knew firsthand loneliness was an ugly companion. "Did you check up on Jill while she was going to school?"

"Sure did. After I'd been gone about seven months, I regretted walking out and wanted her back in the worst way. I knew where she lived so I drove by early one morning as she left for the campus. I saw her walk into the park. I drove around to the other side and saw her cross the street to the university. I've been there every day since. I didn't know she was taking classes. I thought she was working there until a friend told me what she was up to. She saw me one time sitting in my old black truck and walked right up to my door, like you did, and got in my face about spying on her. Said she'd report me as a stalker if I didn't quit."

"Did you? Quit?"

"No way. I smelled her cologne, and all our good times rushed through my mind. I wanted her back even more. Couldn't stop worrying some asshole would harm her. I couldn't stop missing her... loving her. So I went in hock for a new truck, one she wouldn't recognize and parked farther away. Every day I hoped I'd get to talk to her, hoped maybe she missed me." He tilted his head. "But I could tell by her body language—to her I'm yesterday's bad news."

"What kind of body language?"

Randy glanced at the ceiling as if visualizing. "She walked with confidence, like she had a purpose. I figured her mind was on her new career... or maybe a boyfriend, for all I knew. She sure as hell wasn't thinkin' about me."

"Why do you say that?"

He gave a small harrumph. "After I left, I acted like a jerk. Like I was celebrating my new awesome freedom. Ran around with the guys, boozin', pickin' up girls, partyin'. Nearly lost my job. Either she saw me out with the boys or else her friends told her they'd seen me *enjoyin' my life*. Pretty sure they weren't complimentary in the tellin'.

"We bumped into each other once in the grocery store and I tried to talk to her, but she blew me off like the creep I'd turned into."

"Is coming here a good idea? Aren't you afraid you'll upset her?"

He nodded. "Absolutely." He leaned closer to Molly. "But I have to try. She has nobody to turn to—no family in Arizona—except for a no-good brother she refuses to see. I'm all she's got—at least I used to be. Somebody has to help her through this. I hope she'll let me be that person. I'll try hard to calm the water for starters. She once told me hospital patients always need an advocate. Sounds like a good job for me. If she tells me to go away more than once or twice, I guess I'll have to."

He sucked his lip between his teeth. "Do you mind if we don't say I'm her ex-husband? I'm afraid they might not let me in... and the divorce isn't final."

"Let's see how it goes." Molly checked her watch. "Looks like we should head back upstairs."

A small, slight, gray-haired man in a physician's coat walked into ICU's waiting room from a door marked *No Admittance*. He glanced first at Randy who stood a few feet from Molly then studied her. "Are y'all the folks wanting to see our Jane Doe?"

Randy nodded as Molly answered. "Yes," she read his nametag, "Dr. Lange. I'm Phoenix Police Homicide Detective Molly Raines and this is Randy Winslow. We believe there is a good chance he can identify her. He and Jill Bronson married seven years ago, and he thinks your Jane Doe is possibly his Jill. She kept her last name when they married."

Dr. Lange looked Randy over as if Lange were the detective. He faced Molly. "Are y'all vouching for him, Detective?"

"I am." She smiled at the doctor. "Are you from Texas by any chance? Your drawl reminds me of my friend from Dallas."

"That right?" He chuckled. "Grew up in Houston. I'm a proud Baylor Medical School grad."

He gave Randy a quick nod. "Well, how about takin' a look at our patient through the window. We can start there."

"That'd be great," Molly said. "Thank you, doctor."

"Keep in mind, young man, she's been hurt badly, and it'll take a few weeks for the swelling to go down. We have her in an induced coma with IV's, and the tubes and such. It might be shocking to you at first." Lange turned for the door and waved them to follow.

The expansive intensive care unit's rooms had wooden blinds covering the wide windows set in the upper half of their walls along the hallway. It looked like every room was occupied. Dr. Lange led them to a room in the corner of the unit. Randy stepped close.

Dr. Lange's patient was difficult to see because of multiple bandages, the equipment surrounding her bed, and the various lines attached to her body. The head of the bed was elevated, and she was cradled in pillows. She looked as though she were sleeping.

"Is that your wife, Mr. Winslow?" Dr. Lange asked.

Randy wiped the moisture from his eyes. "Yes, Sir. Her bed is close enough to this window for me to make an identification. I have no doubts. I recognize the color of her hair—that little pink streak she put in it a while back. The scar across her eyebrow she got falling off a swing. I see the small dark spot on the back of her hand. She told me she was born with it."

"Yes," Dr. Lange said. "A small collection of melanin."

Randy nodded. "She has a larger one on her right shoulder blade."

Lange smiled. "Right." He placed his hand on Randy's shoulder. "I hope you'll spend all the time you can with her. We get the Dallas Cowboy's games on our TV's, so you can watch their games on Sundays." He grinned then turned serious. "When we bring her out of the coma, it would be helpful to have y'all here. She may need a little assistance waking, and there may be some memory loss due to the blow to her head. You could make a difference."

Randy smiled at Molly then faced Dr. Lange, thrusting out his hand. Lange tentatively shook his hand and Randy thanked him. "I'll come as often as possible, at least once a day. Can I see her now?"

"All in good time. Come with me and I'll get ya set up with our official visitor's identification. Then, if y'all don't mind we'd appreciate your filling out some paperwork. To treat your wife medically, we need to know everything you can tell us."

"No problem, Doc. I'll hang around now; happy to do whatever I can to help."

Dr. Lange turned to Molly. "Next time *you* come, Detective Raines, ask for me, and if I'm not here, ask for Andrea. She'll take ya back to Ms. Bronson's room."

Molly thanked him then turned to Randy, "When you're done here will you please stop by the Maryvale precinct? I'd like you to answer a few questions for me. Do you know where it is?"

He nodded. "No prob. I'll head over as soon as I'm done with the paperwork."

Molly thanked him and headed for the elevators. She found it difficult to get the sight of Jill out of her head. The woman was attached to so many machines; it was hard to believe Jill Bronson would truly wake up.

- 5 -

Warm air washed over Molly when she walked out of the hospital into the late September sunshine. She checked her watch and decided to stop by Granite Hills Park before driving to the precinct. She felt an urge to examine the crime scene once more.

Minutes later she walked around to the backside of the pool building. A fresh coating of colorful fallen leaves scattered the concrete walkway along the back of the building. Scant traces of blood spatter could be seen on the concrete and the structure's block wall if a person knew what to look for. Most of it had worn off in the days following the attack.

The ground in the natural area looked as though caretakers blew the leaves from the concrete into the wooded gardens behind a weathered park bench nestled into the shrubbery at the edge of the walkway. The bench's legs were buried halfway up in fresh and moldering leaves. Molly sat down, placing her evidence bag beside her. She scanned the area to her left and right. Because of the rain and the leaves she doubted the crime scene techs had found any shoe prints.

Patrol reported two men followed the teenage attacker as he ran from the park, but they hadn't appeared to be involved. Were they seated on the bench when Jill Bronson was attacked? Did the men have anything to do with the attack? Other than the bystanders, who shared what they saw with the patrolmen, nobody had come forward to report the attack. Molly wasn't surprised. People typically took the main path rather than circle behind the building.

She stood and as she picked up her satchel, she caught sight of something shiny lying amongst the leaves beneath an oleander. She bent at the waist as she approached for a closer look. She removed latex gloves from her bag and slipped them on. After taking a picture of what might turn out to be evidence, she knelt and cleared away the leaves, exposing a man's brown leather glove. Three half-inch silvery grommets trimmed its wristband. Molly slipped the drenched glove into the plastic sack she took from her bag.

After stowing the evidence, she hastily brushed the disturbed leaves back under the oleander, accidentally exposing a partially disintegrated cigarette butt. She did a double take and almost laughed at her crazy, good luck then wondered who would be so foolish as to throw away the butt if they had something to do with the attack. She looked closely at the cigarette's remains. It hadn't been crushed when it was extinguished, and the burning end appeared to have been tamped out. A tiny, blurred manufacture's logo was printed on the paper, but it meant nothing to her. The lettering beneath the logo appeared to be Spanish. Perhaps the lab could identify it. Securing it as evidence was probably a waste of time. It wasn't much of a clue, if it was one, but better than none. She photographed it, carefully scooped it into a small glycine envelope and stowed it in her bag. As she headed for her car, she thought of the questions she intended to ask Randy Winslow, assuming he showed up at the precinct.

- 6 -

Just before noon, Molly led Randy into an interview room. She invited him to sit at the side of the table, gesturing to the chair without wheels. Molly rolled her chair around to the end of the table and sat down. She turned on her recorder and placed it on the chipped laminate tabletop then opened her portfolio and ran her hand down the empty page.

Molly quoted the date and time along with their names then began. "I'd like to know more about Jill's brother. Did you know him well?"

"I only knew Jerrod because he was Jill's brother. We weren't buddies. Mostly saw him when he'd have a holiday meal with us. We had the same birthday—there was that."

"That's quite a coincidence. Jill marries a guy born on the same day as her brother. Which day? Same year?"

"October eleventh. I'm two years older. Jill saw the humor in it. A couple of times she baked us each a cake with candles. She'd always try to get us to wear party hats, but I wouldn't go along. Now I wish I had."

"Earlier you said Jill refused to see him. Now it sounds like Jill got along with him well enough."

"Only to a point. She tried to have a relationship with him, but eventually gave up. Jerrod couldn't stay out of trouble. Started when he was a kid. By the time he was in his mid-twenties, he'd racked up a dozen arrests for various crimes. That's when Jill gave up on him. Look up his record; you'll see."

"Did he serve time?"

"Juvy a few times then County jail and eventually he did two years in a lockup, near Flagstaff, I think. When he came back to Phoenix, he hit Jill up for money. She gave him all she had—a hundred bucks—and told him not to come around anymore."

"How does he earn a living?"

"He learned to shoe horses while in prison. I understand he's good at it; he works steady. He has five of the large fancy horse ranches around here as clients. Does most of his work for the three biggies."

"Do you know the ranches' names and locations?"

"There's a fancy ranch north of Phoenix. Harmony Farm they call it."

Molly smiled slightly as she jotted the name. Having grown up on her grandparents' Arabian horse farm, Molly was acquainted with the Harmony ranch and Mr. and Mrs. Harmon, the owners. "You mentioned two others."

"I heard Jerrod talk about the Lindsey Quarter Horse Ranch, down the road from Harmony. The other one was Blue Agave Equestrian Center. I have no idea where that is."

"It's okay. I can look it up." She laid her pen down and stared at Randy. "How do you know so much about Jerrod? You said Jill sent him packing after he served two years in jail where he learned to be a farrier."

"Jerrod has a motorcycle pal who hangs out at Doyle's, a biker bar where I used to go. Me and his buddy got to talking one night and he filled me in on Jerrod." He turned up his palms. "Jerrod and I got along okay, but I agreed with Jill. We couldn't trust the guy. One night after he'd left our place, their mother's engagement ring came up missing. Mrs. Bronson had died the year before and willed the ring to Jill. She asked Jerrod about the ring, and he admitted he took it and pawned it. Said he needed quick cash. Showed no remorse at all. That's when I wrote him off."

"Did Jill ever get the ring back?"

"Yeah, I found out where he pawned it and bought it back for her." He smiled. "She was really happy 'til she found out I occasionally hung out at a biker bar."

"What else can you tell me?"

"That's about it." He paused. "He drives a dark green Chevy truck and pulls a small trailer with his tools and equipment. According to his friend, Jerrod's unreliable about paying his rent so he moves a lot. Don't know where he's livin' now."

"Any women in his life?"

"No keepers. Sometimes goes home with biker chicks if he can pick one up, according to his friend."

"Tell me about your job. Do you have to wear protective gear?"

"Just the usual. I'm a house framer, so I wear goggles and gloves. It's usually too hot to wear the stuff you see at Home Depot. Even the goggles bug me after a while."

"What about the gloves?"

"Yeah, but I'm always puttin' 'em on and pullin' 'em off. Too damned hot."

"Do you smoke?"

He chuckled. "Depends on what you mean by smoke. Cigarettes? Never. I tried some weed but didn't dig the thrill. I don't like brain fog. Mostly, I prefer drinkin' Irish stout. That's about it."

"Thank you, Randy, you've been a big help." Molly rolled her chair back and stood. "If I come up with anything I'll let you know." She moved her chair out of the way and opened the door.

Randy skittered his chair back from the table and sauntered out of the room. Molly walked beside him down the short hallway. "Perhaps I'll see you at the hospital," she said. "I plan to drop by whenever I can. If Jill wakes up while you're there, will you give me a call?" She handed him her business card. "Day or night."

"Absolutely. I plan to visit before and after work. Cross your fingers she won't kick me out the first minute she sees me."

"Sure." Molly paused and watched him amble away, hoping crossed fingers would be enough.

- 7 -

After Molly's meeting with Randy Winslow, she prepared lunch at her house for Lawrence Hudson and Tony, his eight-year-old son. Lar had been her first boss, and partner when she moved up to Homicide. When he was bumped up to Assistant Chief, Kelly McMahon was assigned as her partner and supervisor. Lar's wife had passed away a year before his promotion, leaving him to raise Tony who had just begun kindergarten. Three years later, Lar asked Molly out to dinner. They'd been seeing each other steadily ever since.

When they finished eating, Molly invited Lar and Tony to ride over to Harmony Farm with her. "While I speak with Mr. Harmon, you and Tony can stroll the farm and look at the horses. This time of year, there should be foals in the pastures. Tony would love that, don't you think?"

"I'm sure he would, Babe, but I promised I'd bring Tony to my mom's house for an overnight. You go ahead. I'll catch up at dinner. My place? Regular time? Italian food?"

"Good, good, good." Molly ruffled Tony's hair, telling him *bye-bye* then kissed Lar. They walked hand and hand to their cars parked on her driveway. Tony hopped into the passenger seat as Lar slid behind the steering wheel. Tony gave her one last wave.

Molly waited for Lar to pull out then slipped into her car, turned on the radio, and backed into the street. Cardi B with Maroon 5 was singing "Girls Like You." Molly switched to a country-western station and caught Blake Shelton singing his newest release.

Harmony Farm, owned by a retired industrialist, was located south of the old cowboy town of Cave Creek. The farm's lead stallion, Sir Rothman, was a Canadian and US National champion, world famous for producing champion Arabian horses. Before the Harmons updated their breeding program from natural service to artificial insemination, the stallion's stud fee was set at twenty-five thousand dollars. Even at that price, so many mares were sent for breeding to Rothman, the stallion sometimes serviced two mares in a single day. Molly had no idea what a vial of live spermatozoa cost today.

All year long, visitors arrived unannounced at Harmony to see the collection of beautiful mares and stallions, especially the horses on the sales list and of course, the lead stallion. Molly had telephoned George Harmon after leaving the hospital to set up an appointment.

After a short drive, Molly turned off Black Mountain Road and followed the white rail fence that surrounded emerald pastures accommodating two dozen or more mares, some with foals. She pulled in next to the upgraded original barn and parked her car under a giant mesquite. The building still served as the stallion barn and farm manager's office. Mr. Harmon was seated in one of the director chairs on the office's wide front porch. He stood when he saw her get out of her car. He wore a quilted vest over a brown plaid dress shirt, chinos, and shiny brown loafers. Molly couldn't recall ever seeing him in a pair of jeans, let alone cowboy boots.

He raised his hand in a friendly wave, although his face appeared solemn. "Hello, my dear. So nice to see you again, Molly."

"Thanks, Mr. Harmon. I appreciate your seeing me on short notice."

He shook his head in a friendly way. "When will you start calling me George?" He chuckled. "You know how it is around here. I rarely can leave the ranch. You wanted to inquire about our farrier? Is that right?" His voice dropped.

"Jerrod Bronson. Yes, I'm investigating a case involving his sister who recently suffered a serious injury. I'm trying to locate him to inform him of what has happened."

Mr. Harmon's brow rose. "Oh, dear God. I'm very sorry, Molly." He sighed. "Jerrod was found dead yesterday."

Molly's hand rose to her mouth. "Where? Do you know what happened?"

"Here on the farm. He was found near our Artificial Insemination building. I don't know what he was doing there. He doesn't shoe any of the mares in for breeding, and we don't stall any horses there except mares in for breeding. He has nothing to do with our insemination program. Our farm veterinarian, Dr. Spelling found his dead body and called 911."

"Who did police send to investigate the death?"

"Detectives Larry Pilson and Arnie Schmidt. Nice fellas. Do you know them?"

"Yes, we work in the same Bureau. I'll get in touch with them to let them know about Jerrod's sister." She flashed a hand at a fly buzzing her head. "Could you show me where the body was found?"

"Of course. Let's take the golf cart."

Molly smiled as Mr. Harmon helped her into the cart. The sweet, older gentlemen always treated her like a delicate flower, having no knowledge of the men she often came face to face with while on the job. Armed killers and dead bodies had become her stock in trade.

They drove through one of three large metal barns placed side by side behind the stallion barn. Thirty feet beyond them a second row of three identical barns had been erected. All were painted white with forest green trim.

Inside the pristine stable, the air was pungent with the scent of hay, grain, liniment, and fresh manure, rekindling Molly's youthful memories of the years with her grandparents on their ranch outside Kingman, Arizona. That was life as Molly wished it to be—calm and serene. She glanced at her clean hands, the same hands that used to be callused and dirty. Given her line of work, would she ever know serenity like that again?

- 8 -

It was nearly seven o'clock when Molly arrived at Lar's apartment a few blocks north of the Desert Ridge shopping mall. She carried a bottle of his preferred red wine she'd picked up at her favorite wine boutique in Carefree, an upscale, small town north of Scottsdale. Molly tapped twice on Lar's navy-blue door and walked into the small, well-appointed living room. The aroma of Lar's fragrant red sauce floated on the air like a soft Tuscan breeze.

"Is that you, Molly?" he called from the kitchen, "or a bad guy I'll have to subdue before dinner?"

"It's me, but I may need subduing once we open the wine."

The knob on the stove clicked and the light thump of Lar's long-handled spoon smacking against the rim of a pot suggested he would soon appear from the kitchen. Molly wasn't disappointed. He approached her while untying his striped apron, wrapped his arms around her and seriously kissed her hello. She melted against him and returned his kiss. When the moment ended, she asked, "Can we do that for the next twenty minutes or more?"

He grinned. "I like the sound of more. Opening the wine will have to wait." He raised his head, studied her face, and threw his apron onto the sofa. Smiling, he placed his arm across her back and guided her to his bedroom.

On Monday morning, Molly arrived at Phoenix Police Headquarters early enough to catch Detectives Larry Pilson and Arnie Schmidt the minute they arrived. The need to discover more about Jill and her deceased brother, Jerrod, lay heavily on her mind. Standing next to her desk, she spotted the men striding toward the break room. She hurried to catch them as they entered. Their quick stride suggested they were busy, but their otherwise calm demeanor indicated they were not overworked. She crossed her fingers, hoping it was a good sign they'd entertain her idea of her working with them once again. Two years ago, she partnered with them to solve the O'Shea murder case. The deceased, Mrs. O'Shea, was the grandmother of a baseball player who played for the Arizona Diamondbacks.

The break room contained two snack machines, a soft drink dispenser, and two commercial coffee makers, leaving only enough room for a small table with one chair. Pilson laid his portfolio on the table and reached for the orange-collared decaf pot on top of the old appliance just as Schmidt replaced the coffeepot filled with caffeinated sludge. Both turned to greet her.

Schmidt checked his watch. "Hey, Molly, we were hoping to see you. Can I pour you a cup?" he asked, raising the mud-filled pot.

Molly laughed. "Not on your life." She grabbed a mug and a teabag.

Schmidt raised his mug, signaling he wanted to talk to her. "I met with Sergeant Hilliard, and he suggested Larry and I to get with you regarding the case you're working... Jerrod Bronson's sister's assault, I believe."

She grinned. "Great. I updated him on my case yesterday after learning from Mr. Harmon that Jerrod Bronson had been murdered."

Schmidt chuckled. "Hilliard suggested the three of us collaborate. Said he thought you might need our expertise."

Molly glanced at Pilson then back at Schmidt. "He did? That's interesting. He suggested you guys could use my competence, given my experience with Arabian horses—and my law enforcement proficiency, of course."

Pilson cleared his throat. "All right, you two. Cut the crap." He shook his head in mock disgust. "As of now, we're working together. Molly, what about your partner, Kelly?"

"He's leaving on vacation. Has some serious skiing scheduled. That said, Hilliard didn't mention him. All Hilliard said was I should get together with you guys. Said it might ease your caseload."

Pilson turned for the door. "Right, we're close to our limit. Hilliard advised us you would take the lead. Let's grab the conference room and discuss it."

Minutes later, Molly began the conversation by providing an overview of her case, including the poor relationship between brother and sister. Larry Pilson brought her up to date on the Jerrod Bronson murder, saying they hadn't interviewed the ranch staff yet because of being shorthanded.

Schmidt leaned back in his chair and clasped his hands behind his head. "We haven't received the preliminary report from the lab yet either. Seems we're all understaffed. Not much to go on. Both cases are barely underway. I'm wonderin' if brother and sister are into some dirty business together."

Pilson nodded in agreement.

Molly pursed her lips. "I don't think so. According to her ex, Jill sent her brother packing because of his criminal activity. She wanted no part of him."

"Interesting," Arnie Schmidt said. "Still, because of her attack, somebody out there could be thinking she's involved—like somebody presuming on the family connection."

Pilson turned to Molly. "How soon before we can question Jill Bronson?"

"It could still be a week or two before they bring her out of her coma. Her injuries are severe. I plan to visit the hospital several times a week, so I'll keep you both informed on that score. I'm as eager as you to hear what she can tell us."

"Do you believe her estranged husband's story?" Schmidt asked. "Do you think he's on the up and up?"

"I do. As far as I know, he's been straight with me from the jump. I'll arrange a meet so you guys can evaluate him. I think you'll see he's not BS-ing me. He deeply regrets leaving his wife and wants to reconcile their marriage."

Pilson scratched his head. "How did you put this all together, Molly?"

"Actually, it fell into my lap. I followed the few leads I had and got as far as Mr. Harmon at the ranch who told me about Jerrod's murder. So far, we don't have much to go on. I was pleased when Harmon said you guys were working the murder case. I look forward to joining you. We've always had good chemistry."

"That's for sure," Schmidt said. "With the sister's attack to solve, combined with the murder, do you mind taking the lead?"

"No problem. There's a good chance they're connected. Timing of the two attacks suggests it."

Pilson nodded. "Right. Of our three homicide cases, one is wrapping up and the other two are not far behind. I think a threesome's a great way to go."

Molly nodded. "Happy to run with it. Can I take your murder book with me when we're done here?"

"Of course," Pilson said with a nod. "I need to do a little updating then I'll drop it by your desk. As soon as we get the lab report, I'll bring it to you."

Molly headed for the door. "Perfect."

As soon as she returned to her cubicle, she dialed Mr. Harmon's number. He answered on the second ring. They exchanged pleasantries and Molly explained she wanted to stop by the ranch to speak with some of the employees. He sounded pleased she was working the case.

"I can be there by ten this morning," Molly said. "I want to swing by the hospital first to check on Jerrod's sister."

"Not a problem. Come whenever it's convenient. You know farming; we're always here."

- 9 -

Mid-morning at St. James' Hospital, Molly took the elevator up to five and strode into Mathews Neurological Institute's ICU department. She checked in with one of the nurses at their central station, displayed her ID and badge then asked for Andrea. In minutes Andrea appeared carrying a visitor's badge on a lanyard, surgical gloves, and a mask for Molly to put on.

Inside Jill Bronson's room, Randy Winslow sat bedside, holding Jill's limp hand. Andrea lightly tapped the glass with a fingernail. Randy looked their way and waved. Molly returned his gesture.

"It's wonderful how dedicated to his wife he is," Andrea said as she stared at Randy. "Poor guy. Jill's battered face must break his heart. I'm sure she was a beautiful girl before the attack. Her face will need quite a bit of repair." She sighed. "Randy raises all our spirits by simply showing up each morning and after work, and his wife hasn't a clue he's there. Before he leaves, he often comments to us how much better she looks. Wishful thinking I'm afraid."

"Andrea, do you have any idea when she may be brought out of the coma?"

"I don't know. Her doctor will let us know when he makes that decision. However, since Randy provided us with her medical information, we've been able to try additional therapeutics safely. We're encouraged the brain swelling is lessening. But we must still proceed with caution. The rest of her injuries are addressed daily and they're coming along nicely. Her vitals continue to improve which makes us hopeful. We have your contact info along with Randy's so you'll both be informed immediately when her doctor decides to bring her out."

"I appreciate that, Andrea." Molly headed for the exit, peeling her mask and gloves as she strode to the door. "See you soon."

Later that morning, Mr. Harmon met Molly on the porch of the manager's office. A man appearing to be in his forties, dressed in jeans, boots, western shirt and ball cap, stepped out of the office to shake hands with Molly when Harmon introduced them. "Gene's been our ranch manager for several years. If I'm not available, Gene can always help you."

Gene Belmont smiled pleasantly. "I'd be pleased to, Detective."

Molly appreciated his willingness. "Today I'd like to talk to the employees who knew Jerrod... perhaps worked with him."

"No problem," Gene responded. "That would be mostly junior trainers and grooms. He dealt with the farm secretary on occasion, too." He gestured to a conference room adjoining his office. "I'll be out of my office the rest of the morning. Make yourself at home." He jogged down the three stairs and headed in the direction of the AI facility. "I'll send Big Bev to you now, and I'll tell several of the guys to head over when they get a break. I'll let Dr. Spelling know, and the crew teasing the mares, to meet with you when they're done."

"Do you have quite a few mares in for breeding this time of year?"

"We're teasing mares every day. We have to be certain they're ready to conceive before we take them to Rothman. He's collected daily. It's no longer only in breeding season when mares are serviced by Roth. I'm on my way to talk with our lead vet. I'll mention you want to see him, too."

Mr. Harmon swiped a fleck of dust from his sleeve. "My wife's down at the teasing chute as well, Molly, if you'd like to talk to her. She's been recording the mares' evaluation numbers for the past three years. Dr. Spelling relies on her accuracy."

"Thank you," Molly said. "I'll talk to her before I leave."

As Mr. Harmon stood to leave, Molly headed into the conference room. Minutes later, a tall, trim young woman wearing a pink baseball cap over long blonde hair and brown aviator sunglasses, tapped on the open conference door. She smiled. "Hi, I'm Beverly. Everybody calls me Bev. Did you want to talk to me?"

Surprised by her slim body, Molly tried not to stare. "Does everyone call you *Big* Bev?" Molly chuckled. "That's unfair. You could be a runway model." Molly touched a button on her recorder and laid it in the center of the table.

Bev smiled gently as she nodded her acknowledgment. "We have another Bev, also. The Hispanic guys tagged me with the nickname. I've been here for eight years, and *Little Bev* arrived less than a year ago. *Big* was their way of indicating my seniority and telling us apart." She grinned. "But don't be surprised, Little Bev is really little and has dark hair. Maybe stands five feet two in her boots. You'll meet her."

"Yes, I'm sure I will. What is your job here on the ranch?"

"I tend to Rothman, our senior stallion. Probably the most important horse on the farm, if not the Arabian horse world. Some of us call him the *old man.*"

"I'm aware of him… and his reputation. What exactly are your responsibilities for the horse?"

"Pretty much, I do everything. I feed him twice a day, stay with him when the vets come to care for him. Over the last few years, we've discovered there are a few treatments he no longer tolerates. If an outside vet arrives, I stay with him to be sure the vet's aware of what not to do."

"Why would you have an outside vet when you have Drs. Briggs and Spellman?"

"They're in charge of the breeding operation, including all artificial insemination. We use outside vets to worm the horses and handle their shots and vaccinations. That kind of thing."

"I see." Molly paused, marveling at the size of the Harmons' ranching operation. "Do you ever ride Rothman?"

"Daily. After our ride, I take him into the pool to swim. I control his lead-line when he breeds a mare by natural service or when his semen is collected at the AI clinic."

Molly's brow rose. "Wow! Do you spend your nights here, too?" she asked in a playful tone.

Bev's expression remained serious. "I have—when he's not felt well." She gestured with both hands. "He's the heart and soul of this ranch. Without the old man we'd be lost."

Molly paused, studying Bev. "What can you tell me about the murder of Jerrod Bronson?"

"Nothing, really. I hardly knew him. The only time I saw him was when he replaced Big R's shoes." She shrugged. "When he's being shod, I stand at the horse's head, making sure he stays calm while Jerrod works on his feet. It's kinda hard to get to know somebody when all you see is their butt."

Molly chuckled. "I get your point. Thank you, Bev. May I call on you again in the future if I have more questions?"

"Of course. I'll be around. Wherever Rothman is, that's where you'll usually find me." She grinned. "Rothman's *office* is right here, next door to Gene's." She pointed to the far side of the manager's office. Rothman's head protruded through the window as if watching for visitors.

A lean young man of average height approached the porch where Molly waited. He grinned when she gave him a wave. "Thanks for coming to talk with me. I'm Detective Raines."

He extended his hand. "I'm Billy Fenton, a groom and a junior trainer."

Molly shook his hand and invited him to follow her through the manager's office into the conference room. "May I call you Billy?"

"Sure. What would you like to know?"

"What does your job include?" Molly turned on her recorder and laid it on the table.

"I work with the junior grooms, bathing the horses, caring for their manes and tails, getting them ready for the show ring or a prospective buyer. I also ride a few horses in the bullpen whenever I have time. I'm on the learn-as-you-work program. When we're not grooming a horse, we help out wherever we're needed."

"I see." Molly studied Billy for a second or two. "I'm investigating the death of Jerrod Bronson. What can you tell me about Jerrod and how he died?"

Billy rested his forearms on the table and leaned forward. "Not much. Whenever Jerrod was here shoein' horses, it was my job to lead a horse to wherever he'd set up his rig then return the freshly shod horse back to where I found it—one of the barns, a catch pen, or a pasture. Jerrod and me? We never talked much. He was a nice enough guy but not one to bullshit with. He was mostly bent over his work. If he was standin', he was hammerin' on a red-hot shoe or settin' a nail. When he'd finish a horse, he'd swap with me for the next one.

"Whenever Jerrod was here to work, Mr. Harmon gave me a list of horses whose feet needed tendin'. Jerrod learned the horses by name, 'specially the show-string, so it didn't take long to swap 'em out." Billy's hands moved with every word. "Big Bev often helped me bring the horses to him. Jerrod and me, we'd talk a little when we traded horses, but that was about it."

"Did you hang out with him after work? Did he date the girls from the ranch?"

Billy shook his head. "We weren't buddies. We didn't hang out. I never knew him to date any of the girls, but I suppose he could've. The guy you should be askin these questions is Alphonso. He's a junior trainer, like me. He and Jerrod sometimes went riding together on the weekends. They were buddy-buddy."

"Can you tell me how Jerrod died? Do you know why he was over at the AI building?"

"I can't help ya much. When I went that mornin' to feed the mares over there, I saw the area was taped off and a bunch of police cars were parked all around. Dr. Spelling had already fed the horses. That's when I learnt somebody kilt Jerrod durin' the night. I guess you'd have to ask Dr. Spellman or Briggs about Jerrod bein' over there cause them horses don't get foot care—unless they throw a shoe. The horses are there a day or two before they're inseminated and don't stay long after that. If one throwed a shoe or somethin' I'd walk the mare to Jerrod. I never knew him to go to the AI building. Jerrod didn't want to move his truck once he got set up." Billy's tone changed, suggesting he'd said all there was to be said.

Molly stood and thanked him. "Would you please ask Alphonso to come see me?"

"Sure. Do you speak Spanish? His English ain't the greatest."

"My Spanish sucks, but we'll figure it out somehow."

- 10 -

Molly observed the young man who appeared in the conference room's doorway. He could have been right out of central casting. Molly smiled, assuming it was Alphonso who swaggered into the room. Had she not expected him, she might have thought he was a potential buyer shopping for the perfect horse. His freshly dusted black cowboy hat, positioned at a slight tilt, matched the color of his oiled hair and penetrating eyes that roamed up and down Molly's body. Both his black and white plaid Western shirt, with its pearl buttons, and tight-fitting jeans appeared freshly laundered and ironed. Were it not for his large ears jutting out from under his hat, he would qualify for a leading man in a porn movie. His body language reinforced the image he obviously hoped to portray.

Molly held his gaze and Alphonso amused her with a widening grin. "I am Alphonso Munoz; you are the pretty lady, yes?" His English was heavily accented, but understandable. "My English not so good, but I get by." He smiled provocatively.

Molly stared at him as he crossed the room to the long table. *I'm sure you do fine. He either thinks he's cute or clever—or both. Lucky me.* She gestured to a chair. "Please be seated." She touched the button to turn on her recorder. He nodded and sat when she did. "Please tell me about Jerrod. He was your friend?"

"Yes. Little bit."

"How long have you been in the States?"

He flashed a proud grin and raised two fingers. "Two years."

"Do you have a green card?" He nodded.

"Do you ride horses?"

"Little bit. I'm junior trainer."

"Do you ride here on the ranch?"

"Little bit. *Cause I train.*" He tipped his head as if expecting a reaction from her, but Molly didn't buy into it.

"Did you ride in the McDowells? With Jerrod? Molly pointed behind her to the east.

"Yes." He shrugged. "Not much. Two or three times."

"Only two or three times?" He nodded.

"Who would want to kill your friend, Jerrod?"

Alphonso pushed back in his chair and waved her off with his hands. "No. Nooo. I not do. Not see."

"Do you know who?"

He frowned. "I not know."

"Where were you the night he was killed?" Alphonso gave her a blank stare.

Molly reluctantly repeated it in her limited Spanish.

Alphonso smugly grinned. "My grandmother's house for her birthday."

Molly studied him, doubting his veracity. She made a mental note to call on his mother with Maria Carranza, one of Phoenix PD's homicide detectives. The language differences gave Alphonso cover, and he used it to his advantage. Next time she questioned him, she'd turn him over to Detective Carranza. It was said Maria could make a concrete Buddha talk. This punk would crumble like a Girl Scout cookie.

Suppressing the urge to sigh, Molly stood. *"Gracias, Alphonso. Buenos dias."* She waited in place as he smirked, stood, and ran a hand through his glistening hair then slowly reset his perfect hat. *"Adios, Señorita."* He strutted from the room like a one-eyed leopard carrying away his kill. She suspected he was smiling—feeling good about his performance..

Molly followed Alphonso out to the porch in time to see Mr. Harmon heading toward the ranch house. She jogged toward him, calling his name. He turned. "Yes, Molly?"

"Do you have pictures of your employees by any chance?"

"I think so. I'll check with our secretary. Stop by the house on your way out; she'll have them ready for you, if she has any."

Molly stopped instantly; surprised he didn't invite her to come into the house as he always had in the past. "Thank you. The pictures will be very helpful." She turned toward her car, stopped, and glanced back. Mr. Harmon looked in deep thought as he plodded toward the house.

- 11 -

After a fast-food lunch from a nearby sandwich shop, Molly returned to Harmony to interview more of the employees. As she listened to the recording of Alphonso Munoz's interview, a man tapped on the conference room's doorframe. "Detective Molly Raines?"

"Yes. Please come in." Molly gestured to a chair across from where she sat. She switched on her recorder. "Please tell me your name and what your job is at Harmony. . ."

"I'm Dr. Spelling, one of the ranch veterinarians. I understand you wanted to ask me a few questions." He slid his chair forward.

"That's correct." She smiled, hoping to put the man at ease, and introduced herself. "I'm interviewing everyone who works on the ranch." She paused. "What can you tell me about Jerrod Bronson's murder?"

Dr. Spelling took a moment to think and rested his hands in his lap. "Not much. When I drove in, I noticed Jerrod's rig parked in a spot we try to keep open for clients' trucks and horse trailers. I thought it odd he would be at the AI facility, as he'd never been there before. I parked in my usual place and walked over to ask him to move it. When I circled around to the driver's door, I found him lying near his front wheel. I hurried to his side and knelt, intending to help if I could. I checked for a pulse, but he was already dead." Spelling stared out the window for a moment. "Jerrod was a nice guy. It was terrible seeing him like that—skull crushed—face and head bloody."

"What time did you arrive?"

"Around seven o'clock. Sun was up."

"What did you do after you realized he was beyond help?"

Spelling rubbed his hands along his khaki pants as if his palms were sweating. "I took a few minutes to pull myself together. Even though I operate on large animals, seeing Jerrod dead was quite a shock. Not something one expects to see when arriving at work." He squirmed forward in his chair and cracked his knuckles perhaps trying to calm down. "Anyway, I dialed 911. As soon as I hung up, I called Dr. Briggs to tell him. He said he was on his way, and I should feed the mares stalled inside the facility."

"Were you surprised he wanted you to feed the horses? Possibly compromise the crime scene?"

"No, never gave it a thought. The horses would always be our first consideration. We believe it is important to keep to a feeding time schedule for the health of the horses. I'm quite sure, the crime scene never entered his mind."

"Why did you call Dr. Briggs instead of Mr. Harmon?"

He rubbed his neck. "I guess I panicked. I didn't want to be the one to tell Mr. Harmon. He's kinda feisty. Gets upset easily. Besides, we were expecting mares to be delivered sometime in the morning and I was thinking about moving Jerrod's truck out of the way... if I could find his keys. But I remembered you're not supposed to touch anything before the police arrive." He hunched his shoulders. "I figured Briggs would tell me what to do. He's the senior vet."

"Did you feed the horses?"

Spelling pulled a handkerchief from his pocket and dabbed sweat from his hairline. "Yes—hay and grain—like always. We had only two inseminated mares waiting to go home at the time, so it didn't take long. I agreed the mares should be fed right away because once the police arrived, we might be delayed in getting around to it. Couldn't take the chance."

"How long before the patrol officers showed up?"

"About ten minutes, right after I finished with the mares and came outside. One officer checked out Jerrod's body while another talked to me. Asked me questions—wanted to know who owned the ranch, everything I saw when I arrived—kinda what you'd expect. After that I tried to stay out of the way. Once they put up the yellow crime scene tape, it was easier to avoid stepping too close."

"Did they call the Fire Department to come and confirm the death?"

"Right. Two trucks arrived. The paramedics checked the body and one of them confirmed the death. They filled out their paperwork and were gone."

"Did they leave a copy for Mr. Harmon?"

"I don't know."

"Did anyone call Mr. Harmon?"

"Yeah, one of the officers called him."

"Did he come right over?"

Dr. Spelling smiled sheepishly as if enjoying a thought, one he probably shouldn't describe. "Yeah, he sure did. Looked as though he threw on his clothes in a split second and raced over in his golf cart." Spelling's eyes sparkled. "I've never seen him before without his hair combed. It was flying in all directions. We've enjoyed teasing him about his perfect hair. He was quite a sight—like a guy who'd just been wakened from a night's sleep."

Molly chuckled. "Come to think of it, I've never seen Mr. Harmon looking like anything but a perfectly groomed, top-o-the-heap professional." She cleared her throat and changed the subject. "Did you know Jerrod well? Hang out together? Double date?" Molly motioned to his left hand. "I see you're not wearing a wedding ring."

He glanced at his hand. "My girlfriend and I went out a couple of times with him and Cindy. She's the ranch's secretary."

"Had Jerrod and Cindy been dating long?"

"I'm not sure. The few times we were with them they kinda acted like a couple. Although, there was no gossip about them here on the ranch. Jerrod once commented he thought it might be improper to date any girls who worked for his clients. And it's possible Cindy worried the Harmons wouldn't like it if they knew about her and Jerrod. Cindy has a close relationship with Mr. and Mrs. Harmon. Although there were times when she seemed to be the one promoting whatever friendship existed between them." He grimaced. "I don't know, maybe it was just her personality."

"Was Jerrod buddy-buddy with any of the guys on the ranch? Or the young women?"

Spelling rubbed his jaw. "I don't pay too much attention to who pals around with whom. I understand Jerrod and Alphonso often took their horses up to the White Mountains to trail ride on the weekends, 'specially on long weekends."

Molly frowned. "The White Mountains?" Spelling nodded. "Are you sure you don't mean the McDowells?"

He shrugged. "Possibly. But not that I know of."

"Is there anything else you can tell me? Jerrod's habits? His family? How he spent his time? Arguments involving Jerrod?"

"No, ma'am, I'm sorry. I really didn't know him that well. My work with the AI program keeps me pretty busy at our facility. The ranch's stallions are sought after for breeding, especially Rothman, and it seems there's never enough time for anything else." He lowered his head and glanced at her from beneath his brow. "I'm sorry about Jerrod. He was a nice guy. Didn't deserve to die that way."

Molly stood. "Thank you, Dr. Spelling for sharing your valuable time. I appreciate it." She handed him her business card. "If you think of anything, anything at all, no matter how small, please call me."

As Dr. Spelling left the room, Molly gathered her things and headed for the main house to talk with Mrs. Harmon and the farm secretary, Cindy. It was hard to imagine how a young woman could work so closely with Mr. and Mrs. Harmon and at the same time, date an ex-con.

- 12 -

On Monday afternoon, Mrs. Doris Harmon opened her door and her arms when she saw Molly standing on her sprawling porch. Molly didn't hesitate to accept the warm embrace. They hugged each other and rocked from side to side like girlfriends irrespective of age. When Doris loosened her grip, she leaned back, studied Molly, and smiled. "I was hoping you'd stop by. George has mentioned your recent visits. Sad you have to come here under such terrible circumstances." She took both of Molly's hands. "Can you stay long enough to have an iced tea?"

"Of course. I love your tea. It's always perfectly sweetened." Molly followed Mrs. Harmon into the kitchen.

"Have you seen Jimmy since he returned?" Mrs. Harmon asked.

"No. I thought I'd see him around here, but I haven't."

"I'm not surprised. He probably slept for twenty-four hours after returning from Australia. I think he only spent a day or two checking the training progress of the clients' horses before he had to run up to Flagstaff to do a three-day workshop. It had been on his calendar for more than a year. After Jerrod's body was discovered, Jimmy thought of cancelling, but knew he couldn't. Too many people had signed up for the workshop by then. We talked quite a bit about what he should say if a guest brought up Jerrod's death."

"Of course. Knowing you and Jim, I'm sure you came up with just the right thing to say." Molly smiled sweetly. "I'm happy for him. He has a good career in the Arabian horse business; of course, he's earned it with all his hard work."

"So true."

Mrs. Harmon was of average height and pencil slim. She wore her gray hair in a stylishly cut and the little makeup she wore was applied perfectly. This afternoon she wore no jewelry, not even her ring with its four-carat diamond flanked by one-carat emeralds, a ring she had sworn to Molly she'd never take off. Mr. Harmon had given it to her on their forty-fifth anniversary. Molly recalled Mrs. Harmon complaining it trapped food in the settings when she cooked. Avocado and ground meat were the worst. And there was the evening when she laughed and joked it was simply one more aggravation married women had to put up with.

Molly stared at Mrs. Harmon's left hand. "You're not wearing your beautiful diamond ring," she blurted.

Mrs. Harmon sighed. "I know. I misplaced it a few days ago." Her eyebrows squeezed together. "I'm sorry, I'm very distressed over it. I thought surely I'd come across it by now. I can't imagine where I left it."

Molly's heart went out to her, knowing well the stress of losing something so precious. Painful images returned of the search she'd made three years ago, trying to find her mother's heirloom necklace, a gift Molly treasured. She felt the misery as if it were yesterday and the struggle to reconcile the loss. It took Molly months to accept the truth.

"I'm so sorry. I know losing something so beautiful causes terrible pain."

Mrs. Harmon reached for Molly's arm and directed her into the kitchen. "Yes, it's difficult." She forced a smile. "But I'm sure it will turn up. Now, how can I help you?"

"Do you have time to answer a few questions regarding Jerrod Bronson?"

Mrs. Harmon's right hand fluttered to her throat. "The poor dear. Such a terrible thing."

"Yes, I agree. I'm told he was nice to everybody. Did you know him well?"

"Not really. Sometimes he'd bring me his bill for shoeing, and we'd talk about the horses and some unimportant things. He liked baseball, and you know how much I enjoy it. So he'd start a conversation about the Diamondbacks. He'd grin if they were in a winning streak and frown if they weren't." She paused. "Usually he dealt with Cindy, our secretary."

"Do you suppose I could speak with her before I leave? Maybe she can tell me more about him."

Mrs. Harmon handed Molly her glass of tea with a lemon wedge perched on top. "I doubt it, but worth a try. Cindy is such a nice girl. Comes from a lovely family. She came here to work with the horses, but when Shirley, our long-time secretary moved back to Missouri, we asked Cindy to fill in until we could hire a replacement. Cindy did such a good job, we asked her to stay with it. She's lightened my workload by half. Cindy's been our secretary for three years now."

Mrs. Harmon carried a glass of tea in each hand. "I fixed a glass for Cindy. We usually have a beverage about this time," she said as she led the way toward the guestrooms that served as offices for Cindy and herself. She stopped and turned back to Molly. "Is there something in particular you wanted to ask me, dear?"

"Yes, actually. Do you have photos of all of the people who work here?"

"Why, yes. Would you like to see them?"

"I would. Some of the images might be helpful to my investigation. Could I possibly borrow a few?"

"You can take them all. I have a huge album chuck full."

"That's perfect. I'll return them."

She followed Mrs. Harmon down the hallway to the first door and entered the well-organized office.

Cindy looked up from her work and smiled. "I thought I heard your footsteps."

Mrs. Harmon introduced Molly, explaining she and Molly's family were long-time friends. "Molly has a few questions to ask you regarding Jerrod." She handed Cindy her glass of tea and took a sip from her own then turned for the door. "I'm going to hunt up some pictures while you girls visit." She turned to Molly. "When you're finished, come find me in the kitchen."

"Thanks. Will do."

As soon as Mrs. Harmon was out of earshot, Molly closed the door and sat in the guest chair. "Cindy, I'm investigating Jerrod's death and I understand you were friends." Molly placed her recorder in her lap and set it to record. "How well did you know him? Did you see him outside work hours?"

Cindy's eyes widened. "Jerrod? Not well at all. He worked here eight to ten days out of every month. With the number of horses we maintain, he'd usually come twice each month. We rarely spoke. He'd bring his billings to the door. I'd enter his work in our records then cut him a check before he left. He'd either pick it up or I'd carry it to his truck and leave the envelope on the driver's seat."

"Did you ever date him?"

"Heavens no. I could lose my job. The Harmons have a rule against dating fellow employees. Everyone knows that."

"I see. Did Jerrod pal around with any of the men who worked here? Perhaps stop in for a drink with them after work?"

"I don't know."

"Mrs. Harmon tells me you came here originally to work with the horses. Do you ride?"

"I used to, but I haven't for quite a while."

"Did you go riding with Jerrod? I know he enjoyed riding in the mountains on the weekends."

"No. I no longer own a horse."

"Couldn't you borrow a ranch horse?"

"We don't keep casual riding horses. The feed bill is huge as it is. Our horses are either part of the show string, on the sales list, or in performance training. That doesn't include the outside mares here for breeding. The Harmons would never allow me to ride any of those horses. Our broodmares are typically in foal or have a foal at their side. All the others you see belong to clients. I used to keep a gelding, but I sold him to a client for their daughter to compete in the western classes."

Cindy glanced down at her manicured nails. "I wish I could tell you more, but I really didn't know much about Jerrod." She looked at Molly with tears in her eyes. "I hope you find whoever did this to him."

"I'll keep working at it. One last question: Did you know Jerrod's sister by any chance?"

Cindy shook her head. "I'm sorry. I wish I could be more help."

Molly nodded as she stood, stopped her recorder, and slipped it into her bag then handed Cindy her card. She picked up her nearly empty glass. "I appreciate you giving me your time. Call me if you think of something."

Remembering Mrs. Harmon asked her to come to the kitchen, Molly retraced her steps. The smell of frying onions filled the air as she approached the large kitchen. Mrs. Harmon turned off the gas burner, picked up a manila envelope and offered it to Molly before giving her a goodbye hug. Molly set her glass on the counter and took the envelope.

Mrs. Harmon said, "There are one or more pictures of each employee, plus I put in a couple of people who quit the ranch a week or two ago." She patted Molly's back. "Please tell your grandparents and your mother I send my best wishes. I miss them and the good times we once enjoyed." She gave Molly's arm a little shake. "And you, my darling girl, take care of yourself—stay safe." She kissed Molly's cheek.

"I will, I promise. Thank you for the pictures. I'll review them when I get back to the office."

As Molly walked toward her car, Gene Belmont, the ranch manager, trotted after her. "Molly, wait up," he called. He covered the lawn that separated them in three bounds, his hand extended toward her. "I was searching my directory for a phone number and accidentally came upon this one." He handed her the note.

"This guy owns a motel with a barn where people can put up a horse or two while overnighting at the motel." The corner of his mouth rose in a slight smile. "I believe Jerrod used this place on his weekend rides. A while back, he happened to mention it when we were talking about his activities."

Molly studied the number, thinking the area code might take in the Payson area. She smiled at Gene. "Thanks a lot." She rattled the notepaper in her fingers. "This could be very helpful. I'll definitely look into it."

"Let me know when you're coming our way again. I'd like to take you to coffee. You have an interesting job. I'd like to hear more about it... and you, too."

She smiled. "I haven't talked to every employee, so I'll be back—either tomorrow or the next day. Just depends."

He turned to go. "Let me know in advance and I'll pull together the employees you'll want to have available." He waved as he jogged away.

Molly watched him run, wondering what his motives might be.

- 13 -

The next morning, Molly walked into the office carrying a doughnut box from The Little Dutch Girl coffee shop. People she passed were quick to comment about the tempting fragrance radiating from the box. She invited them to help themselves in the coffee room.

After dropping off the pastries, she took a bite of the maple bar she carried with her as she headed for Schmidt and Pilson's cubicles. When she approached Pilson's cubby, he stood. "I smelled your little goodie before I saw your face. Did you bring us some?" She nodded. With a chuckle, Pilson peered over the partial wall into Arnie Schmidt's domain. "Molly brought doughnuts."

"Great," Schmidt called out. "I'll be right there."

Molly said, "Let's head for the conference room and catch up on our cases. Swing through the break room and grab a doughnut before they're gone. We could be a while." She gave them a wave. "I'll see you there."

Minutes later, they sat around a table with coffee and pastries resting on napkins in front of them. Larry Pilson tapped his pen against his notebook. "Molly, I know you said you were going to arrange a meet for me with your victim's ex, but I got an early start yesterday and dropped by the hospital on a chance of running into him. I met him, Randy Winslow, as he was leaving the ICU heading to work.

"We talked as I walked with him out to his truck. Like you, I got the sense he was being straight with me." Pilson stared at his pen and notebook, tapped his pen a couple more times. "After he drove off, I returned to the ICU and talked with your victim's nurse. She vouched for him, exclaiming his good qualities. For now I'm inclined to think he's trustworthy. The minute he slips up, I'll be all over his ass. When I asked about Jerrod, Randy bluntly told me he didn't care for Jerrod because of how he treated Jill, Randy's wife, and Jerrod's sister."

Molly nodded. "So, you didn't pick up even a *little* stink of a lie?"

"Not once."

"Okay then. You and I are on the same page with Randy. I'll continue giving him the benefit of the doubt—until I no longer trust him."

Schmidt said, "I've spent all my time working to close one of our cases, so I haven't anything to add. Although I've not met the victim's estranged husband, hearing you guys, I'm optimistic. Molly, have you turned up anything at the ranch?"

"The usual." She smirked. "I've run into more than one liar. I'm quite sure a couple of employees out there at Harmony Farm will be helpful in the future. I've asked all the starter questions of the people I interviewed. Once I've talked with them all, I'll be better prepared to dig deeper. Mrs. Harmon provided me with pictures of all the employees, but I haven't had time to go through them."

"Who are your liars?" Pilson asked.

"The ranch secretary, for one. She knows stuff she doesn't want to share, and there's a junior trainer, Alphonso—*Mr. Slick* with his big ego who tries to skirt the truth. So far, none of the people I've talked to have been much help."

"What about the ranch manager?" Arnie Schmidt asked. "When we were there the morning the body was found, I picked up some mixed signals coming from him. Could be something—or nothing."

"Right," Molly agreed. "I haven't had a chance to spend much time with him and I have a feeling he could be helpful. As I was leaving yesterday, he gave me a phone number for a motel where Jerrod may have stayed while weekend riding. I checked out the area code and it's for Pine, Arizona. I'll call the place this morning and let you know if it's worth driving up there. Could be another dead end."

As Molly headed for her cubicle, she wondered what was around the Pine area of the White Mountains that would attract a person enough to pull a horse trailer that far north. The McDowell Mountains were much closer to the ranch. Plus, they offered plenty of trails to ride. Perhaps she and Lar could take a drive up north to Pine over the weekend.

When Molly reached her cubby, she remembered another detail and returned to Pilson and Schmidt's cubicles. "There is one thing that keeps nagging at me. Mrs. Harmon has lost a four-carat diamond and emerald ring—a gift from her husband. She once swore she'd never take it off. Yesterday she told me she'd simply misplaced it. I'm not buying that answer."

- 14 -

Molly left headquarters early to get a jump on the commuter traffic. She looked forward to working in peace and quiet at home to do the serious research she could only do there. After her last conversation with Pilson and Schmidt regarding Randy Winslow's credibility, negative and vexing thoughts interrupted and destroyed her concentration.

She recalled her mother's advice. "Never ignore what astrology has to say about people you've encountered, especially those who trouble you." Like Randy Winslow. Although Pilson's positive impression of Randy helped sooth her worries, she couldn't eliminate the niggling. He had adamantly claimed to worry about Jill's safety, but he was in a perfect position to know all of her moves and schedules. He could easily have been her attacker.

At home in her breakfast room, Molly adjusted the shutters preparing to work seated at the table.

She poured a glass of iced tea and pondered Pilson's opinion of Randy. After several sips of tea, she stood and headed for the attic. With a small flashlight snugged into her waistband, she entered the bedroom hallway and lowered the drop-down ladder to the loft. Although it had been quite a while since she searched her mother's astrology texts for information, it didn't take long to access the old trunk that held the books and files collected over her mother's lifetime.

Molly held the flashlight between her teeth and used both hands to rifle through the texts until she found the beginner's book. Moments later, she sat at her breakfast table and opened the Handbook for Humanistic Astrology by Michael Mayep and turned to the chapter on Libra, remembering Randy shared an October eleventh birthday with his deceased brother-in-law.

Because their birth years were different, some planets would reside in different houses and their resulting charts would be dissimilar. But most of the aspects would be the same. Molly didn't have the time of birth for either man so she couldn't construct a personal chart on either of them. It didn't matter. All she wanted was to gain a little insight into Randy Winslow's psyche.

Two hours later, Molly pushed her book and note pad to the side and contemplated what she had learned. *Libra was an air sign, blessed with constant mental stimuli, strong intellect, and a keen mind, but on occasion, to their detriment, they could act impulsively.* Like Randy's decision to leave his wife.

They loved to read, enjoyed challenging discussions and people who had a lot to say. They were fond of material things. Like Randy's new truck. Molly recalled Randy's lengthy story describing the failure of his marriage and why he walked out on Jill. Then there was the impulsive purchase of his new truck.

Libras have a heightened social consciousness, comparing and evaluating people and situations. Perhaps Randy was inclined to over-think things. Maybe he was too judgmental when it came to Jill.

Libras are social animals with a definite set of values, ideals, and social standards. Libras typically search for a partner who will set clear boundaries. Had Randy expected too much from Jill? Perhaps it wasn't in her nature to set standards, but she didn't hesitate to tell her brother to stop coming around, cutting him out of her life.

Finding peace and harmony in a love relationship is a very important goal. No wonder he was determined to win her back—and to be with her every day at the hospital even though she had no idea he was there.

Despite all the women he'd chased after leaving Jill, she was apparently the only one who had provided him a deep, meaningful relationship along with clear boundaries, something he understood, and he needed. Sad he was too immature to recognize it during their marriage. The cliché of not knowing what we've got 'til it's gone came to mind.

Molly stood and stretched. She'd just spent two hours researching what might make Randy Winslow tick and hadn't reached any conclusions. She still believed he was trustworthy; the negatives in his horoscope didn't amount to much. Of course, she hadn't enough info to help her dig very deep. Basically, all she had was a broad overview. When she thought of drawing a contrast with Jerrod's Libra chart, she realized she was out of her depth. All in all, her knowledge of astrology was not much help. If only she could discuss it with her mom.

So be it. Time for dinner and she was hungry. Tidying her work area, her thoughts went to the leftovers waiting in the fridge. Her cell phone rang as she headed to the kitchen.

"Detective Raines? This is Dr. Dressner from the M.E.'s office. The preliminary report on Jerrod Bronson is ready if you'd like to pick it up."

"Great! I'm out of the office, but I'll stop by in the morning on my way to work."

"I'll leave it at the front desk."

- 15 -

The next morning Molly arrived at the Medical Examiner's office at five past eight and was greeted by a tall young man seated at the front desk. Molly introduced herself and explained the reason for her visit. He smiled and in a surprisingly loud voice said, "I have the report right here."

Molly stepped back and watched as the fellow searched through the stack of papers and envelopes in his in-basket. "Ah-ha! Here it is." He glanced at her and asked, "Molly Raines, right? Never mind; I know, I know; you told me." He handed her the manila packet.

Molly thanked him and headed for the door. Another voice called her name.

"Hang on, Detective Raines. May I have a word?" Dr. Dressner asked as he hurried toward her. "I heard Lenny here call your name."

Like duh. She recognized the sound of his voice and turned around. "Of course."

"You'll see in the report the mention of blunt force trauma to the head which probably resulted when the deceased fell. We weren't able to link it to an implement used to strike the skull.

He may have struck his head on a nearby rock or possibly against his truck. However, the only blood we found was beneath his head. More importantly, I want you to know about something you won't find in this report.

"I thought of it in the middle of the night. I noticed a very subtle dark stain on the skin next to the deceased's knife wounds. He was stabbed multiple times. The wounds were oval shaped and deep enough to kill him, but the head wound was the cause of death. The stain appears only on two wounds.

"The body arrived dirty in places from lying on muddy ground and, as a result, the stains were barely visible when the body was washed. I didn't give them much thought at the time. Mostly chalked it up to bruising. To tell you the truth, I'm probably making too much of it, but it's been on my mind ever since I woke in the night."

Molly made eye contact with him. "What do you think it might be?"

"That's just it. I haven't a clue, but I hope to know before long. Some kind of a liquid is my best guess. I'll delay my final report until I have more information. I plan to run some tests on the tissue. I think it was the unusual appearance of the stains that caused them to stick in my mind."

Molly nodded. "You've piqued my curiosity, that's for sure. Will you please call me with your findings?"

"Of course. It's important I get to the bottom of it. Kinda like solving a mystery. You would know about that." He smiled. "To be sure, I'll be calling you."

Molly thanked him and left. As she headed for police headquarters, she changed her mind and direction, traveling instead to the Harmons' ranch. She drove to the side entry that served the AI building, parked her car, and walked into the AI facility through the main entrance. Dr. Spelling must have heard the door and greeted her with a mug gripped in his right hand.

"Hello, Detective." He gestured with his coffee mug. "Care for coffee?"

Molly smiled. "No thanks. I came to take another look at the scene of the crime."

He grinned. "Just like in the movies."

She glanced up at him. "You're jovial this morning."

"We delivered a foal early this morning. Always puts me in a good mood." He glowered at the glass door and pointed at it with his mug. "Until I'm reminded of poor Jerrod. He was a nice young man, and life hadn't treated him well. He didn't deserve what happened to him."

"Yes, murder is a terrible thing." She stared out through the glass. "I'm wondering if I missed something when I was here. Do you have time to come along and show me exactly where you found the body?"

"Happy to."

They crossed the concrete sidewalk that circled the building to the steps leading down to the parking area. Spelling stopped on the lowest stair and pointed to the row of rocks surrounding a flowerbed of recently planted pink oleander. He raised his hand and pointed. "See the sixth rock over? Jerrod's head, extended right arm, and hand were about two feet from that rock. The truck's front bumper was near that spot. I noticed the tire marks when his truck was hauled away. It's just a guess, but that's how I remember seeing it when I first found him."

Molly counted the rocks and her eyes settled on the sixth rock. "I see. Be careful, Dr. Spelling. Don't step too near to where the body rested."

Dr. Spelling lagged behind as she slowly moved closer to the body's location.

"If you don't need me, Detective, I'd like to get back to work. We're going to collect Rothman's semen in a half hour, and I need to get everything prepared."

"Certainly. I'll be here a while. No need for you to hang around. As soon as I've finished, I'll be on my way." Molly watched Spelling enter the building then turned to her task. She circled the area where the body had been, looking for marks in the ground that was now dry to the touch. She recognized the spots that suggested he'd been dragged from his truck. The ground where he and his attacker had scuffled looked the same as before. She found footprints of what could be a work boot with a thick, notched sole. She believed the crime scene technicians had taken pictures of the print, but she bent down with her camera and took several just in case.

When she approached the area where Jerrod's head and shoulder had lain, she knelt to study the scratch marks in the dirt where Jerrod's hand would have rested.

At first glance the scratches appeared to be nothing more than marks left from a clawing hand. Jerrod must have been in great pain. The more Molly studied the marks a design began to form in her mind. She leaned back and refocused for a clearer view. As she stared at the scrambling of lines an image appeared. She blinked several times then squinted at the scratches. The image might have been a tree with branches arching out on both sides. An acacia? A palm? A mesquite? What could it mean? Molly studied it a little longer on the chance it would take on a different image but all she could make out was the suggestion of a tree. She took pictures from three different angles to show Pilson and Schmidt. She crossed the parking area to the passenger's side of her car to stow her bag on the seat.

Near her front tire she eyed two heel prints of what might have been from a woman's shoe or boot. Chances are the techs saw no reason to investigate this far away from the body's location. Could one of the two Bevs or Cindy have been here when Jerrod was knifed to death? Working quickly, she took a twelve-inch ruler from her evidence bag, laid it near the depressions and snapped a couple of pictures of each heel print then left the ranch.

As she drove to police headquarters, it was the picture scratched in the dirt she couldn't get out of her mind. Other things she'd noticed might be clues, but the tree scratched in the dirt dominated her thoughts. At a couple of red stoplights, she studied the *tree* pictures on her digital camera. Her investigating partners would probably laugh at them. They weren't sharp and the tree she thought she'd seen wasn't clear either. It required some imagination. Molly sighed. It was one of those *you had to be there* scenarios.

She parked toward the back of the parking lot at police headquarters and headed into the building. She took the stairs to the second floor, strode toward her cubicle, past Larry and Arnie's workstations. Schmidt gave her a wave while Pilson was on the phone. "Hey," she said to Schmidt. "I have something I'd like you to see. I need your opinion. Can you meet me in the conference room as soon as Pilson is off the phone?"

"Sure," Schmidt said. "I'll grab him and meet you there. Were you out at the ranch?"

As Molly walked away, she said over her shoulder, "Yeah, I just came from there. I'm going to drop off my stuff and grab a beverage. I'll leave the door open."

Molly stepped into her cubicle, placed her briefcase and handbag on her desk, and switched on her computer to check email. Her eyes ran down the list of seven messages, stopping at Randy Winslow's name. She opened and read his message. Jill's doctor intended to bring Jill out of her coma around seven this evening. *At last.*

Molly ambled into the break room for a cup of tea and helped herself to a cruller from a box somebody was kind enough to share. It wasn't a maple bar, but it was frosted with chocolate and that was just fine. With both hands filled she went to the conference room.

Pilson and Schmidt walked in five minutes later wanting to know what was up.

She chuckled when she noticed they each carried a doughnut. "Between the three of us, I think we killed the pastries."

"It's our job, right? What have you got?" Pilson asked with a look of expectation.

She pulled up the pictures she'd taken at the crime scene and handed her camera to Pilson. "There are six images there, three of which were scratched in the mud, I think by Jerrod Bronson just before he died. I'll double check if the crime scene techs made castings of the boot prints you'll see in the others." She glanced from man to man as Pilson handed the camera to Schmidt.

"Looks like there was a woman around there," Molly said. "Of course, no telling when she might have left that print. What do you think Jerrod was trying to draw or say when you look at those pictures?"

Pilson frowned. "Holy crap, Raines, all I saw was a bunch of scratches—like he was reacting to pain. What do you think you saw?"

Molly stared at Schmidt, waiting for him to say something and hand back the camera. While he continued to study the images, he glanced at Molly for a moment, pursing his lips. "I do think I see something there. Not sure what, but something. What were you thinking, Molly?"

"My only thought was possibly a tree, even though the trunk is narrow enough to suggest a leaf. Could be either, but whatever it is, it might be a clue. I know it sounds farfetched, but after checking out Jerrod's astral chart last night, I believe he was smarter than people gave him credit for—perhaps even a deep thinker. He may have tried to send us a message with his scratching."

"Ah c'mon, man," Pilson muttered. "Astrology is bullshit. Don't even go there."

Arnie Schmidt sat up straighter and stared at Pilson. "Don't *c'mon* Molly! She's had past success with help she got from astrology." He turned to Molly. "What else did you discover about him?"

"Not much. I didn't have birth time, year of birth, or birth location, so I had no way to look up the negative aspects that may be in his chart. Libras tend to get close to people who set parameters. It's possible somebody was giving him orders."

Pilson raised his finger. "Maybe he didn't follow the orders as given."

Molly nodded. "Good thought. That could be. But I'm just guessing."

"Well," Schmidt said, "It's possible he was in the middle of double crossing the guy giving the orders and he was found out."

"What do you think, Mol?" Pilson asked.

She shrugged. "It's all speculation based on weak but possible clues. Anything's conceivable at this point. All I've got to go on is what his scratching may mean. My hunch is Jerrod was trying to tell us something. On my way home, I'm going to run by that nursery on North Tatum and look at all the pictures of trees they have on display. Maybe I'll have some luck narrowing down what kind of a tree Jerrod had in mind."

Molly eased back in her chair. "How are you guys doing with your cases?"

Schmidt answered. "We closed one and the other is on hold until the suspects, a man and wife, are found and returned to Arizona. We have BOLOs out to all western states plus New Mexico, Montana, Idaho, Utah and Colorado. So, while we wait, we can help you run down witnesses and leads."

"Great," Molly said, "I can use the help. By the way, Jill Bronson's doctor told Randy, he's going to bring her out of her coma this evening. I plan to be there."

"That's some good news at least," Larry Pilson said.

Molly stood and smiled. "I think so. I'll find out tonight when we'll be able to talk with her."

As Molly watched the two men leave the room and turn in the direction of their cubicles, she punched Lar's number into her phone.

There was a happy sound in Lar's voice when he answered. "Hi, babe, what's up?"

"I'm going to stay in town for dinner." She shared the news about Jill, saying she'd grab a sandwich at a nearby shop.

"I can do you one better than that. How about I meet you at Nick's Trattoria on Indian School? I know how much you like Italian cookery. We can have a glass of wine and a comfortable dinner. Five-thirty?"

"I'll be there. Love you."

"Back atcha, kiddo."

Molly walked to her cubby intending to check messages and let Randy Winslow know she would meet him at the hospital a little before seven o'clock. The thought of bringing Jill Bronson out of her coma raised the hair on Molly's arms. Randy would be a mess if it turned out Jill's brain was damaged.

- 16 -

A few minutes before seven, Molly donned the mask and gloves she received from a nurse and followed her back to Jill's room in Mathew's ICU department. Randy glanced up and looked through the window at Molly, stood and came out of the room.

"Hey, Detective, it's good to see you. Obviously, you got my message."

"I did, Randy. Thanks."

Dr. Lange spoke as he approached from behind Molly. "Hello, Randy, Detective Raines, I wondered if I'd see you this evening."

Molly's brow rose. "I couldn't miss this. We've all waited for quite a while to have Jill wake up."

"Don't expect much, Detective. Patients often respond differently. I'd like you to watch from here. Randy, you come with me, and we'll get started. She's been without sedation since this morning so there's a good chance the sedative has cleared her system. But no promises. She may need a few more hours. Or she may be tired and fall into a natural sleep. If that's the case, be patient... she'll probably be able to speak to us tomorrow."

Molly remained at the window, viewing the activity inside. Randy held Jill's hand, softly stroking her arm as Dr. Lange walked into the room, lowered the lights to a soft glow and moved to the other side of Jill's bed. He left Jill's door ajar, allowing Molly to hear the verbal exchanges.

"Jill? Wake up, Jill. Can you open your eyes?" Dr. Lange asked. He raised his voice slightly and called her name. "Jill? Jill? This is Dr. Lange. Can you hear me?" He took her hand. "Squeeze my hand, Jill, if you can hear me."

Jill must have applied pressure to the doctor's hand because he smiled at Randy.

"Good girl," Dr. Lange gushed. "Now, try to open your eyes; even a little if you can."

Molly thought Jill's lashes fluttered but she didn't see them open.

Dr. Lange stroked Jill's hand. "Jill, dear, I'm here with Randy. He's holding your left hand. Will you squeeze his hand?"

Jill remained still for a moment then, without opening her eyes, turned her head a few degrees to the left then the right and back to the left. Her eyebrows pinched together as if she was confused or possibly trying to remember something. She slowly sucked in a breath and slightly raised her chin. If she moved her hand, Molly didn't see it.

Randy pulled himself more erect. He grinned as tears slipped down his face. He lifted Jill's hand toward his face as he tipped his head and kissed it. She didn't appear to resist. "That's great, Sweetheart. Great. Please try to open your eyes."

Molly leaned closer to the glass. Jill's lashes fluttered, but only for a moment. Molly crossed her fingers. Then it happened. Jill opened her eyes, turned her head and looked at Randy. She pulled her hand from his and her facial expression became more relaxed. She seemed to take another deep breath then closed her eyes.

"She has fallen asleep," Dr. Lange said to Randy then turned to give Molly an okay sign. "Randy, she'll probably sleep until early morning. If you come by on your way to work, there's a good chance she'll be fully awake."

It was nearly nine that evening when Molly arranged a conference call to Pilson and Schmidt. She described her hospital visit, suggesting they might be able to speak with Jill Bronson in a few days. They expressed their pleasure and thanked her for the call.

"Don't hang up; I have something I want to tell you." She didn't pause long enough for them to comment. "I went out to Harmony Farm to look at the crime scene again—as you know. It dawned on me as I drove home just now, although we have a mold of the shoe or boot print, nobody noticed tire tracks—other than Randy's truck. I have no doubt the crime scene techs did a careful search of the area, and if they didn't spot any treads, they had no reason to mention it. Anyway, I'm going to go back in the morning just to double-check for my own piece of mind." She paused to grab a breath. "Here's the deal, I haven't been able to complete all the employee interviews. Could you guys meet me there in the morning and lend a hand?"

"I can be there by nine," Pilson said. "I'll come straight from home."

"Me, too," Schmidt chimed in.

"That's great. If we don't find any tire marks, we'll know whoever dragged Jerrod out of his truck had to be on foot and not concerned about being seen at night on ranch property. Most likely an employee."

- 17 -

On Thursday morning, Schmidt and Pilson drove into Harmony Farm and parked behind Molly's car near the outdoor riding ring. Like Molly, they had stopped along the way for coffee. Steam rose from their paper cups as they walked to the front of Molly's ride where she leaned against the front fender. The breeze cooled her face and rustled her auburn hair.

She grinned at the men as they balanced their cups in front of them.

"Hey guys. I stopped at Nordale's Nursery, the place I mentioned to you yesterday. The tree wholesaler who supplies Nordale was there. He looked at my pictures of what I thought was a tree but, couldn't come up with anything. He thought it was more likely a leaf. So we struck out there."

Molly sipped her coffee and threw the last of it into the weeds near the fence rail. "I also talked with George Harmon. He told me we can use the conference room next to the manager's office in the stallion barn, plus a couple of rooms in the main house." She swatted at a troublesome fly. "If you don't mind, I'd like the conference room. Mrs. Harmon is expecting you at the house. You'll like being there. She'll treat you like invited guests... that's how she rolls. I want to talk with both Dr. Briggs and the ranch manager, Gene Belmont, and be certain we are not overheard."

"All fine by me," Larry Pilson said. Schmidt nodded in agreement.

"Mr. Harmon prepared a list of the employees I haven't talked to yet." Molly tore the notepaper in half and handed the lower portion to Schmidt and the upper to Pilson. You'll each have three employees. She tapped on Schmidt's wrist. "Arnie, you have Jim Harmon on your list, only child of the owners. He's a nice guy and he'll have answers for all your questions. We should be done by noon. Let's keep in touch by text."

Molly waited by the fender of her car, watching the two detectives stroll toward the Harmons' personal residence. After they walked into the house, she headed across the graveled lane and entered Gene Belmont's office.

"Good morning, Gene. Can you spare me a few minutes to answer some questions?"

Gene's face lit with a friendly smile. "I've been expecting you. Mr. Harmon alerted me this morning that you'd be along. How are you? It's nice to see you again."

"I'm fine. This investigation is keeping me busy." She motioned to the conference room door. "Can we talk in there? I want to be certain our conversation confidential."

"Not a problem." He stood and followed her.

Molly set up her recorder and placed it on the table before she sat down. As soon as Gene was seated, she pressed the record button, stated the date and their names then began the interview.

"When did you first meet Jerrod Bronson?"

"I met him when he pitched us to use him as our farrier. He's been shoeing horses for us about eighteen months. He was skilled and I liked him well enough."

"How did you find him?"

"Alphonso Munoz recommended we give him a chance. I asked him to make a regular shoe and a corrective shoe, which he did. The sample shoes he made were damned impressive."

"Did you spend much time with the man?"

Gene shook his head. "Nah. He'd check in with me when he arrived in the morning. I'd give him the list of horses Mr. Harmon had prepared, and/or the list the trainers wanted shod. Jim Harmon was the only trainer allowed to request a corrective shoe. Jerrod and I would extend pleasantries, and he'd go to work. That's about all."

"The other day you mentioned he often rode into the mountains. Which mountains?"

"Dang, you have a good memory. The Whites. He'd pull a horse trailer up to either Pine or Payson and ride for a couple of days. Somebody told me Jerrod had some forest land up there and in good weather he liked to camp out. Alphonso went with him fairly often, but I'm not sure he was into camping."

"You gave me the phone number of a motel in Pine where he would sometimes stay. Do you know anything about the place?"

"Not really. I learned about it from Alphonso. Want to know anything 'round here, ask Alphonso. He told me they had a barn, so the horses didn't have to stay in the trailer overnight. He was probably afraid I wouldn't lend him my horse if he didn't tell me about the horse barn."

"You loaned him your personally owned horse?"

"To Alphonso? Hell yeah. He's a super horseman. Some of our best young guys have come up from Mexico. He maybe our best junior trainer."

"You ride much?"

"Did a fair amount until last year. Took a hell of a nasty fall—messed up my knee. Since then, I've ridden only in the larger round bullpen a few times." He chuckled. "I don't want my horse to forget me. I've only been here a little more than a year; he's the only friend I've got."

"What do you know about Jerrod's forest land? When he bought it? Why he bought it? Strikes me as strange he'd want to spend his money on a land parcel when he's starting a new business. I wonder how he found it and the money to buy it."

Gene shrugged. "I don't know the answers to *any* of those questions, but I see your point. I never thought about it. Maybe it was his parents. He might have inherited."

Molly stared at Gene, contemplating the idea Jill's family may know about the land. She made a mental note to follow up. "I heard he and Cindy were romantically involved. What can you tell me about that?"

"Not a damned thing. That shouldn't be happening. If the Harmons find out about it, they'll can her ass." He glared at the wall behind Molly. "Who told you that?"

"I'm afraid I can't say. All my interviews are confidential." She cleared her throat. "How well do you know Cindy?"

"Not well. She pretty much stays at the house. A while back she used to ride her horse in the outdoor arena, but I haven't seen her there for quite a while. She did say the workload had increased a lot in the last year because of the international semen shipments. Mrs. Harmon has assigned her the job of preparing all the stallion breeding reports for the American Arabian Horse Registry. Having six breeding stallions makes for a lot of work when it comes to the annual report."

"I'm curious. Do you ship a lot of semen overseas?"

He nodded. "Quite a bit. It's been a good market for us."

"Which countries?"

"England, Spain, and Portugal. We also have buyers in the Middle East, South America, and Australia." He smiled. "One of our junior trainers landed a job with a big Arabian horse ranch in Argentina. He's been gone nearly a year. He says he loves it there."

"How do you keep the semen viable while in shipment?"

"The vials go out in a small cooler with dry ice. Works well. Haven't had many problems."

Molly smiled. "Amazing how far the Arabian horse industry has come—shipping stallion semen around the world. I remember when artificial insemination wasn't allowed."

"Yep. And now it carries a live foal guarantee if inseminated by a licensed Vet. It's very popular these days. Saves the mare owners a lot of money they don't have to spend on travel, lodging, and time away from work." He gave her a soft smile. "If you have time, I'd like to take you for coffee. We could speak more about it. Of course, dinner would be better. Would that work?"

She smiled gently. "I appreciate the invitation, but because I'm working on Jerrod's murder here at the ranch, it would be a conflict of interest."

"Not surprised. Maybe sometime in the future. I like talking to you."

Molly stood, believing it was time to end the interview. "Thank you, Gene. May I call on you with future questions? I have no doubt I'll have more to ask." She dropped her recorder and phone into her bag and turned for the door adjoining the office.

Gene remained standing by his chair. "Of course, anytime." He paused and smiled at her. "Maybe then I can convince you to go to dinner with me. I like you, Molly. I'd like to know you better."

She smiled a kindly smile. "I really can't."

He grinned. "Can't blame a fella for trying."

- 18 -

As Molly and Gene left the conference room, he cut through his office to the back door adjoining the stallion barn. Molly walked out to the wide front porch to wait for Dr. Briggs. According to her watch, he should arrive in less than five minutes. Relaxing in a director's chair, she watched one of the trainers work a western pleasure horse in the outdoor training ring. In a nearby pasture to her left, mares and their foals grazed on the abundant grass. It was pleasant for the first five minutes then her impatience began to spike. She glanced again at her watch. Briggs was ten minutes late.

She dialed the number on Dr. Spelling's card to inquire about Briggs, but before he picked up, Dr. Briggs rounded the corner of the building in his electric golf cart. The motor was so quiet she hadn't heard it coming. Briggs parked the cart and bounded in her direction.

"Sorry, ma'am. Seems there's always something gettin' in the way." Briggs introduced himself and handed Molly his business card at the same time. He was a big man, nearly six and a half feet tall. Molly guessed he weighed around three hundred pounds, although he moved like a man half his size.

His blue eyes glittered when he smiled and when they shook hands, her hand disappeared in his gentle grip.

"We can use the conference room," she said as she turned to lead the way.

When they were seated with Molly's recorder operating, she asked, "How long have you worked here, Dr. Briggs?"

"Please, ma'am, call me Mitch. I've been here 'bout four years. Mr. Harmon gave me the pleasure of setting up the AI system. That's artificial insemination."

"Yes, I know what it is."

"Of course. I even designed the building. The lab has all the latest technology, and next year we're plannin' a state-of-the-art operating room. We don't have a lot of trouble with horses colicking, but we do have our share. With the new operating facility, we'll be able to operate in time to save more horses than we do now. To lose a horse to colic is heartbreaking."

"You're proud of the facility you've created, I see."

"You betcha. Would you like a tour one of these days?"

She laughed. "You betcha." Molly teased. "As my grandma used to say with a gleam in her eye." Molly picked up her pen. "Seriously, I would like to see your facility." She paused. "Where did you go to veterinary school?"

"Lexington Large Animal Veterinary College after four years at University of Tennessee." His face registered the pride he took in his educational history.

"That's a beautiful part of the country."

"Yes, ma'am."

Molly cleared her throat. "Now, what can you tell me about Jerrod Bronson?"

"I didn't know him. That is, I knew who he was, but I had no dealings with the fellow. Dr. Spelling did on occasion, but not me. We don't shoe horses at the AI facility. They hafta be walked over to Bronson's rig for shoein'. That's why it was such a surprise to learn Bronson's truck was parked in front of my building when he was killed." He raked his fingers through his gray-tinged hair. "We sure didn't need something like this happenin' right now with all the work we've got on our plate."

"Are you usually busy this time of year?"

"Not like this year. My guess is our program has caught on throughout the industry—throughout the world. We're shippin' more semen this fall than the last two falls combined."

"Where were you when you learned of Jerrod's death?"

"Still in the rack, tryin' not to wake up right then. I'd been late gettin' back from Casa Grande the night before. Allowed myself a little extra snoozin' that morning. Spelling woke me up, callin' to tell me what happened. Got my ass in gear the minute I hung up the phone. Sure as hell, never expected to wake up hearin' about a murder. Do you have any idea who did it?"

"It's too early in our investigation. Along with Dr. Spelling, who else helps with the work you do?"

"I work alone in the lab most of the time. Get help now and then from Spelling. Big Bev walks the stallions over when it's time to collect 'em. We collect Rothman regularly, the other stallions not so much. They usually cover the mares. A one and done, if you get my drift." Molly nodded, and Briggs continued, "Billy Fenton, one of our junior trainers, handles the collection sleeve for me. See I'm too big to get out from under a horse before he comes down from the breedin' dummy. Sure don't want a flying hoof to knock my brains out.

"I also call on a junior trainer or two to help out if the stallion's a little on the green side. The young colts need time to acquire experience for doin' their part. First in my mind is keeping all of us safe—don't want nobody gettin' hurt. And sure as hell, don't want to harm a stallion cuzz of a silly-ass accident." He spread his long arms wide. "So ya see, we simply do what we have to do to get the job done. And around here, we do it pretty damn well."

"What about Rothman?"

"He's a dream. Knows his job like the pro he is. He's taught me a lot. When he walks into the collection arena, he's ready to deliver."

Molly nodded. She'd lived around horses long enough to be familiar with the vernacular.

Briggs looked at his watch. "Far as ole Jerrod's concerned, I'm afraid there's not much I can tell ya."

"I have one more question. How do you go about shipping semen? I understand it travels in dry ice, but do you simply take it to the post office?"

"No, ma'am, a commercial carrier comes here to the ranch and picks up the out-going product. They provide the efficiency we need. Prompt delivery is an important part of the process."

"Thank you, Dr. Briggs. You have been very helpful." She handed him her card. "If you think of anything, anything at all, please call me."

"Yes, ma'am, I sure will. Maybe next time you come our way you'll tour our facility. I do love showin' it off."

Molly extended her hand. He took it in both of his. "I enjoyed our visit, Detective." His voice moved up an octave. "Ya'll come back now."

"You can count on it, Dr. Briggs."

Molly left the conference room and headed for her car. On her way her phone buzzed. Schmidt's text read, "I just finished last interview. Mrs. Harmon wants to talk with you. I think it's important. Pilson isn't done. So no hurry."

Molly headed for the house. She couldn't remember a time when Doris Harmon wanted to talk with her about something important.

- 19 -

The late afternoon sun cast long shadows across the lawn. Mrs. Harmon opened the door before Molly finished knocking.

Mrs. Harmon said as she backed up, "Molly, sweetheart, c'mon in. Thank you for coming," she whispered. "That nice detective said he'd get hold of you."

Molly dropped her voice. "What is it? You look upset. Is it about your lovely ring?"

Mrs. Harmon frowned. "No—well, yes. But there's more." She reached for Molly's hand. "We need privacy."

Doris Harmon led Molly across a small, landscaped area to the guesthouse and locked the door once they were both inside. "Sit down, dear. I have an awful thing to discuss with you. Simply awful. I know it probably isn't your area of endeavor, but I need your advice." She paused. "Am I keeping you? Do you have time?" She headed for an overstuffed sofa, sat, and patted the cushion beside her.

Molly sat where Mrs. Harmon obviously wanted her. "I'm not on the clock. Take all the time you need. My gosh, what is it?"

"I'll start from the beginning. You know we must record all the information regarding a mare that is serviced by one of our stallions, you understand?"

"Yes."

"Each stallion has his own report identifying the mares he has bred. Once a year all the stallion reports are sent to the American Arabian Horse Registry. They confirm the sire's name and registration number when the resulting foal is registered with them."

"I understand." She reached for Mrs. Harmons' hand. "I can see by your face how upset you are. What is it?"

Mrs. Harmon dropped her voice nearly to a whisper. "For each vial of Rothman's semen we send to a breeder for artificial insemination, we are paid $25,000. We charge less for other stallions. A licensed veterinarian must send us a signed statement indicating he or she administered the insemination if it isn't done here. If a live foal does not result for any reason, we rebreed the mare the next year. If Rothman isn't available, we substitute one of our other stallions and adjust pricing if the mare owner agrees."

"Okay, I see."

"Well, two nights ago, around nine o'clock, I couldn't recall if I'd told Cindy about a semen shipment that was sent to replace one that wasn't delivered in the time allotted. I went into her office to leave her a note and noticed the stallion report for Rothman was on her computer screen. I don't know why she hadn't shut down her computer. It's a rule around here. Privacy is important. I always close mine in my office. Cindy usually closes hers, too.

"Because I'm the treasurer for all our farm business, and I still do the ranch accounting prep and pay the taxes, I always know how much money has been earned by Rothman's breedings to date, as well as the customers who purchased each vial. I discovered there were three more breedings than we have been paid for. That's a lot of money not accounted for. I can't explain it to our accountants."

Molly stared at her. "$75,000, wow! She glanced at the small, beautiful statuette of an Arabian foal standing in the center of the coffee table. "Are you sure about this? Is there any way you could be wrong? Have you checked with your accountants?"

"No, but I plan to, although, there's no reason I can think of how they'd be helpful. I work with Gene and Cindy on it. But we do send all our info to the accountants at year end for them to do our taxes—then I write the check. We have always used a dual-entry accounting system. I account for sales income in a different ledger than breeding income. Rothman has his own ledger because of his breeding success. I also have a ledger for our auction sales. When checks or payments for breeding fees come in, they are recorded in the appropriate ledger then deposited in the bank ASAP. We certainly don't keep that kind of money here in the house. There is no doubt in my mind three breeding fees are missing, because there is no mention of a cash sale or installment contract in Rothman's ledger under the names of the clients listed on Rothman's stallion report."

Molly nodded. "I see." She reached again for Mrs. Harmon's trembling hand. "I don't have an answer for you, but I will speak to my boss about it in the morning. I've never handled this type of investigation; you need to discover what has happened. Any fraudulent business activity would require a forensic accountant to investigate. I *can* say you should continue to pay close attention to all breeding and financial transactions. Check at the end of each work day if that isn't your habit."

"Oh, I will."

"Have you asked Cindy about it? She's in charge of the stallion reports, right?"

"Yes, but not income received. That's my job. Cindy said she handles all the breeding reports the same. She didn't seem to think we should be concerned."

"Does George know about this?"

"No, not yet. I haven't wanted to tell him because I worry he'll become so upset he could have another heart attack. It's big money, sweetheart. Our overhead is surprisingly large. Besides the cost of horse feed—it is enormous, there's maintenance, and utilities for this big place. You'd die if you saw our electrical bills. We have travel expense, entertainment expense… well, you can imagine, what with the auction expenses. Besides, you know what it costs just to enter a horse in the different classes at the shows." She rolled her eyes. "And our show string has had so many horses these past few years. Seventy-five thousand sounds like a lot of money, and it is, but without it we'll be in a world of trouble."

"I know you're right. I haven't shown a horse in ten years, but even then, the cost to ship a horse, rent stable space, cover hotel and meal expense, decorate our stalls, and enter all the classes I wanted, took every dime I could scrape up. If Mom hadn't been able to make my show clothes, I could never have afforded to show my horse."

Mrs. Harmon reached for Molly and hugged her. "Oh, sweetheart, we're so lucky to have you in our lives. It's like having a daughter. God bless you, my darling."

Tears came to Molly's eyes. "I know you're worried, and rightfully so, but we'll figure it out. First thing, promise me you'll tell George tonight. After dinner, pour him a double scotch—from his best bottle, and tell him he must remain calm when he hears what you have to tell him. Let him know you've talked to me and I'm seeking proper help."

Mrs. Harmon's hands trembled. "Oh, my dear, what would I have done without you?"

Molly glanced at the clock on the fireplace mantle. "My detectives will be ready to go soon. Tell me, what's new with your missing ring? Have you found it?"

"No, that's another thing I'm going to have to confess to George. I'm afraid my darling husband will think I'm turning into an addlepated old woman. How could I lose a four-carat diamond?"

"Gosh, Mrs. Harmon, you have had a terrible run of bad luck in the past few weeks. I'm so sorry. Why don't you hold off on telling George about your ring in hopes it turns up soon."

"You're right, sweetheart. That's what I'll do. I'll discuss the missing fees with George and postpone worrying him over my ring."

Molly caught up with Pilson and Schmidt sitting on the back bumper of her car. "I'm sorry. I hadn't expected my visit with Mrs. Harmon to take so long. Let's get together at headquarters and discuss what we've learned today. I must talk to Sergeant Hilliard about another matter and want to catch him before he leaves for the day."

- 20 -

As planned, Molly met with Schmidt and Pilson in the Violent Crimes Bureau conference room. Their meeting followed Molly's conversation with their boss, Sergeant Hilliard, regarding her suspicion someone was embezzling large sums of money from Harmony Farm. Hilliard said he would notify the Financial Crimes Detail and request they contact the Harmons.

Molly shared with her partners the facts behind Mrs. Harmon's discovery of missing breeding fees. "There's a good chance this fraudulent activity may be connected to the murder of Jerrod Bronson. It may also overlap his sister's attack. Or the crimes may not be related at all."

Larry Pilson said, "So far, we're looking at a case for fraud and a case for murder, plus the attack on Jerrod Bronson's sister, Jillian. We really don't have anything yet to support the sister's connection. Have you seen her, Molly, since she came out of the coma?"

"I'm going to the hospital later today. Did either of you come up with usable info from the ranch hands you interrogated today?"

"I may have a couple of leads worth following," Arnie Schmidt said. "I spoke with two trainers and a groom, as you know. They told me the ranch's head trainer is the Harmons' son, Jimmy. Where is he in all this?"

Molly stared at Arnie. "I'm sorry, I should have mentioned it. Jimmy Harmon was in Australia when Jerrod was murdered, teaching a trainers' clinic. He arrived home a day or two ago. On my first trip to the farm, George Harmon, his dad, mentioned Jim was gone. I crossed him off my list of people to question since he was out of the country, and I forgot about him."

"Understandable," Schmidt muttered. "Should we put him back on our list?"

"Yes. Considering what may be going on with the international semen sales, we should—if only to clear his name." She shook her head, annoyed with herself for overlooking Jimmy. "What else have you learned?"

Schmidt tapped his notes. "According to the two trainers and groom I spoke with, the Harmons' son is very good at his job. Apparently, they weren't blowin' smoke. Mrs. Harmon showed me the collection of Arabian National trophies he's won. I counted eight National Championships and two Reserve National Championships." He turned to Pilson. "Winning reserve means you placed second. Get it? Winning at the National's, or taking second, is really a big deal."

"It sure is," Molly agreed. "I've known Jimmy Harmon a long time. He's a world-class trainer. Did you learn anything else about him?"

Schmidt shrugged. "Not really. I got the impression he doesn't spend much social time with the crew. He's too busy. Besides training horses for the farm, he trains for others, too. It appears the ranch has a barn full of outside horses in for training. Now I understand why they have the number of trainers they've hired. Jimmy sometimes hangs out with Big

Bev after hours, and it's not unusual for him to take the training staff out to dinner occasionally—probably to make up for the little time they spend socializing. In all my discussions, the unpaid semen sales never came up. I doubt the crew knows about it."

"Anything else?" Molly asked.

Schmidt said, "A junior trainer, John Atchison, said Jerrod was seeing the ranch secretary, Cindy, on the side, but they both were very discreet because of ranch rules. He gave me the name of the place where they frequently met." Schmidt scribbled *Whistler's Grill* on his notepaper and pushed it to Molly.

Molly tucked the note into her portfolio. "Is the place patronized by other ranch employees?"

Pilson gave a nod. "I heard *Whistler's* mentioned by one of the grooms. Sounds like it's too pricey for the barn crew, but some of the trainers go there. That's where Jimmy Harmon took the trainers to dinner occasionally. Are you planning on talking to him, Molly?"

"Yes. I don't expect to get much from him. He wasn't home when the murder occurred. What about Mrs. Harmon's missing ring? Any mention of it?"

Pilson shook his head. "Nope. I asked all three guys, and none knew it was missing."

Molly turned to Schmidt. "How about you?"

"No. I asked about the ring, but nobody had an answer. The three guys on my list are married. Occasionally the three couples go out with the others to local bars on the weekends. They mentioned a place called *Dempsey's Off Shea.*" Molly noted it in her phone. "I asked about other employees and discovered we have a few liars in the crowd or they're not in the know. It was unanimous Alphonso Munoz flirts with all the girls and can't pass a mirror without admiring himself. No crime in that. Gene, the ranch manager, is liked. He's fair-minded in the way he deals with staff, does his job, but doesn't socialize with employees much. Probably too busy. One of the grooms said Gene divorced a couple of years ago. Didn't know why."

"I heard that about Gene, too," Pilson said. "You talked to him today, Molly. What did you find out?"

She shared her conversation with the ranch manager, mentioning the forest land Jerrod owned. "It may be nothing, but I plan on asking Jill Bronson about it when I see her at the hospital later today." Molly glanced from Pilson to Schmidt. "We should interview both vets regarding the questionable semen sales—Gene and Cindy, too. I also think Alphonso needs to tell us a lot more about his activities with Jerrod Bronson."

Molly raked her fingers through her hair. "I have a nagging suspicion this semen issue is related to the murder—and Jill's attack. We're talking seventy-five thousand dollars—maybe more. And that's just recently." Her brow furrowed. "I mean—for some people, what's a murder or two when that kind of money is at play?"

- 21 -

Molly arrived at the hospital a little before five o'clock, signed in at the ICU nurses' station and asked for Andrea, Jill Bronson's care nurse. A few minutes later, Andrea hurried toward her, waving both hands in a friendly gesture..

"I thought I might see you today." Andrea smiled.

"I'm sorry I didn't come sooner; it's been a busy day. How is Jill? Can I talk to her?"

Andrea motioned Molly to follow her back to Jill's room. "She's doing as well as expected. She's sore all over, of course. We have her on painkillers."

As they approached Jill's corner room, Andrea said, "No more than five minutes."

Molly opened the door and walked softly into the room. It saddened her to see Jill so helpless. Jill's tubes were as numerous as before and her bandages appeared to be fresh. The only encouragement Molly took from Jill's appearance was the energy that shown in her eyes. Jill watched in silence as Molly approached. Molly slowly moved closer and introduced herself. "I can only stay a few minutes. Would you mind if I asked you a few questions?"

Jill raised her hand, beckoning Molly to come closer. "Randy told me you'd be here," she said just above a whisper.

"Does Randy come often?"

Jill gave a barely noticeable nod. "I tell him he doesn't have to, but he comes every day before and after work. He brought all those flowers you may have seen at the nurses' station. They won't let me have them in my room. He's so kind. Says the nurses like having them. He's going to bring me milkshakes." She chuckled.

"Are you in pain?"

"Not too bad. They give me pills for it."

"I'm investigating what happened to you. Do you remember your attack?"

"Not much. I think the man was young. He had black hair on his arms.

"Perhaps he's Hispanic. Did you see his face?"

"I don't think so. It happened so fast. I didn't have time to really look at him. But then, I don't think I could have raised my head; he'd hit it so hard." She paused. "I think he was kinda tall. I don't think he was fat."

"Did you see his clothes?"

"Not really. Jeans and a T-shirt, maybe. I'm not sure." Her eyes brightened. "I remember his shoes. They were ugly—red, green, and yellow. The band around the bottoms used to be white—when they were new." Jill spoke so softly, Molly worried she wasn't hearing her correctly.

"His shoes were dirty?"

"Yes. Old. I think his clothes were old, too. I tried to keep my head down, so I mostly saw the stuff on the ground." Again, she brightened. "I think one tattoo was new. There was a bandage over part of it."

"What did it look like—the part you saw?"

Jill spoke more rapidly. "I'm not sure. An animal maybe. Could have been a dog's head. I remember its ears. One was pointed and the other was broken... or missing. I don't know."

Molly stepped closer and tenderly touched Jill's ankle. "Are you happy to see Randy?"

"Oh, yes. I feel safe when he's here." She pointed to her facial bandages. "He tells me not to worry about my face. Says I'll always be pretty." She stared up at Molly. "But I still worry. I'm afraid he'll think I'm ugly when he sees my face. There was so much blood.... A plastic surgeon is coming tomorrow. I don't want him to come when Randy is here. I don't want Randy to see me."

Molly struggled to keep her tears from falling. It appeared Jill was still in love with her husband. "I'm so sorry this happened to you." She lightly stroked her ankle. "Believe your doctors. I'm sure you'll be as beautiful as the picture Randy showed me."

"Pink cap and ponytail?"

Molly's heart thumped. "That's the one."

"It's his favorite. It used to be in a little frame next to his bedside." She paused. "I'm so lucky Randy's my husband. He's always so kind. If only he'd been with me, this wouldn't have happened... and I wouldn't be in this place."

"Do you see your brother, Jerrod, often?"

"Not anymore. I told him never to come to my house because he stole from me. He was in jail for a while. I couldn't trust him."

"What do you know about Jerrod's forest land? How he came by it?"

"I've never heard of any land."

"Did he like to ride horses? Did he own any?"

"I don't know if he owns a horse. When we were kids, Mom would take us to a riding academy where we could ride. Jerrod liked that."

Molly stepped back. "I can see you're tiring. This is enough for today. I'd like to visit with you again if you don't mind."

"I'd enjoy the company, but I don't remember much about what happened."

"Sometimes it's the little things that make the difference. I would like to bring my partners the next time I come. I'll see you again in a few days." Molly smiled and turned for the door.

Molly's sadness lifted as she pulled into the parking area of Lar's apartment house. If she were lucky, little Tony would be there, too. He was such a spunky child. Seeing them was just what she needed to lift her spirits. Even though she'd spoken only briefly with Jill Bronson, it was hard to shake the blues after seeing how injured she was. How could one human wreak such violence on another? Perpetrators of pure meanness must have a missing link in their psyche. Molly felt more hopeful when she recalled the way Jill spoke of Randy. Jill must not remember they were in the process of divorcing.

Molly parked in the last row of vehicles across from the apartment building and stepped from her car, the keys clamped in her hand. She smile at the thought of seeing Lar, recalling the warmth of his arms when he held her. If there was ever a time she needed his hug, it was now. As she stepped back to shut the driver's door, she glanced toward his navy-blue door. A petite woman walked out of his apartment with Lar close behind. The late afternoon sun glinted off a gold clip she wore in her long black hair. The woman turned back to Lar and embraced him. They kissed with an apparent level of passion... not fit for his mother to see.

The keys slipped from Molly's hand.

- 22 -

Molly picked up the car keys and looked back at Lar's closed door. She wanted to face him and demand answers, but hesitated. She didn't want to appear desperate, or worse, needy. She paused to think it through before whispering to herself, *no way in hell*. She unlocked her vehicle, slid behind the wheel, and piled her hands on the steering wheel. She rested her forehead on top of her hands. *Who was that woman?*

Sadness overwhelmed her. Did relationships always have to end this way? The woman's hair was dark like little Tony's, but she wasn't Tony's mother. Lar's wife had been dead for several years. So where did this woman fit in Lar's life? Did it matter? *Hell yes, it mattered.* Relationships were meant for two, not three. Molly had been through this before, and by damn, she wouldn't go through it again.

Heartache gripped Molly like a mighty fist. Clamping her jaw, she accepted what she'd seen. She wiped away a tear, refused to cry, started the car, and headed for home. There was one never-fail cure for heartbreak. *Speed and chocolate.* When she got home she'd make fudge—rich, gooey fudge. She loved to cook. It was the only thing she'd found that blocked the invasion of unwanted thoughts. She stomped on the gas and sped from the scene. Tomorrow, she'd face the sonofabitch.

Molly spread the pictures Doris Harmon had given her in even rows across her breakfast table. She started with the Harmon family, followed by trainers and grooms then all the ranch hands. The last row contained the stall cleaners and groundskeepers. She bit into her third piece of candy as she rearranged the photos.

When she picked up Gene Beaumont's picture, she wondered how long ago he'd divorced. Next, she inserted Cindy's picture, placing it next to Gene's. They were both attractive. Had they been involved? So far, nobody had suggested that might be the case. She'd bring it up to him next time she saw him. Maybe going out for coffee as he suggested could make a difference. They could talk about staff in a more casual setting.

With so many young men and women working closely together six days a week—sometimes seven—it wouldn't be the first-time jealousy caused a murder. It dawned on her she didn't have a picture of Jimmy Harmon then remembered there was one of her with him on her personal phone. She'd print it and add it to the group. Jimmy was another guy in which Cindy might have an interest. Trainers and Arabian horse owners across the United States and in Europe admired and looked up to Jim. Besides Jimmy's broad personal reputation in the horse industry, Cindy might find his being the owners' son even more attractive.

Molly studied the photos, contemplating who would have something to gain by being involved in the crimes committed. At five past ten that evening she gathered up the pictures in order, placed them in the manila envelope and stored it in her evidence bag. As she carried her plate, dotted with candy crumbs, along with her empty milk glass into the kitchen, she thought of the personal questions she hadn't asked during the interviews.

Sleep didn't come easily. Images of Lar and the woman outside his apartment door spun in her brain as if in a never-ending loop. At two a.m. she threw back the covers, ran fingers through her tousled hair and angrily padded to the kitchen. She poured a half glass of milk, munched down another chunk of fudge and swore off men.

The next morning as Molly dressed for work, her cell phoned played *Mac the Knife*. The caller ID window displayed Lar's name. At first she ignored the call then changed her mind. She tried not to sound upset with him when she answered, but it was a challenge.

"Hey, babe, I thought you might have come by last night. I cooked a few of your favorites."

"I did come by then changed my mind."

"Really? Why?"

"I saw you kissing that woman outside your door. It was obvious she wasn't your sister and certainly not your mother."

Lar hesitated before saying, "I can explain—"

"I'm not interested." Molly smacked the button ending the call.

She finished dressing and dabbed on a little makeup. Her phone's timer buzzed, reminding her she was about to be late and propelled her out the door. It was important she be the first to show up for her shift.

By the time she arrived at the precinct, weariness had set in, slowing her steps. She dragged herself inside and, still in her coat, sat in Pilson's desk chair to wait for him. Ten minutes later, Pilson entered his cubicle and stopped short. "Molly? What's going on? Are you okay?"

"I'm fine," she grumbled. "OD'ed on chocolate last night. I do that sometimes."

"You sound angry. Depressed even. What's happened? Why are you sitting here, still in your coat?"

"Wanted to catch you the very minute you arrived. Listen, we have to be overlooking something in the Jerrod Bronson murder case. I don't know what, but something. We agree we've been lied to. It's time to cut through the lies. As soon as Schmidt gets here. Sooner the better."

Molly stood, stepped around Pilson, and headed for her cubicle. She'd taken only a few steps when her cell phone vibrated. It was Lar.

- 23 -

When Schmidt joined Molly and Pilson in the conference room, Schmidt looked at Molly and did a double take.

"What the hell happened to you? You look terrible."

She waved him off. "Had a little trouble sleeping last night. I'm fine." She glanced from one man to the other. "We're nowhere with the Jerrod Bronson murder. I'm serious. We have to change our approach."

Pilson frowned. "What do you suggest?"

"I'd like you to go out to the ranch and wander around, talk to anybody you encounter. My gut tells me there is something going on out there that we're missing. Take the casual approach. See if it adds to what we already know. Most of these people are still kids. Talking to a cop in a formal setting might be intimidating. While you admire all the pretty horses, see if you can get some information on who runs around with whom; is anybody in a serious relationship; has anybody recently suffered a breakup? If so, with whom? Has anyone been fired recently? Does anyone suddenly have a lot of money to spend? You know, the kind of gossip young people thrive on.

"While you're doing that, I'll check out the two restaurants Schmidt came up with. See what I can find out."

"Right," Schmidt said. "I hope to visit the hospital—talk to Jerrod's sister. Do you think it's too soon?"

Molly paused. "I'll call ahead to Andrea, Jill's care nurse, and let her know you want to stop by. If Jill isn't up to visitors today, it'll save you a wasted trip."

"Great," Schmidt said. "Text me and let me know. If it doesn't work, I'll also spend some time at the ranch."

She stood and picked up her bag. "Let's meet back here around four o'clock."

Molly drove by *Whistler's* restaurant and realized it was open only for dinner, so she drove on to *Dempsey's off Shea*. According to their sign, they were open for lunch. Molly suspected someone would be there by now, prepping for the lunch crowd. She parked her car next to the building and walked around to the front door.

An older woman who identified herself as Linda Thoms, owner/manager, greeted her. Molly introduced herself, showed her ID and asked if Linda could spare several minutes of her time to answer a few questions.

"Of course. How can I help you, Detective?"

"I'm investigating a murder case and I'm wondering if you'd be kind enough to look at some photographs and tell me if you recognize anyone... possibly diners who frequent your restaurant. It's my understanding some, or possibly all, of the pictures are of people who spoke about coming frequently to your restaurant for dinner, maybe lunch as well."

"I'll do my best; these old eyes still work pretty good if there's adequate illumination. The lights are dimmed only slightly for the lunch crowd so it shouldn't be a problem. Still, I can't guarantee my accuracy. You know, getting older isn't a picnic, and I ain't lying."

Molly spread the photos Doris Harmon had given her across the nearby table. "I understand. But you don't look very old." Molly smiled at the woman. "Take your time and if you recognize anybody for any reason, please tell me."

Linda slowly studied each image. She did not react until she saw Alphonso. She laid a finger on the photo. "I've seen *him* in here, that's for sure. Mostly for lunch but a dinner or two."

"Did he come in alone?"

"No, usually with a lady. But a couple times he came in with one or more men. I remember him cause he flirted with me, if you can imagine that, and the other girls as well. They loved it, of course."

Molly turned Alphonso's picture face down. "Any others seem familiar?"

Linda tipped her head. "Let me see." She pointed to Cindy's photo. "She's the gal who usually came in with that other guy."

"Right," Molly replied. "Did they come in often?"

"About once a week, usually on Wednesdays." Linda continued to stare at the remaining photos. "This girl has been in with that same guy." She pointed to the picture of Big Bev. "Only once, I think. I remember her because I used to wear my hair like hers. You know that long ponytail." She smiled wistfully. "I used to have beautiful hair until I bleached the hell out of it." She chuckled and moved on to the next picture.

"Oh my, I recognize this fellow. I don't know his name, but he made a big deal of signing the check. I can't remember them all, though I do most regulars. I wouldn't call this guy a regular." Linda talked faster. "I remember him because I love men with salt and pepper gray hair. But what stands out in my memory was his beautiful wristwatch. I figgered he got it in Alaska somewhere. You know the kind—the fancy band. His had white ivory squares with engraved symbols on them. Maybe he got it in the Orient. It had a diamond in place of each number on the face with a gold nugget bezel. That's why I thought Alaska. You know—the nuggets."

"Did you talk with him about it?"

"Oh, no, I just took his order. I would have loved to talk with him though. He's my type—big, strong, all man. You know what I mean?"

Molly chuckled. "Yes, I do." She nodded to the last few pictures. "Anybody else?"

Linda tapped one with her finger. "This fellow comes in; often brings a handful of young guys for lunch. Sometimes there's a couple girls with him—that gal I already picked out and a younger one. I noticed them because they're all dressed in sloppy clothes and half dead boots. One kid's boots were held together with duct tape." She laughed and tapped the photo. "He wasn't dressed much better."

Linda glanced over the photos remaining face up. "Sorry I can't help you with the others. Did one of these people murder somebody?"

"The investigation is ongoing so I really can't talk about it."

A group of diners strolled into the restaurant and Linda waved to them. "I'll be right with you." She turned back to Molly. "I hope I've been helpful. Would you like to stay for lunch? On the house, of course. I enjoyed talkin' with ya. We serve a great Ruben sandwich."

"The Ruben sounds perfect, but I'll pay for it. I'll need the receipt." She turned for a table near a window. "I'll sit over there. The light's good. I can make some notes of our conversation."

The sandwich turned out as tasty as Linda said. Molly took her last sip of Coke, stuffed her notepad and pen into her bag and headed for the door. She stopped on her way out to pay the young man at the cash register and Linda approached her.

"Thanks for coming in, Detective," Linda said.

"Thank you for your help. The Ruben was perfect." She shook Linda's hand and headed out. It was nearly one o'clock when Molly left the parking lot.

Next stop, Whistler's Grill. She hoped she'd have as much success there.

- 24 -

Molly parked in the strip center's large lot and headed for the stand-alone building that was Whistler's Grill. It was always a little surprising to find an upscale restaurant located in or as part of a strip mall. But these days it was commonplace. Before leaving her car, Molly made the promised call to St. James Hospital then texted Schmidt. *Jill can see you today at Mathew's ICU. Good luck.*

The restaurant's front door was locked. Molly cupped her hands around her eyes and peered through the glass at the dim interior. Somebody moved around inside. Molly rapped her knuckles on the upper glass portion of the door next to the restaurant's logo, a silhouette of a whistling gentleman in overcoat and fedora, strolling with hands in his pants pockets.

The man inside acknowledged her pounding with a wave as he moved toward her. Seconds later, he opened the door and smiled. "Hello, can I help you?"

Molly returned his smile and explained who she was and why she was there. "Can you spare a few minutes to talk to me?"

"Of course. Always pleased to help." He pushed the door wider for her to enter. As she walked past him, he said, "By the way, my name is Curtis. I own this place."

The restaurant was well-laid out with a beautifully decorated interior. Molly silently vowed to bring her sister here for her next birthday. "Thanks, Curtis. I have a few pictures I'd like you to look at. Is there a place where we might have more light?"

"Yes ma'am. By all means. Let's go into the bar. I'll flip on the overheads."

The barroom smelled of disinfectant, more than the dining area had. When Molly placed the photos on the dark wooden bar, she felt a slight dampness on the highly varnished surface. "You must have recently cleaned in here," she remarked.

"Right. My cleaners at night do a good job, but I always redo the bar. People like to rest their forearms on a bar. Sure don't want it sticky. Check out my foot rail. I shine the brass every morning." Curtis smiled a wide happy smile. He was a tall man with the build of a football player. All in all a likeable guy.

Molly was tempted to ask if he'd played ball and where but thought better of it. "You're proud of your business I can tell, and it shows." She laid her hand next to the pictures. "Let's go from left to right. If you see someone you think you recognize, please let me know."

Curtis focused on each photo then tapped on Dr. Briggs' picture. I recognize this guy. He comes in two, three times a month. Nice guy."

"Does he bring anyone with him?"

"Yep, I see this little lady with him most of the time." He pointed to Cindy's face. "I've seen her in here quite a bit the last several months. She's becoming a regular. Brought several women with her the last time. But mostly, she accompanies a man."

"Always with the same man?"

"Oh, hell no." He pointed to Alphonso. "I've seen her come in with this guy a lot lately. And this guy, here." She tapped Jerrod Bronson's photo. "She used to come in with him a lot before the other guy."

"Did you get to know him?" She pointed at Jerrod's photo.

"Not really. He looked to be a workin' man. Never could quite get his hands washed clean."

"Interesting you noticed his hands," Molly said. "How did they act when they were together?"

"She treated every guy she came in with the same." He paused and stared at Molly. "She liked to cuddle, if you get my drift." He frowned slightly, acknowledging some discomfort with the conversation. "None of them guys minded."

"I suppose not." Molly cleared her throat. "Do you recognize anyone else?"

He pointed at Jim Harmon's picture. "I like this guy. I think he owns a ranch somewhere. I got the impression he brought people he wanted to treat, entertain, or impress. I could tell by how he dressed and acted. He knew how to be a host, if ya know what I mean. I liked that about him. He often ordered food for the entire crowd instead of having them order individually, same with the wines. He knew a lot about wine and good food." Curtis grinned as if remembering Jimmy's refinement. "The young man had class; I'll say that for him. My waitstaff could learn a thing or two from the guy."

"Did he ever bring a date with him?"

"I guess. Sometimes it would be him and a girl. Whenever he brought in a mixed group there was always a young woman sitting next to him."

"Do you see her photo here, Curtis?"

He chuckled. "This one; the one who liked to cuddle, and her. He brought the cuddler only once as I recall. The other woman came more often. She seemed like a sweet girl, soft-spoken and pretty in a country-girl way. Beautiful long blonde hair."

"Did you ever overhear their conversations?"

"Yeah. Couldn't help it. I'd come around with food or refill wine glasses and they'd be talkin' about horses. This guy seemed to be the horse-guru no matter the group."

Molly nodded. "I'd say that's accurate. You mentioned this man earlier." She gestured at Dr. Brigg's picture.

"Yeah, I think he is a veterinarian of some kind. He liked to put on the dog—pardon the pun. Seemed like he enjoyed the dazzling, wealthy, well-connected gentleman. You know... the big show. So did the Hispanic kid. But this fellow wasn't the flirty type; he acted the role of the man-about-town. Wore this big ole ring made of ivory with a diamond embedded in it. I recall the ivory had yellowed some, probably with age.

"He liked expensive scotch whiskey and, oh yeah, expensive champagne on some occasions. He'd order the fancy bottles with a kind of a dramatic flair. It seemed to be all about impressing the ladies. He liked to smoke cigars; that was his big deal. I'd pour the champagne and he'd light up this big ole cigar—like he was some important dude. And I'll tell ya, he dressed like one."

"Isn't your restaurant a non-smoking establishment?"

Curtis grinned. "Oh, yeah, but we got a private room, The Blue Velvet Room, off to one side of the building, with extra-good ventilation. We allow smoking. Only room we do allow it. We put a humidified cigar room in there alongside the wine cellar. Cigar smoking's never been a problem." He chuckled. "The cuddler especially liked the velvet room. She really turned it on back there."

"How do you mean?"

"Well, there's one big table in the center of the room and it seats up to fourteen—four on three sides. On the fourth side of the table there's a chaise lounge instead of chairs. Diners reserve the room and specify their menu choice ahead of time. It all comes for one set price and the room is theirs for the entire evening. He and the cuddler always sat on the chaise lounge. A couple times I walked in on them, and she was… let's say more sprawled than upright. The big shot looked kinda annoyed I had interrupted the business he was doing."

"It sounds like you don't care much for him."

"Correctamundo. I don't care for guys who throw their weight around tryin' to impress… especially around other men. When his group was all men, his voice always rose above the others. My mom used to say, 'If you're too busy talkin', you can't be learnin.'"

"Good advice. Would you take one more look at the pictures?"

"Sure." He focused on each remaining picture. "This guy came with the big fella a lot of the time, especially when they brought men from foreign countries. He talked like he was a veterinarian or something, too. He was a good bit smaller than the big guy."

Molly didn't comment.

Curtis chuckled. "There was one group… I couldn't recognize the foreign accents, but I'm pretty sure the men were Middle Eastern. There was one time a guy came with the group wearing a turban. You shoulda heard the talk back in the kitchen after the waiter turned in their specific food requests."

"Like what?"

"Dietary rules. Certain spices. I think they followed a certain religion that told 'em how to eat."

"Anything else you can tell me?" Molly asked.

"Not really." He paused. "There was a woman the smaller vet would bring in when he came by himself. Tall and dark haired. She was classy. Polite, always acted like a real lady. I seem to remember I heard him call her Julia one time. I couldn't forget *her* name."

He paused, placed his hands on his hips and faced Molly. "That's all I got. I'm sorry I can't help you more."

"You've been very helpful. Your insights are useful, and I appreciate your time."

"Let me give you my card." He reached into his shirt pocket. "If you ever come here for dinner, tell them when you make your reservation Curtis invited you. Meal's on me. We do a steak and lobster you'll dream about later." He lowered his head and chuckled.

"Thank you, Curtis, you're very kind. I'll tell my friends about your lovely restaurant." She laughed. "Don't think I'll mention The Blue Velvet room, however."

He laughed and extended his hand. "Don't blame you... although it's very nice for private parties—serves up to fourteen, or sixteen if we swap out the lounge."

"Thanks again." Molly shook his hand, picked up the line of pictures and left.

As she walked around the building to her car, she tried to recall if and where she'd heard Julia's name mentioned. She gave up as she unlocked the car and stowed her bag. Her trip had been successful. She learned a lot. She now saw a different side of Cindy, the *sweet* girl who worked for the Harmons. It wasn't surprising to hear of Jimmy Harmon entertaining guests, probably potential horse buyers or people interested in breeding their mares to Harmony stallions. But why would the vets be entertaining the people she'd just heard about? Molly sighed. Probably didn't mean anything... but it might.

Molly spent the better half of the afternoon working on her notes to share with Pilson and Schmidt later that day. As she wrote about Cindy, her reflections kept going back to Lar. What was she going to do about him? Once upon a time, she thought they would have a future together. *What a joke that was.*

He'd tried calling several times, but she hadn't picked up. Why would she? She wasn't ready to hear what he had to say. Molly tried not to think his explanation of *the kiss* would be lies, but what else could it be? Each time she refused his phone call, she thought of calling him back then couldn't imagine how she might start a conversation. Why did relationships have to get so messy? Painful and messy.

Painful and messy? Words she often used when discussing a murder case.

Molly, Schmidt and Pilson sat down for their meeting at exactly four o'clock. Molly explained her findings at the two restaurants then asked Schmidt what he'd learned.

"I spent time talking with Briggs and Spelling, both smart guys. They place high value on their jobs with Harmony. They believe it's one of the finest breeding operations in the United States and one of the best managed. Spelling holds Gene, the manager in very high regard, and his admiration for Mr. and Mrs. Harmon, for what they've created over their lifetime, is obvious."

"I spoke to each of the vets, also," Pilson said. "They were very generous with their time. Briggs strikes me as a bit of a stuffed shirt whereas Spelling is more down to earth. However, it's clear Spelling respects Briggs as his boss."

"What did you learn about Cindy?" Molly asked.

"Not a lot," Schmidt said. "It was clear she had dated Alphonso. Of all the grooms and junior trainers I spoke with, none of them thought she'd dated anyone else on the farm. Big Bev told me Cindy had quit seeing Alphonso after only a couple dates. In a roundabout way, she said Cindy told her Alphonso was too sleazy for her taste. Said he was all hands—her words."

Molly sat straighter. "Let me get this straight. Cindy told Bev that Alphonso was too aggressive for her?"

Schmidt nodded. "That's what Bev told me. Why?"

"I got a totally different impression from the Whistler's manager when it comes to *sweet* Cindy."

Pilson rubbed his hand along his jaw. "Like what?"

"Well, I'll put it this way. If my mother heard what I heard today about Cindy, Mom's word choice would be *tramp.*"

"Okay. I can see that," Pilson said. "I spoke with Little Bev, and she sort of alluded to Cindy being a girl who found it hard to say *no* when it came to men. Her impression was Cindy didn't care for young guys, preferred older men, yet she was known by a few to have dated Jerrod Bronson. Like so many places with a variety of employees, the ranch is certainly a gossip mill."

Molly jotted a note. "Did either of you get even a hint of something illegal going on with the breeding program?"

"I didn't," Schmidt said. "When I was in the AI facility my questions had more to do with ranch employees in general and their contributions to the overall success of the ranch. The Harmons have put together a terrific staff. Pilson and I agreed before we got there, I would spend the bulk of my time with the training staff and groundskeepers while he hung out with the vets."

"That's right. I spent most of my time with vets," Pilson said. "Briggs didn't have a lot to say. He spoke about his background and how he spent a lot of his time with Mr. Harmon because Harmon's knowledge of bloodlines goes way back to at least five or six generations, maybe more, depending on if they're talking Egypt, Russia, Spain, England, or Poland. Apparently, Mrs. Harmon is as sharp as her husband when it comes to selective breeding. She advises clients on their choice of sires based on their mare's bloodlines and confirmation, just like her husband. According to Briggs, the clients often sing Mrs. Harmon's praises when it comes to matching mare to stallion."

"What about Dr. Spelling?" Molly asked.

Pilson scratched his head. "Spelling mostly talked about his workday, what he does when not helping collect the stallions or inseminating the mares. He told me Dr. Briggs prefers to manage the collection side of the activity and have Spelling take responsibility for inseminating the mares with the designated semen."

Pilson looked from Schmidt to Molly. "You remember telling us about the breeding income not matching the stallion Breeding Reports? Well, this may be nothing, but it caught my attention. According to Spelling, he isn't involved with the AI bookkeeping done there at the insemination facility. Briggs does all the AI charting and record keeping after hours and keeps his journals in a locked document safe in his private office."

Molly frowned. "I was under the impression Doris Harmon and Cindy did those bookkeeping jobs."

"I hadn't heard that. Maybe they're using some kind of a cross-check system, or dual entry, that kinda thing."

Molly mentally ran through her notes. "Don't the vets have an assistant who would do that job?" Molly asked.

"Not that I know of," Pilson said. "When I think about it, there isn't an office area for a clerical assistant that I've seen in the AI building. And I've never met such a person." Pilson slid back in his chair. "The way the vets talk, there wouldn't be much for an assistant to do because the vets don't have a private practice. So, there's no billing or record keeping for a clerk to do. Cindy handles the phones in general and we understand Mrs. Harmon and/or Cindy do all the financial bookkeeping—bill paying, taxes, that kinda stuff. No need for an AI assistant to answer vet phone calls; the vets use cell phones. Briggs even packages the semen vials himself for the delivery people to pick up."

Molly shook her head in mild disbelief. "Wow! I've got to talk with Mrs. Harmon and also our Sarge. If a forensic accountant hasn't been assigned by now, we need to push hard for it." She raised a finger, pointing toward the ceiling. "Have either of you heard of a woman by the name of Julia? I understand she leans toward the elegant side."

"I haven't," Larry Pilson said.

"Me neither," Schmidt agreed.

"Her name came up in a conversation about the vets. We need to find out more about her and where she fits."

- 25 -

Molly began her day at Harmony Farm. Her first stop was at the main house. Mrs. Harmon's face and waving hand appeared in the window of her back door before Molly crossed the porch. Mrs. Harmon opened the door and hugged Molly. "You're here bright and early. Come in, come in. The coffee's fresh and hot."

Mrs. Harmon gestured toward a chair at the breakfast table. "Would you like to sit down?"

"No thanks. I can't stay. I have a million things to do. I wanted you to know you'll be receiving a call from a member of the police department who specializes in forensic accounting. He'll set up a time and date to meet with you."

"You must be a mind reader. I just hung up from the police department's forensic accounting department. I have an appointment with Detective Fielding at the first of the week. He sounds very nice."

"Oh, good." Molly paused, studying Mrs. Harmon for a moment. "Now, tell me. Have you had that difficult conversation with your husband?"

Mrs. Harmon's eyes glittered. "I have. George, bless his heart, was wonderful about everything. He plans to sit in the meeting with Officer Fielding. We're both very concerned about the missing income. George was quite alarmed when I explained it to him, so he doesn't want to miss a minute with the detective."

"Of course. What about your ring?"

Mrs. Harmon's brow rose. "Well." She grimaced. "It still hasn't turned up. I'm afraid it never will." She shook her head. "George tells me not to worry about it; says it's just one of those things." She paused. "He such a dear. He said he was glad it was the ring and nothing bad happened to me."

"I guess that's both good and bad news." Molly tipped her head. "Tell me, have you ever heard of a woman named Julia by any chance?"

"That's Dr. Spelling's daughter. She's a pretty girl. The only time we see her is if we're having a social get-together and he brings her along. I like her; she's quite bright and owns a charming ladies' boutique on Tatum just north of the freeway. You know, the Desert Ridge Mall." Mrs. Harmon laid her hand over Molly's arm. "Tell me, dear, why do you ask? Is Julia okay? She hasn't been harmed, has she?"

"Oh, no. It's not like that. She was mentioned in one of the interviews. Is Spelling not married?"

Doris shook her head. "His wife, Alice, died of cancer about five years ago."

"Oh, I'm sorry. That explains how close he and his daughter seem to be."

After leaving Mrs. Harmon, Molly settled into a chair in front of Gene Belmont's desk in his stallion barn office. "Thank you for seeing me without advance notice," Molly said.

He smiled. "Always a pleasure, Molly. It's okay if I call you Molly, right?"

"I guess so. When we're alone, but not around people here on the ranch."

He grinned. "You're all business this morning. How can I help you?"

"I'd like you tell me all you know about Alphonso and Jerrod's weekend rides into the High Country. Payson or Pine, right?"

"Yes. Both towns, actually."

"What do you mean?"

He raised his palm. "My understanding is they sometimes stayed in a motel over- night in Payson, but when Jerrod went alone, he would camp on his forest land outside Pine. Alphonso told me early on he didn't like to camp, so even when they rode together, he would still use the motel while Jerrod camped on his property. Stalls are provided at the place in Payson for the horses. Alphonso knew better than to put the horse he borrowed from me at risk by keeping them overnight in the trailer."

"Have you ever been up there?" Molly asked.

"No. No reason for me to go. I do have a map I marked up for Alphonso to find the place the first time he went along with Jerrod." Gene leaned down and opened a lower desk drawer. He removed a well-worn map and spread it on his desk. Molly stood for a better view and leaned over the desk as he showed her the approximate forest land location. The motel's address was printed on the side in line with Payson's dot on the map. Pine's location had been circled and compass points jotted at the margin.

Molly looked closer and pointed at the dot indicating Pine. "Can you read the number on that road? It's probably Bureau of Land Management land."

"I think it is BLM-owned. Looks like number 1410."

Molly leaned closer to Gene. "I think you're right. Looks easy enough to find."

"Are you planning to go up there?"

"Oh, I'll definitely go. Just a matter of when."

"Want some company?"

Molly smiled. "Not the first time. I'm sure one or both my partners on the case will want to see it for themselves. We'll probably do a day trip."

Gene shared an easy smile as he refolded the map and handed it to her. "Well, let me know if you change your mind. You shouldn't be wandering around in rough forest land by yourself. Want to borrow my horse? Mr. Harmon tells me you're an excellent rider—and you used to compete."

Molly smiled. "A lifetime ago. And no, I don't want to borrow a horse. I expect there's a road into the land Jerrod owned. If I'm wrong, I may take you up on it next time I go."

Molly caught up with Pilson and Schmidt in the second-floor conference room at police headquarters. They each had carried a cup of steaming coffee into the room.

"What's up?" Schmidt asked as he rolled a chair closer to the table.

Molly glanced from man to man. "Can you clear your schedule tomorrow? We need to make a trip up to both Payson and Pine. We've put it off long enough. So far, our leads have turned out to be weak. We have to do better. I've requested a four-wheel drive police truck."

Pilson sipped his coffee then swiped a hand across his mouth. "I can make it. Have you been certified at the driving track for a four-wheel drive truck?"

"Yep. End of last week. I did a walk-in and they agreed to test me, then and there. Coincidentally, I was out that way, so it saves us a bunch of time. We'll pick it up at Deer Valley Airport on our way."

Pilson gave a small bob of his head. "Are you plannin' to go early so we can get back in time for dinner? It's important to me."

Molly nodded, wondering why it was so important. Larry Pilson was a single guy. Maybe he had a date. *It could happen.*

Schmidt said, "I have something on my schedule, but I can rearrange it. Have you let the Coconino Sheriff's office know we'll be in the area?"

"Yep. Just before I returned to headquarters. I doubt anybody will show up. The sergeant I spoke with wasn't curious enough to ask a single question."

"What do you expect to find, Mol?" Schmidt asked.

She shrugged. "I'm hoping to find something to give us a better direction. This is the slowest investigation I can ever remember." Her shoulders slouched. "We're dealing with all this crap, and we a don't have a decent clue as to the why of it. Not any of it.

"I'm hoping there might be something about Jerrod's forest land that will have meaning." She rolled her chair back, stood, and paced the width of the room. "There must be some reason Jerrod drove up there as frequently as he did. Often enough to have a regular place to stay all set up." She paused in thought. "I saw something on a BLM road on the map Gene Belmont gave me. It looks like there is a road into his land. If he could drive into his parcel, why would he take a horse to ride?"

Pilson shrugged. "Maybe it was his preferred way *to get away from it all.*"

"Maybe," Molly muttered.

- 26 -

The following morning, they arrived in Payson a little past nine o'clock, used the drive-through at the first Starbucks they came to then continued to The Horseman's Hotel, a rather dilapidated motel on the highway.

Mrs. Tillie Gull introduced herself as one of the owners when they approached the registration desk. "Lookin' for a room, are ya?"

"No, Mrs. Gull." Molly introduced her partners and herself. "We'd like to talk with you regarding Mr. Jerrod Bronson and Mr. Alphonso Munoz. I believe they've stayed with you several times. Always arrived with a couple of horses needing stalls for the night."

"Why, yes, I remember those fellers. They took good care of their horses, brought their own feed and everything. You know, we offer horse feed at no extra cost to the customer. I hope those fellers ain't in no trouble." Her eyes moved slowly from Pilson to Schmidt and back to Molly. "Are they okay—them two guys?"

"I'm sorry to tell you Jerrod Bronson has died. Mr. Munoz is doing well."

Gull's hand fluttered to her chest. "Bronson's dead? I'm so sorry. Had he been ill?"

Schmidt cleared his throat. "No, ma'am, Bronson was killed. We're investigating his murder."

Tillie shrieked, "Murdered? Oh, my Lord."

We'd like to ask you a few questions if you don't mind," Schmidt said softly.

Tillie turned pale as she stood staring down at her registry book, her hand having remained over her heart. "Oh, my. That's just terrible. Murdered. He was such a nice feller. Did you say the other guy's okay?" The detectives all nodded. "Well, I suppose that's somethin'." She pulled a hanky from her sleeve and dabbed her eyes. "Oh, my God," she muttered. "Murdered? Whaddaya want to know?"

Molly stepped closer, resting her arm on the elevated counter. "We understand Jerrod Bronson owned some forest land around here. Do you know anything about that?"

"Can't say as I do. Didn't talk to him much. Stanley, that's my husband, he talked to him more 'en me. I remember they asked for directions to find a certain spot in the forest the first time they come around here. Stanley told 'em to talk to old man Conklin. He lives above the tire store down the highway to Pine. Used to be a huntin' guide.

"Conk knows everthing when it comes to the woods in these parts." She paused. "On the other hand, Stanley also told them boys, 'if you don't want to be bothered with Conk's bullshit, take the highway to Pine then go on to Strawberry and grab the highway north.' I remember him sayin' they should go past the road to Happy Jack—that goes into the Coconino National Forest. Go about a mile and a half and look for the road number they wanted. Stan said it weren't hard to find."

"How long would it take us to reach Road 1410?" Pilson asked.

"From Pine? About half an hour, give er take." She gestured across the room. "Hep yourself to some cookies and coffee. Both fresh—just made 'em."

"We have coffee in the truck but thank you," Schmidt said.

Leaving Payson behind, they agreed to put off finding Conklin unless they had no choice. Molly was surprised to discover Tillie Gull's directions were accurate, something she hadn't expected.

At the quaint little town of Strawberry, they turned north onto Highway 87 and followed it to BLM, Bureau of Land Management, Road 1410. There, they entered the forest and rode in silence as Molly steered her way around and through the multitude of potholes.

Several trails leading deeper into the forest were marked along their way. They traveled less than a half mile when they spotted a shingle bearing the name *Bronson* nailed to a pine tree. Molly turned right onto the trail and slowly drove to where the road ended at a small clearing.

Schmidt was the first to speak. "What the hell? No cabin? Not even a tent. All I see are trees, tall friggin trees." They got out of the truck and ambled into the clearing.

"I can see why Bronson hauled a horse or two," Pilson said. He pointed to the far side of the clearing where a patch of wild green grass and weeds grew in stark contrast to the clearing's hard brown dirt. "Bronson probably pitched his tent over there. Looks like he built a small fire pit." Pilson crossed the clearing, glancing in all directions then pointed. "I found a scrawny trail. Appears to be heading northeast. Looks to be tough going for a hiker but a horse would handle it easy enough." Pilson didn't wait for anyone to comment as he plunged onto the brush-lined path and disappeared out of sight.

"Should we go with him?" Molly asked Schmidt.

"Not me. He won't go far. He'll probably be back in five minutes. Don't know what he's going to find other than trees and more trees." He grinned sneakily. "Maybe he'll get chased back by a bear."

Molly frowned. "Don't even joke about it. If he comes running back, screaming *bear!* I'm diving into the truck. You can fend for yourself." She turned and stared at Schmidt. "Of course, knowing you, I'll probably reach the truck after you, and have to wait while you unlock the door."

Schmidt's face lit with glee, but his laughter was cut short when Pilson shouted. "Hey! You guys? Ya gotta see this!" He waved a broken branch with his floppy hat on the end of it over his head to signal his location. "Do you see my hat?" he shouted. "Take the little trail. Don't step off it. Got to avoid the Poison Oak. I'm waiting for you."

Molly and Schmidt jogged to the start of the trail and picked their way through a stand of second-growth timber with bushes and brambles covering the ground until they linked up with Pilson.

"Do you hear that?" Molly asked. "It sounds like a stream or maybe a river. I wonder if this trail picks up on the other side."

"I checked it out," Pilson said. "It does continue on the other side. It's more like a wide stream rather than a river. Surprising how noisy it is." He pointed to his left. "Follow me—it's not far." Pilson turned onto a sliver of a trail. Molly doubted they would have noticed it.

They hiked about twenty-five yards. Pilson pushed the branches of a tree aside, exposing a narrow, but elongated, clearing where Pilson pointed to his right. "Take a gander at that . . ."

Molly gasped.

Schmidt blurted, "Holy shit!"

- 27 -

They stood side by side staring at the scene. Pilson's fists rested on his hips. Schmidt's arms were folded across his chest, his feet wide apart. Without realizing it, Molly held her breath as she stared in silence at the site, her mind reeling. Pilson and Schmidt also remained silent, gazing at the panorama as if they didn't know what to say.

With a small shake of her head, Molly muttered, "I wouldn't have believed this if you'd told me. I thought I was going to see a dead body or maybe a crude grave. But a marijuana field never crossed my mind."

"How has he gotten away with this?" Pilson sounded as astonished as she felt. "The forest rangers must patrol these trails. They must know about it."

"How big is it do you think?" Molly asked.

Pilson answered, "Half a football field."

"It's pretty well hidden this deep in the forest," Schmidt said.

Pilson moved closer to the tall plants. "This is amazing. The plants look healthy; check out their flowers." He rubbed his fingers along a leaf. "These plants may be ready to harvest—or almost so." He studied the rows of marijuana, glanced around the general area then kicked over a clump of dirt. "Look at this. He's put in an irrigation system." Pilson turned in each direction then pointed into the distance. "I'll bet that crossing pipe runs to the stream we heard up the trail."

Molly walked beyond Pilson to the start of one of the rows and studied the ground. "Take a look at this." A crude drawing had been made in the dirt, about fifteen square inches in size.

Arnie Schmidt joined Molly. "I see what you mean. A human hand drew that. It looks like the lower part of the drawing was rubbed away but what's left could be the top of an animal's head." He pointed at the image. "See there, that could be an ear. And look, that could be a broken ear—flopped over. What's between the ears?"

"Looks like a crown." Schmidt said. "On the other hand, it could be numbers." He paused. "I think I can make out a three and a six. Ah, what the hell," he muttered. "It could be anything."

Molly knelt close to the image in the dirt. "I can make out an eight next to the three. At first, I thought it was a crown between the ears," she pointed, "but that looks like an upper case 'A'."

She pivoted around and stared up at Pilson. "Jill Bronson described a similar image the first time I talked to her, but she mentioned only the dog's ears. It was a tattoo on the arm of the guy who attacked her. I'll ask her about it when I see her."

Schmidt gestured to the field. "I think this marijuana is important to our case. We may be looking at our first connection—a decent clue to follow."

"Yeah, great," Pilson muttered. "Do the words *gang-related* come to mind?"

"Always possible," Molly muttered.

"If that drawing is similar to what Jill described, it's more solid evidence than anything we've found so far," Schmidt said.

Molly took several pictures with the camera whose strap she'd hung around her neck before leaving the truck. "We should probably head back."

"Want to follow that water pipe to know for sure it runs to the stream?" Pilson asked.

Schmidt chuckled. "You're really into Mary Jane horticulture, aren't you? You must've grown some in your past."

"Hell no." Pilson shot back then laughed. "I did some research for a case I had two years ago." He looked to Molly. "Following the pipe's not necessary; I thought it might be one more question answered." He cleared his throat. "Seriously, Molly, how do you think this marijuana field fits into this ever-growing, crazier-than-hell puzzle?"

Molly pursed her lips. "You got me." She raised her hands and counted on her fingers as she reviewed out loud. "First Jill Bronson's attacked... nearly killed. Her estranged husband could be involved somehow. Her brother Jerrod is murdered at Harmony... We've got a possible embezzlement of ranch funds, Mrs. Harmon's expensive ring goes missing, and now we've got a marijuana crop on our hands... and not a small one... owned by the murdered guy. Next, we have another image scratched in the dirt—but it doesn't resemble a tree like what Jerrod scratched while dying."

"Don't forget, the marijuana's growing on federally owned land. Are you thinking what I'm thinking?" Schmidt asked Pilson.

"Yeah. More legwork."

"Actually," Molly said, "Jerrod Bronson privately owns this plot, but it is undoubtedly surrounded by government land. He probably had to cross federal land to reach his water source. His sister, Jill may know something about it, unless that memory was erased by her amnesia. I asked her about Jerrod's forest land, and she said she'd never heard of it. But I'm hoping

her memory continues to improve. I'll ask her about it again."
She turned to Pilson. "Do you know anything about the process
of buying Bureau land? I don't want to involve the Feds if we
can avoid it."

"I've had no experience with it—never bought anything
from the government."

"Maybe it has no bearing on our case at all," Molly said,
turning to Schmidt. "What do you think?"

"No clue." He rubbed his jaw. "Where do we go from here?"

Molly smirked. "Alphonso Munoz. If the three of us sit
down with him, perhaps he won't act like the fool he truly is,
and between the three of us we'll get him to talk. I believe he
knows more than he's letting on."

They took a variety of pictures then headed back to The
Horseman's Hotel to ask more questions. Stanley Gull was
working the registration desk and welcomed them with a smile.
Molly handled the introductions as each detective showed their
ID.

After Molly explained their reason for coming to his motel,
he smiled broadly and asked, "What can I do for you? "Ain't
every day I get to chin with detectives. So, how can I help ya?"

Schmidt asked, "Have you been up to see Bronson's forest
land lately?"

"Nope. No reason to. Why do ya ask?"

"Somebody's farming it. I thought you might know who."
Schmidt pressed.

Stanley cocked his head and squinted as if he was in some
kind of negotiation. "Can't tell ya. Never been there. Never
goin' there. I take care of Munoz's horses when he stays here...
nothin' more, nothin' less. Mostly, I've only dealt with the
Mexican guy. So ya can quit askin' me things cause I got better
things to do." He turned on his toe and left the desk, striding
out through a nearby arch.

Pilson raised his eyebrows and glanced at Schmidt. "That was short and got us nowhere. Good job, chief. Masterful interrogation." He glanced around the reception area then headed for the coffee stand. "Tillie's put out more cookies. Anybody want a coffee and a snack for the road?"

Molly sighed loudly. "No. Let's go. I want to get to Alphonso before he leaves the ranch."

- 28 -

It was after four o'clock when they drove onto Harmony Farm's picturesque property. Molly steered the truck to Gene Belmont's office in front of the stallion barn and parked across the road next to the outdoor arena.

As they walked toward Gene's office, he appeared on the porch, smiled at Molly, and waved. "Whoa, looks like you brought backup. Should I be worried?" He laughed and waved again. "Howdy, detectives. Nice to see you. What can I do for you?"

Molly preceded them up the stairs to the porch, shook hands with Gene and asked, "Is Alphonso around?"

"I'm afraid not. He asked for a few days off. Said his grandmother was ill and needed his help. He also wanted to give Jerrod's brother-in-law a hand making funeral arrangements. I guess Jerrod's sister is still in the hospital."

Disappointed, Molly glanced at her two partners. "That's my understanding. I have it on my schedule to drop by to see her tomorrow morning. I'm really disappointed we missed Alphonso. How soon before he returns to work?"

"Three, four days, maybe a little more."

"Do you have time to answer a couple questions?"

"Sure." He waved for them to follow him inside to the conference room. "Take a seat. Did you find that forest land okay?"

"We did," Molly responded. "That's what we would like to talk to you about."

"I don't think I can be of help when it comes to Jerrod's business or his hobbies."

Schmidt asked, "Did Jerrod talk about the land as if it were a hobby?"

Gene shook his head. "No, he didn't talk about it at all."

Pilson raised a finger as if an idea had just come to him. "Tell me, Gene, do you have much trouble among your employees, here on the ranch, with drug use of any kind? Marijuana in particular?"

Gene's brow shot up. "No—not that I'm aware of. Have you found something indicating we have a drug problem? We can't have people involved in drugs around the horses. It could lead to somebody getting hurt—or hurting a horse. What do I need to know?"

Molly spoke up immediately. "Don't worry, Gene. If we found you had a drug problem, we'd tell you right away. We found marijuana growing on Jerrod's forest land. Because of his murder, we are investigating everything. You know what I'm saying... following every lead. Schmidt's question was one we had to ask. I'm certain there'll be others."

"Well, I must say, you gave me quite a scare. Drug use on the ranches around here is not unusual. A few terrible accidents on several of the ranches have resulted in injuries to both ranch hands and horses. Years ago, George Harmon instituted a zero policy against drugs of any kind. The kids—the employees are told about it when they're first hired and reminded often. We will not put up with it. We assure everyone when hired it will result in their being fired immediately. To my knowledge, our staff is clean."

Molly and the men stood. "I'm sure you're right. Everyone working here strikes me as dependable and loyal to the ranch," Molly said. "If we should discover anything to the contrary, I'll contact you." She turned to leave then paused. "Thanks for telling me about Jerrod's funeral. It's possible Jill is not aware of her brother's death. I'll contact her husband and offer my help."

Randy Winslow answered his phone on the second ring. Molly explained she'd learned he was arranging Jerrod's funeral. "That's very nice of you, given the circumstances."

"I felt Jill would want me to. If she knew about his death."

"You haven't told her?" Molly asked.

"No. She's way too fragile to hear that news. I'll tell her in good time, probably when she's up to visiting his grave. Is there something I can help you with, Molly?"

Memories of her suspicions about Randy flashed through her mind. What a change. "No, I was calling to offer you my help. What have you planned for the funeral so far?"

"Jerrod was not a religious man. It wasn't his thing. But there is this biker, a guy by the name of Robert Pennington, who is strong in his faith. I thought we could have a service at the Mortuary up at Pinnacle Peak whenever I can secure a date and time, and I'd ask Pennington to officiate. The chapel holds upwards of eighty folks, and I've already discovered the ranch people from Jerrod's customers do want to attend, besides the bikers, of course. I plan to invite a few people to gather in a local restaurant following the service—not too many. I figure the ranch owners who hired him, and his closest friends in the biker crowd."

Molly grinned at the thought of the ranch owners mingling with the bikers. "Sounds just right. Would you like a suggestion for a restaurant?"

"It would help."

Molly told him about Dempsey's off Shea. "I'll go with you when you talk to the owner. She'll remember me. I think they have a room to one side that might suit your needs."

"That would be great. I'd appreciate your help. I've never had to plan a funeral before." He chuckled. "I'll probably make lots of mistakes, but Jerrod won't care. Just imagine, me arranging a funeral."

"Jill will thank you."

"That's why I'm doing it... not to be thanked, but because Jill can't and there isn't anybody else."

"Let's keep in touch. By the way, be sure you write down the addresses of each facility you decide on. People will ask where to send flowers."

"Geez, I hadn't thought of that. Great. I'll do it. I'm sure you know, Jill and I would be pleased if you'd come. Well, that is, Jill will be happy when I tell her you attended."

"As soon as you have time and place, let me know."

Jerrod's funeral was a week later at 11:00 a.m. at the mortuary Randy had in mind. Molly hadn't expected to see such a large gathering. Schmidt agreed to go with Molly when Pilson said he had an important meeting that would finally wrap up his other case.

Randy stood at the door to the sanctuary, greeting the guests and offering them a vellum handout prepared by the mortuary staff. The chapel was larger than Molly expected and devoid of religious symbols. A raised dais filled the front of the room. Upon it and to the right several baskets of flowers sat below a draped table bearing a single tall candle and a black leather Bible. Standing candelabras were placed near each end of the table. A handsome walnut podium sat to the left.

Piped in soft music played until Mr. Pennington, in black leather with a matching brimmed hat approached the podium. He removed his hat, cleared his throat, and spoke in an admirable baritone voice.

Molly and Schmidt sat at the back of the room. Ranch owners, including Mr. and Mrs. Harmon, in business suits, sat among bikers in black leather and do-rags. Some women were dressed in dark toned dresses and others in perfectly tailored, lightweight wool pantsuits. The biker chicks had arrived in full makeup, including false eyelashes, and glittering fingernails. Like their counterparts, most wore black leather with lots of fringe. A few wore pastel cowgirl hats.

Molly searched the seated crowd while keeping an eye on those still arriving, in hopes of spotting Alphonso. So far, he had not appeared.

Drs. Briggs and Spelling had arrived in business suits. Briggs came alone, but a pretty, dark-haired, beautifully dressed young woman clung to Spelling's arm. Molly studied her as they walked up the aisle to two available seats. Could she be the mysterious Julia?

Mr. Pennington did a fine job of presenting Jerrod as a standup, hard-working man. He emphasized Jerrod's love for the horses and the tenderness he brought to his job. When the service ended, the crowd of strangers talked quietly as they left the sanctuary.

Molly and Schmidt walked directly to their car and drove to Dempsey's. Molly intended to arrive ahead of the crowd to make sure the restaurant was fully prepared for Randy's invited guests. Randy met Molly and Schmidt as they approached the door, and they walked in together.

Molly asked Randy, "Did Alphonso Munoz give you a hand arranging everything for today?"

Randy looked puzzled. "No. Who is he? I don't know anybody by that name. He wasn't invited to come here."

The guests arrived and spoke politely to one another, even though it was obvious they'd not met before. Molly found it curious to watch strangers from entirely different worlds speak easily and kindly to one another. The variety of races and cultures in the gathering appeared to be unimportant as strangers spoke to strangers like friends. It warmed Molly's heart. She hugged Mr. and Mrs. Harmon and thanked them for attending. Schmidt shook hands with them and expressed his gratitude for their cooperation during the daily interruptions of an unpleasant investigation.

The last guests to arrive were Drs. Briggs and Spelling. Briggs straightened his tie when he noticed Molly, smiled with a slight bow of his head. When Dr. Spelling saw Molly, he reached for his companion's hand and walked to Molly with a wide grin. "I'd like you to meet my daughter, Julia Spelling."

Molly smiled at the young woman, offered her hand, and said, "It's very nice to meet you. I've enjoyed knowing your father." She turned and reached for Schmidt to bring him into the group. "This is my partner, Homicide Detective Arnold Schmidt."

"Did you know Jerrod well?" Julia asked, directing her question to both detectives.

"I'm afraid not," Molly said. "I'm acquainted with his sister and her husband." Molly stepped a little closer. "I'm sorry, I don't mean to stare, but I must say, your emerald stud earrings are the most beautiful I've seen. Are they a family keepsake? Were they your mothers? They are lovely."

Julia's hand slowly rose to touch her earlobe. "No, I received them from a friend."

Schmidt, who had been staring at the woman from the moment he was introduced, said, "Molly's right. Those emeralds are beautiful... very clear. I shopped for months to buy my wife an emerald ring. It's her birthstone. I never found one as clear as those you're wearing."

Julia smiled. "I don't know much about jewelry; I wear very little. But I must admit, I've enjoyed these."

Molly nodded her approval. *I'll bet you have.* "If you'll excuse us, Arnie and I need to speak to the caterer.

- 29 -

Molly and Schmidt wandered in the direction of the bar following their brief conversation with the Spellings. When Molly felt they were far enough away from them, she asked softly. "Were you as surprised as I to see those earrings on Julia Spelling? And, how about Randy's never having met Alphonso? Gene told me Alphonso was helping Randy arrange the funeral."

Schmidt grinned. "We may have just fallen into the butter tub, as my mother liked to say. I doubt Miss Spelling knows anything about Mrs. Harmon's ring. If she did, I'm sure she would never have worn those earrings here today. Are you thinking the stones were removed from the ring? Or just a coincidence?"

Molly raised her brow. "Mrs. Harmon's ring was my first thought the minute I noticed the emeralds. Once you've seen that ring, you don't forget it. The emeralds Julia is wearing appear nearly identical in size and color as those in Mrs. H's ring. It's not in my nature to waste time on coincidences. We're going to have to dig deeper into Spelling and his daughter."

Schmidt stopped in front of the bar, asked for a couple of Cokes, and turned back to Molly. "I agree. There could be a connection to the murder."

"Right. If someone removed the emeralds, what would they likely do with the diamond? It was huge, four carats."

Schmidt shrugged. "Hide it for the future? Have it set in another ring or pendant? Maybe they pawned it."

"Right." Molly picked up her soft drink and took a sip. "We're going to have to call on an outrageous number of jewelry stores and pawn shops if the buying pawnshop involved hasn't registered their purchase with the police. Tomorrow, I'll check with the pawnshop detail at the Property Crimes Bureau."

"Good idea, but don't look for any help there when it comes to canvasing the shops. The bureau's overworked with too little help."

"True, but maybe they can advise us where to start our search. We can't ignore it, even if it's only to return the stolen ring to Mrs. Harmon. I still think it's connected to Jerrod's death, given the timing. The murder and the theft happening so close together might not have been coincidental. I'll talk to the boss when we get back to the precinct. Maybe he'll assign us some help."

"Good luck with that," Schmidt said quietly. "What about Alphonso?"

"Tomorrow lets you and I pin him down at the ranch. We'll get Pilson to go with us. He can be damned intimidating. If Alphonso has no choice but to face all three of us, he may be more forthcoming."

Schmidt started to speak but stopped, placing a hand on Molly's shoulder. "Looks like the Spellings are heading out. What say we meet them in the parking lot? I want to know who gave her those earrings."

"Me, too. Let's go."

Molly led Schmidt out a side door that opened into the parking lot. She spotted Dr. Spelling and Julia walking between a row of parked cars at the rear of the lot. She broke into a run with Schmidt following. Schmidt sprinted passed her and yelled, "Dr. Spelling! Hold up, will you?"

The Spellings stopped and turned toward them. Schmidt waved. "I want to ask you something," he said as he jogged over to them.

"What is it?" Dr. Spelling asked.

Schmidt took a few seconds to catch his breath. "Actually, it's Julia we want to talk to." He glanced at Molly, and she nodded.

The early afternoon sun glinted off Julia's beautiful black hair. She seemed annoyed while staring at Molly.

"Julia," Molly began, "we would like you to tell us who gave you your lovely earrings. It could be important to the investigation of Jerrod's murder."

Julia blushed and looked away. "I don't see how my earrings could have anything to do with a murder."

"We'll be the judge of that," Schmidt said then smiled.

Molly gestured with her hand toward Julia's dad. "If you'd be more comfortable speaking to us in private, we can arrange that."

"Julia?" Dr. Spelling said. "It may be important. I'm happy to walk away, give you and the officers all the privacy you need." He raised his hands in a placating manner, indicating she should remain calm, and it would all be okay. Without another word, he turned and walked back toward the restaurant without waiting for her reply.

"The stones in your earrings may be connected to a theft or burglary as well as a murder," Molly said softly. "Knowing who gave them to you might save more lives."

"I'm not comfortable having people, even my dad, know my personal business. Obviously, I'm not fourteen anymore."

"We'll respect that," Molly said. "But please, it's terribly important."

Julia wrung her hands. "It's really none of your business."

Schmidt inched closer to her and spoke above a whisper. "That's where you're wrong. We're investigating a murder. Give us the chance to prove there is no connection to your beautiful gift. Don't make the mistake of obstructing us from doing our job."

Julia's eyes widened. "I'm sorry, that wasn't my intent. If it's that important to you, it was Jim Harmon. They were a birthday gift. We've been dating off and on for about a year. But I'm sure he's not involved; he would never do something like what you're talking about."

Molly nodded. "Do you mind telling me, are you seeing him on a regular basis? You must have missed him terribly when he went to Australia."

"I knew he wouldn't be there long."

Molly gave her a hint of a smile. "Thank you, Julia. You've been very helpful."

Julia nodded, despite the unhappy expression on her face, turned and walked toward her dad.

- 30 -

The following day, Molly parked her car in the small parking lot on East Union Hills Road and walked into PPD's North Resource Bureau. She made her way into the Property Crimes' office. A Sergeant Hancock greeted her with a pleasant smile. After she showed her badge and introduced herself, he asked, "How can I help you, Detective?"

Molly explained her reason for being there. "I'm hoping you can tell me if you've recently received a buy/sell report on a four-carat diamond."

"I'm sorry, Detective. We receive reports of purchases over twenty-five dollars from every pawnshop in the Valley every day. There are over seven thousand pawnshops and second-hand dealers in Phoenix alone. So, you can imagine what our filing cabinets look like. We're slowly converting to digital but it's going painfully slow. We're still using paper."

"Oh my gosh, I had no idea."

He chuckled. "Yeah, it's something, isn't it?" He smiled. "You can understand why I wouldn't know about that monster diamond you're looking for." Surprise and disappointment caused Molly's heart to quicken. Hancock tilted his head. "I can see you're not pleased. Don't blame you. Here's what I can do for you: I'll give you the names of the six pawnshops that are known for buying high-end items, plus a couple others who would like to gain that part of the market."

"That would be great. Hopefully, I'll save a lot of shoe leather." Molly's rapidly beating heart slowed, but only a little. She had hoped for greater help. But she was thankful for Sergeant Hancock's cooperation. She recognized it was the best he could do under the circumstances.

The sergeant stepped to his computer, typed in the information, clicked the mouse, and seconds later his printer whirred into motion.

Molly walked back to her car with a tight grip on Hancock's printout containing the names and addresses of eight pawnshops in the greater Phoenix area.

She left the Bureau and drove to the hospital hoping to speak with Jill Bronson. While parking in the designated spot, her cell phone rang.

"Hey, Mol, it's Lar—please don't hang up. Are you free to talk? I have something to share with you."

Fearing what Lar might say, Molly's pulse raced. "I'm working."

"I know. This is a work-call during your shift. I've been reviewing your current murder investigation. You guys are doing a good job, but you have a lot of balls in the air. I'm wondering if you could use more help. I'm happy to supply it... just say the word."

Molly drew a deep breath and tried to control her voice. "We may need some help. Our investigation has developed a variety of facets we didn't see coming when we first took on the case. I'll call you if it gets out of hand."

"Yes, I noticed. Have you heard back from the forensic accountant?"

"Not yet. I'm on my way to talk to the attack victim... hoping to get more info from her regarding her deceased brother." Molly checked the time on the dashboard. "Thanks for the offer of help. If it becomes more than the three of us can handle, I'll let you know."

"Great. Now can we talk about us?"

Molly's heart dropped to her stomach as she held her breath. "Not on the phone. Maybe this weekend." She hung up.

The bandages on Jill's face from her recent surgery left enough space between them to see the rosy cast to her skin.

Molly walked to the side of her bed, smiled, and squeezed Jill's hand. "You look a lot better. Most of the tubes are gone. Feel like talking?"

Jill tried to smile but the tape fought back. "I'm going home soon. They say I'll be a day patient from then on. Still don't know when I can go back to work." She touched the bandage along her jaw. "My reconstructive surgeon, says I'll probably be discharged in a couple days after my next surgery. They're going to touch up around my left eye tomorrow. That's how plastic surgeons talk—*touch up*. The skin graft next to my eye seems to be attaching well."

"That's great news. How are you doing with the rest of your injuries?"

"A little stiff and sore, but better every day. I get around quite well. I walk several times each day."

"And Randy?"

"He's wonderful. We're talking of getting back together. Did you know we were getting a divorce?" Molly nodded. "At first, I didn't believe him because I didn't remember any of it. He was *sooo* timid when he told me what happened between us, I felt sorry for him. To convince me, he brought his copy of the Decree of Divorce he'd recently received. He said I could read it myself. Ever since then, when he comes to visit, we talk, talk, talk." She laughed.

"You sound very happy."

"I am." She folded her hands. "Now what would you like to talk about?"

"Are you aware Jerrod owned a plot of land in the National high-country forest around Strawberry, Arizona?"

"No. He never mentioned it to me—unless that's one more thing I've forgotten."

"Probably not. Is it possible your parents owned it and gave it to Jerrod?"

"No. My mom died after my dad. If she had property in the forest, I would know about it because I managed her affairs. She and Jerrod had a difficult relationship. I'm afraid she'd given up on him. Jerrod didn't inherit it from her."

"You sound convinced. Do you recall if Jerrod smoked marijuana or used other drugs?"

Jill's eyes widened... as much as her several bandages would allow. "I remember smelling it on him once when he came to my apartment—and one other time. But that's old news; I haven't seen him in months. I'm sure you know he was in jail."

"Yes, I know. Did you ever meet Jerrod's friends? Hispanic friends?"

"No. I never saw an Hispanic person with him. He ran with a bad crowd—bikers and thugs, people like that. He knew better than to bring them around me. The last time I saw him was the night he stole my mother's ring." She hesitated. "I was so angry. I'm terribly sorry. I'm afraid I can't help you very much. Do you think you'll find the guy who hurt me?"

"I'm hopeful. I work on it every day." Molly stepped back. "When do you and Randy plan to get back together?"

"Not till I'm bandage-free, but he's coming home with me when I'm discharged from here." She attempted another smile.

"It will be so nice having him there with me again. I tell him to quit apologizing; I swear he tells me how sorry he is every time he comes here."

Molly laughed. "That's great. When you see him, tell him hello for me?" She patted Jill's hand. "I must go. Take care of yourself. It's important." She waved goodbye and left the room.

- 31 -

As she drove back to headquarters, Molly couldn't get the idea out of her mind of Randy and Jill getting back together. It seemed too soon, given Jill's health issues. Was Randy the good guy he seemed to be or a well-disguised abuser? She sighed, guessing only time would tell.

When she walked through the squad room, Larry Pilson saw her, waved, and followed her to her workstation. Molly dropped her bag on her desk chair and picked up a stack of paperwork from the side chair. She stepped aside for Pilson to join her. "Have a seat," she said. "You look good. Have you joined a gym?"

"You're kidding, right? No—no gym. I closed that case I told you about and my stress level is much improved. We're sending it to the county attorney's office." He raised his arms and stretched. "Got the best night's sleep I've had in weeks." He exhaled a whoosh of air. "What have you got to say for yourself?"

"I saw Schmidt's car when I pulled in just now. Let's grab him and get caught up. I could use a coffee. How about you?" Molly asked.

"Sounds good. I'll grab Arnie and meet you in the coffee room, or do we need the conference room?"

"Coffee room's fine."

Molly poured creamer into her coffee and leaned against the small refrigerator. Pilson and Schmidt stood facing her. "I don't have much to share," Schmidt said. "How about you, Molly?"

"I ran out to the Property Crimes Bureau. That was a first. I swear we never stop learning while on the job." She repeated her conversation with Sergeant Hancock and followed it up with what Jill Bronson told her. "She either didn't know about her brother's forest land or lost her memory of it. So Jerrod's marijuana field continues to be a question mark, but we know he was a user—if that makes a difference. Probably minor, but a user just the same. As far as Jill and Randy getting married, I don't know what to think about that. I've believed right along he was a good guy. I sure as hell hope I'm not wrong."

"You're not," Pilson said. He turned to Schmidt. "What have you got?"

"I started looking into the process of buying BLM land. Like all things Federal, there're papers to sign and a dozen hoops to jump through. I suspect Jerrod bought it from a third party and paid some professional to make it happen. His purchase is legit. My guess is his sister now owns it through inheritance laws."

Molly's jaw dropped. "Oh, no!" She laughed. "*Katy, bar the door* when she and Randy hear that! I can see their faces when they get a look at the marijuana plants they now own, all standing so straight and tall."

Schmidt shrugged. "Jill's his nearest relative, so she will inherit unless he had a will giving it to someone else. It'll all come out in the wash—that'd be my guess, anyway." He faced Molly. "So what's next, boss?"

Molly smirked. "I expect Jimmy Harmon is back from Flagstaff and at work on the ranch. I plan to call him when we're done here and invite him to join me for a drink. We've been friends since we were kids. I'm pretty sure he'll go for it." She tossed her paper cup into the trash and turned for the door. "Then I'm going home and wash my hair—among other things."

Pilson chuckled. "Can I come, too?"

Molly lowered her head and looked at him from beneath her brow. "Depends on if you're talking about my hair or Jimmy. Forget about it. In both cases, the answer's *no.*"

- 32 -

Molly drummed her fingers on the desktop waiting for Jim Harmon to answer his cell phone. When he came on the line, she heard music before he said hello.

"Hey, Jimmy, it's Molly Raines. How are you?"

"Molly! Great to hear your voice; it's been a while. Dad said you were working this terrible murder case. Talk about bad juju."

"That's why I'm calling. Is Alphonso there today?"

"Yep. I'm watching him right now work a client's horse; the mare is just coming off a stifle injury. He's being very careful with her."

"Could you spare him for about thirty minutes to speak with me this afternoon, around three o'clock?"

"Don't see why not. I'll have Gene make sure Alphonso is in the conference room at three."

"Great. I'd like to talk to you, too. I've a couple of questions unrelated to Jerrod's murder. How about after I interview Alphonso?"

"Of course. Let's make it around four-thirty. We can do some catchin' up at the same time. Do you know Dempsey's Off

Shea? I'd like to get off the ranch for a while. Be a nice change of scene. Otherwise, it's going to be another long day."

"Sure, I know the place. Time's perfect, too. See you there."

Molly crossed the large room of half walls to Pilson and Schmidt's cubicles. "I made an appointment for us to talk with Alphonso later today. I'm thinking we go out to the ranch at three o'clock. I also have an appointment with Jim Harmon at 4:30 at Dempsey's Off Shea. Said he wanted to get away from the ranch for a while."

"Why's that?" Pilson asked.

Molly shrugged. "I didn't ask. He sounded tired over the phone. "After we interrogate Alphonso, I'll either head for Dempsey's restaurant or stop in on Mrs. Harmon if I have the time."

"When you see young Mr. Harmon, are you going to quiz him about the earrings?" Pilson asked.

"Sure as hell am. Mostly to cross his name off the list. But he does have some explaining to do."

"Do you get a sense he's mixed up in the murder or the theft of semen... or both?" Pilson asked.

"I doubt he'd be involved in either," Molly answered. "Jimmy is one of the most honest, stand-up guys I've ever known. But those earrings have gotten under my skin. There's gotta be something going on."

Molly glanced at her watch. "I'm going to check out a few pawnshops this afternoon." She handed Pilson a copy of the list Sergeant Hancock had printed for her. "Why don't you guys take the bottom three shops on the page? See what you can find out. Maybe they have video of the people coming into the shop with stuff to sell around the time Mrs. Harmon's ring went missing. Then meet me at 2:45 at the ranch."

Both men nodded. "You know," Schmidt said, "we may have time to call on some of the businesses around the north end of the park where Jill Bronson was attacked. They probably all have security cameras. We could get lucky."

"Sounds good. I'll see you at the ranch."

- 33 -

The afternoon had cooled, and rain threatened the Phoenix Valley as Molly drove into Harmony. She parked in her usual place next to the outdoor riding arena. Big Bev, riding a beautiful bay stallion in the training ring, waved to Molly as she stepped out of her car. Minutes later, Schmidt and Pilson pulled in and parked behind her car.

They walked together into the office. Gene approached them as they entered, shook hands, and exchanged a few minutes of small talk. He opened the door to the conference room. "I wiped off the table. The outdoor arena keeps us well supplied with dust. Stay as long as you like. I made a fresh pot of coffee. Help yourselves; it's all there on the sideboard."

"Thank you, Gene." Molly took her small digital recorder from her bag and placed it on the table. She turned it on to be certain she had plenty of battery life and discovered, for some reason, it wasn't working properly. With a small, annoyed shake of her head, she replaced it with the second recorder she always carried.

Schmidt placed his bag on one of the chairs and helped himself to coffee, filling a paper cup from the stack. Without they're asking, he filled two more cups and handed them to Molly and Pilson.

Molly nodded her thanks at the same time Alphonso arrived at the open door of the conference room. As always, he wore fresh clothing and his dusted black cowboy hat. Molly glanced his way. Alphonso smiled when their eyes met. Then his eyes cut to the two detectives across the table and his smile flipped to a frown.

"Come in, Alphonso." Molly said as she stood and pointed to the open chair. "Have a seat." She closed the door and gestured to her partners seated across from him. "I'm here with Detective Pilson and Detective Schmidt. They have a few questions for you." She returned to her place at the head of the ten-person conference table.

She reached forward and turned on her recorder. Although neither of the other detectives displayed a phone or recording device, Molly had no doubt they were operating in the men's jacket pockets.

Detective Schmidt asked Alphonso. "We understand you and Jerrod Bronson were close friends. Is that right?"

"No mucho."

"Speak English, Alphonso," Molly said.

He nodded.

Schmidt continued. "You must have been close friends to spend all those weekends riding in the mountains together. Where did you go to ride?"

"White Mountains."

"You told Detective Raines you rode in the McDowells. Which is it, the Whites or McDowells?"

"Maybe both. I not remember."

Schmidt scowled. "Of course, you remember. Don't lie to us. It won't go well for you."

Moisture formed at the top of Alphonso's clipped mustache. "I don't lie." His voice bore a defensive edge.

Pilson asked. "How often did you go with Jerrod to the high country?"

"Not many—now and then."

"Not many? How many is that? Three, four? Five? You were Jerrod's good friend. You rode together every weekend. You borrowed your boss's horse every weekend. Wasn't it more like ten or twelve times?"

Schmidt leaned forward, sliding his forearms closer to Alphonso. "Don't lie to us! You went several times a month in the summer. It was nice to get away from the heat in Phoenix. You lied when you said not many. You went much more than that."

Alphonso pursed his lips and repeated, "I don't lie."

Pilson pressed. "So, you agree you went many weekends. Mr. Gull at The Horseman's Hotel said you came regularly, nearly every weekend. Tillie Gull referred to you as that handsome young man, *Alphie*. Sounds like you and the Gulls were friendly. They thought of you as their son. You must have been there more than *now and then*."

Schmidt cleared his throat. "Tell me, young man, did you spend time with Jerrod on the land he owned in the Coconino Forest? He liked to stay there. Did you stay there, too?"

"I don't like to camp in the woods. I stay at the motel with the horses."

Schmidt's brow rose. "But Jerrod kept the horses with him when he camped in the forest, didn't he?"

"Sometimes yes; sometimes no."

"Jerrod needed the horses to ride in the forest and you rode with him. Did you bring the horses each morning from the motel in the trailer?"

"Yes."

"So when you rode in the White Mountains, where did you go?"

"The Rim." He raised his hand as if confused. "The trails. I don't know the names."

"The Mogollon Rim?

"Yes. People say that. I forget."

Schmidt leaned across the table. "Jerrod owned land in the Coconino Forest. Did you camp there with him? Ride the horses there?"

"I no like to camp. Never go there. Only Jerrod camp there."

"Well then, where did you stay if you don't camp?"

"I say before, the motel on the highway. It has a barn for the horses. I ride Mr. Belmont's horse. He say his horse have to sleep in a stall—no trailer."

Schmidt nodded. "I see. Jerrod camped on his forest land, and you slept at the motel with the horses in a stall. Right?"

"Yes. Sometime Jerrod come to motel, too."

Schmidt raised his chin. "When Jerrod didn't sleep at the motel, you drove the horses to the place where Jerrod camped. His forest land place?"

"Yes."

"Well then, you lied to me." Schmidt tapped the table with his forefinger. "You said you never went to Jerrod's forestland. But you went there every time you and Jerrod rode horses on the Mogollon Rim."

Alphonso's face darkened. "I don't lie," he insisted. His eyes narrowed in anger.

Schmidt tapped his finger again. "But you did lie. I'll have Detective Raines play it back for you." He turned to Molly and pointed at her recorder. "Detective, please?"

Alphonso threw both hands into the air. "Okay! I go there a little bit."

Schmidt smirked. "Now we're getting somewhere. When you were there, did you see the pretty garden Jerrod had planted?"

"No, no. I see only trees... bushes and pinecones. A river, too."

"I see. You saw the river nearby, the trees and bushes, but no garden."

Schmidt leaned farther over the table and glared. "You saw all that? If you saw the river, you had to see the garden." He shook his head. "You keep lying to us."

Alphonso shook his head rapidly. "No lie. I see no garden."

"Did you carry water from the river?" Schmidt asked.

"Yes."

"You're a lying sonofabitch, Alphonso." Schmidt fumed. "You couldn't miss the garden. It's huge. You couldn't go to the river without seeing it. Almost his entire land was his garden." It was because of the big garden you carried pails of water. Many pails of water, right?" Schmidt hammered the table with his fist. "What was growing there, Alphonso?"

Schmidt pointed his finger at Alphonso. "Don't you lie to me anymore!" he warned. He gave a small wave at Molly and Pilson. "We all saw the garden. You saw it. What was growing there?"

Alphonso stared at his knees in silence, as if refusing to answer. His chest expanded with each breath he took.

Schmidt relaxed back into his chair. "Do you know the penalty for lying to the police, Alphonso?"

Alphonso glanced up but didn't answer.

"We're prepared to arrest you right now. You lied to Detective Raines when she interviewed you a few days ago. Now you've lied to me more than once." He paused, glanced at his fingernails, and muttered, "I hate a liar." His voice grew louder as he spoke. "Especially a dirty, rotten liar." Again, he shook his finger at Alphonso. "Look at me! I've a notion to arrest you right now and haul your punk-ass to jail. Is that what you want me to do?"

Alphonso's eyes widened. He shook his head. "No, Mister, no."

"Then tell us what Jerrod was growing in his garden!"

Alphonso stared above Schmidt's head and set his jaw. He spoke just above a whisper. "Marijuana. But I not his partner."

At the mention of a partner, Schmidt's eyes widened. He slapped the table hard, making Alphonso and Molly flinch. "That's right. Marijuana. If you weren't Jerrod's partner in the marijuana, who was?"

"I don't know. He not say. I not ask."

Schmidt waved him off. "Don't tell me that. You know. We all know you know. Alphonso, you've got to quit lying. You're in deep shit here. Jerrod is dead, and you don't look so good. Don't make it worse for yourself. Who owns the marijuana? Jerrod or someone else?"

Alphonso leaned his elbows onto the table and gripped his head in his hands. "Okay, okay. Miguel, from the cantina, tell me his *amigo* has a *jefe*, a boss, who wants to grow weed in Arizona. He pay big money. He pay me to find someone to do it. I talk to Jerrod. He say okay. I bring Jerrod to meet Miguel and they make bargain. Jerrod get a lot of money to grow it. When it is cut, he gets more. That's all I know. I don't lie to you. I tell the truth."

Schmidt said, "Except it's not cut, and Jerrod's dead. Who's going to cut the plants and take them away?"

"I don't know. Maybe Miguel know."

"Where do you meet Miguel?"

"We go to Cantina de Carlos. Miguel tell me his boss is very happy. Jerrod's weed *es mucho grande. El Jefe...* the boss even pay me a bonus for helping. He want Jerrod to grow more for him, but Jerrod say no more. The boss not like that."

"Then what happened?"

The boss tell Miguel to tell Jerrod he better do what he say or else. I tell Jerrod the boss is dangerous, but he no care. He say his horse shoeing business too important, too big now. No time to grow weed." Alphonso slumped back in his chair as if a weight had been lifted from him. "That's what I know. I tell you all."

Alphonso turned to Molly, a pleading expression on his face. "Now, I no go to jail?"

Molly turned off her recorder. "Maybe. Maybe not. We'd like you to help us. Somebody murdered your friend, Jerrod. We think maybe you. You're in serious trouble." She counted off the list of offenses on her fingers. "First, you lied to police, and there's the marijuana field. There's Jerrod's murder, and his sister's attack." She paused and stared at Alphonso. "It doesn't look good for you. Do you understand?"

Alphonso raised his head, his eyes wide. He gave her a small nod.

Molly leaned toward him. "If you help us, we can help you." She spoke softly.

Alphonso sat a little straighter. "What do I do for you?"

Molly moved slightly back from him. "Talk to Miguel and tell us what he says. Find out when they plan to harvest the plants. If you work for us, you could be a hero who brings down a drug ring. The boss you're talking about may have more people growing marijuana for him in Arizona, New Mexico, and maybe California. We want to know all about his operation. If you can do this for us, we'll keep you out of trouble and we'll pay you for your work."

He rubbed his hands over his hair. "I can't go to jail. I love the horses. I must be with the horses." Alphonso gripped her hand between his. "For you, I help. *Gracias*, my angel, I do it for you."

She smiled at him as she slipped her hand from his. "You made the right decision. We'll keep you safe." She handed him her card. "I want to see you before you talk to Miguel again.

We'll decide what you're going to say to him." She stood. "We're finished for now, Alphonso. You can go back to work."

As he left the building, heading toward the barns, he moved like a man totally defeated. When he was out of earshot, Schmidt exhaled loudly. "What do you think?"

Pilson smiled. "I think it was a good interview. If he follows through, we could land a big one. Maybe bigger than we could have guessed." He asked Molly, "Why didn't you tell him he'd have to wear a wire?"

"I was afraid we'd spook him. I'll explain just before wiring him up." Molly picked up her bag and turned for the door. "We're going to have to surveil this fellow, Miguel. He could be central to it all. When Alphonso goes to the cantina to meet Miguel, I want to be there outside listening." She ran a hand across the back of her neck. "I meant it when I said we'd keep Alphonso safe."

- 34 -

Late in the day, Molly walked into Dempsey's Off Shea a few minutes early and was surprised to see Jim Harmon already there, waiting for her in the entry area. She smiled at the sight of him. He stood, chuckled, and hugged her. "My God, Molly, how long has it been?"

"Three, four years? I'm not sure." Molly, still in his arms, leaned back and studied his face. "You don't look a day past fifty-four!"

"You are so bad… same ole Molly." He shook his head as he slid his hands down her arms to her hands. "Let me look at you. You never change… still twenty-two, right?"

Molly smirked. "Right. And we're both lousy liars."

"Yeah, but it's fun. Where would you like to sit? Want to go in the bar?"

"That's fine."

Minutes later, the server placed a red wine in front of Molly and a scotch and water in front of Jim. They reminisced about the years they'd spent competing in horse shows up and down the West Coast, including Molly's regional win in English Pleasure on her beautiful gray mare, Crazy Girl.

He rubbed his chin. "I remember that night at the Regionals. Your horse performed perfectly, but more than that, I can still see your beautiful navy saddle suit with the silver vest your mom made for you. You and your horse were a picture to behold." He reached for her hand. "Do you miss it? Even a little? You were on your way to some big wins when you decided to retire from the ring."

She smiled. "Do *I* miss it? A little. You flatter me, but it was sweet to bring up my regional win. I never competed at Nationals. And how about all the National trophies you've raked in over the years? Your winning reputation is known around the world. How have you managed to keep your head on straight?"

He grimaced. "Good genes. I may have a positive reputation around the world, but the ranch's reputation is in trouble because of this murder case. Dad is worried sick. Can you tell me anything?"

"Not much, I'm afraid. We're following the clues. Did you know Jerrod very well?"

"Not really. He was an excellent farrier; I really admired that about him. We had him try his hand at some corrective shoeing and he was a natural. For selfish reasons, we miss him, but we were all saddened when we learned of his death. He was well-liked. I hoped he would continue with us for years to come. He was humble about his skill set; I admired that a lot."

"Did you talk with him about things other than shoeing?"

He grinned. 'You'll like this. He loved baseball as much as you do. Often when I made it a point to stop and say hello, it was always baseball he'd bring up—a batter's homerun, an outfielder's great catch. After that, we talked about the horses he'd be working on, of course."

"You know about the loss of your mom's anniversary ring, don't you?"

He glanced down. "I do. She thinks she misplaced it, but you and I both know it's worse than that. She's heartsick over it. If I mention it, she tells me she's sure she'll find it... almost like she can't bear to think somebody would actually steal it from her."

Molly sipped her wine. "That brings me to a question I'm sorry I have to ask you."

"What's that?" His brow rose. "How bad can it be?"

"I understand you've been dating Julia Spelling lately and you gave her a lovely pair of earrings for her birthday."

"That's true. We're not serious. Julia is pleasant to be around; we enjoy each other. But truth be told, it's not going anywhere."

Molly, surprised by his words, stared at him. Who gives costly earrings to a woman when he knows *it's not going anywhere?* "I'm sorry, I'm afraid I don't understand. I'm sure the stones were very expensive. How can you brush it off so lightly?"

He responded with a sardonic smile. "I bought them in Hawaii, on my return from Australia. They caught my eye as I walked past a jeweler's window. They weren't cheap, but they would have been out of my price range had I bought them here at home." He took a swallow of scotch. "What are you getting at?"

Molly stiffened. Why was he acting so flip over such a serious matter? She frowned as she pressed him again. "The stones in Julia's earrings are a close match to the emeralds in your mother's ring—in size, clarity, and color. They're each the size of a one-carat, brilliant-cut emerald."

A grin crossed his face then disappeared. "They are, aren't they? It was the first thing I noticed about them when I saw them in a jeweler's window in Honolulu... how much they resembled Mom's. Lucky for me, they were advertising a going-out-of-business sale. I thought Julia would like them."

"Believe me, she does. Do you have a sales receipt?"

"Of course. Not sure where it is, but I kept the paperwork. I'll hunt it up if you'd like to have it." He stared sternly into Molly's eyes. "Are you thinking I stole my mother's ring? Do you really think I'd do that? Good God, Molly, if I asked her for it, she'd rip it off her finger and give it to me."

Molly's pulse throbbed in her ears. She shook her head. "I'm sorry, Jimmy, I know you're right. Please forgive me. But it's my job to ask these questions. If I don't, my investigating partners, who also saw Julia's earrings, would have. I see now I should have left it to them to talk to you, but I thought it would be easier if you heard it from me."

"I think you're right about that," he mumbled. He slipped his arm around her shoulder and pulled her closer to him in the circular booth. "It's all right. I understand."

She took a deep breath. "If you could provide me with your sales receipt and any other documents you have for the file, it will no longer be an issue and I'll never bring it up again." She reached for her wineglass, wishing she were anywhere but there.

He nodded. "I'll get you all the documents ASAP."

He smiled in that way she remembered from years ago—whenever she and Crazy Girl worked perfectly in the show ring and won. The kindness in his eyes that always accompanied that certain grin was there now. "Would you like to hear about Australia?" he asked quietly.

She smiled but her regret for prodding him remained. "Of course. I want to hear all about it."

They spoke about the Australian ranchers, the quality of their Arabian horses, the number of AI breeding contracts he'd carried home, and the success of his workshops at the various ranches across the continent.

When the server appeared and asked if they'd like another round, they both shook their heads.

"No thank you, I really have to go," Molly said.

"Me, too." Jim picked up the check. "I promised Mom I'd help her get together the menu and guest list for her annual Thanksgiving dinner for the ranch crew and their families."

"Your mom always did look out for the ranch employees."

"Yep. She worries the kids who come here from Mexico to work for us will be homesick. They're excellent horsemen and she wants them to feel comfortable for as long as their visas allow them to stay."

They walked to Molly's car without speaking. Standing near the driver's door, he smiled. "I wish it had been under different circumstances, but I enjoyed having a chance to spend time with you again. When I saw you at the ranch a few days ago, I realized how much I've missed you. Even though we were teenagers and competitors, being together was always special."

"Teenagers? You were an old man."

"Old man?" he huffed. "I was nineteen, and you were fourteen."

She laughed. "I could always get under your skin." She studied his face. "It has been nice getting together today, in spite of it all."

He casually dropped his hands into his pants pockets, took a step back, and studied her. "By the way, Mom's having a few people over to the house Saturday night for Doc Briggs' birthday. Want to come? I know she'd love it if you would. It won't be a large group."

"I wouldn't want to intrude, and I'll have to clear it with my boss. The department frowns on even the least appearance of conflict of interest."

"I hadn't thought of that. Please try. You're like a daughter to my folks. It'll make us all happy."

Pleasant memories flooded Molly's mind. The Harmons were like family. Her face warmed. *Why not?* "All right. I'll run it by my sergeant. If he says it's okay, I'd love to. Will Julia be there?"

"She'll undoubtedly come with her dad. Is that a problem?"

"No, of course not. Just curious."

They hugged each other then Molly slipped into her car, closed the door, and rolled down her window. "Jimmy, please get me those receipts from Hawaii as soon as you can."

"Absolutely." He grinned as he studied her face. "Back on the job?"

"Always. It never ends."

Jimmy and their teen years filled her thoughts as she drove home. Recalling he was the very first guy she'd had a crushdated on made her smile. To see him socially again would be nice. *If only.*

As fast as a bullet and equally jarring mental pictures of Jerrod Bronson's dead body pushed all thoughts of Jimmy aside.

- 35 -

Molly tapped her fingernails on the tabletop, waiting for Lar to answer. He picked up on the third ring. There was an apprehensive quality in his voice when he said "Hello, Molly."

She went straight for the reason she'd called. "I wondered if you were going to be home this afternoon. If so, I'd like to come by. I think we should talk."

He was slow to answer. "Sure, it's a good idea. Can you come around four this afternoon?"

"Yes, that's fine. I'll see you at four o'clock."

Her knocking made a hollow sound on Lar's door. She wondered if Lar's words would be as hollow. He opened after three quick taps, studied Molly for a moment then stepped back. "Hello, Molly. Please come in. Would you like something to drink?"

"No thanks. I can't stay very long. I'm meeting Pilson for a stakeout tonight—the Jerrod Bronson murder case."

"I see. Well, I'm guessing you want to talk about the other day. Let's sit down." Molly wanted the conversation to be short.

She hated confrontations. She took the few steps to the sofa and perched on the edge of the corner seat. Lar sat on the end of the coffee table, facing her, their knees nearly touching.

Molly studied his eyes. "I want you to explain who the woman was and why you were kissing outside your front door. Had she been with you all afternoon?"

"I don't know where to start." With his elbows propped on his knees, he lowered his head and rubbed his jaw. "I met Marcie in college. We dated for a while then went our separate ways. She recently moved to Phoenix from Chicago. It's been twenty-four years since we've seen each other."

"How long had you dated?"

"About a year and a half."

"That's hardly *a while*. It must have been serious. The kiss I witnessed looked seriously passionate. Have you been seeing her since she arrived here?"

"I'm not going to lie to you, I—"

"Well, that's good to know."

"Yes, I've been seeing her—the past two weeks. Look, Molly, I'm sorry. I feel very close to you, and I feel awful hurting you. I never wanted to do that."

"Also, good to know."

"Marcie was that person who walked into my life when I badly needed someone. We were a couple until we graduated and went our separate ways. I never forgot her. She has come back into my world and the memories are strong. I want to see where it takes us."

Molly stood. She studied Lar for a long moment. "Thank you for being honest." She stepped around the coffee table and opened the front door then glanced back at him.

"I'm not hurt as much as you may think... or thought I might be. I figure it's a lesson learned. I've learned a lot from you. Goodbye, Lar."

As Molly walked toward the stairs down to the first floor, she glanced at the cars parked belo. Adrenalin filled her bloodstream. If anyone noticed her, she hoped she acted ordinary—nothing to see here—in control, not a silly female, falling apart at the seams. She grabbed a breath of fresh air. She wanted to run—to escape—but the stairs were just ahead— out of sight from Lar. Thank God. She couldn't bear to have him see her in this state of torment. Her emotions assailed her. Disgust. Anger. Sadness and disappointment. Tears filled her eyes. She tried to blink them away, refusing to raise her hand to brush them aside. *Just keep walking.*

At the bottom of the stairs, she paused, pulled a tissue from her purse, and blotted her eyes. She took a deep breath, fished her key fob from the bottom of her handbag, and strode to her car. She slid inside, gripped the wheel., and stared straight ahead.

It's over.

Done.

- 36 -

A little past seven-thirty that evening, Molly picked up Pilson at his home and drove to the Cantina de Carlos on Indian School Road. She parked east of the front door in their parking lot. Pilson craned his neck from side to side, checking the cars on either side of them and those behind.

"Thanks for shaking loose tonight. Your Spanish is a lot better than mine, and I expect these guys won't speak English" She glanced from side to side. "What do you think of where we're parked?" Molly asked.

Pilson shrugged. "This is a good place. We're not too far from the door. We can see them if they come out, and I don't think we'll be noticed. Are we close enough to pick up their voices on the equipment?"

Molly handed him a set of ear buds. "The cantina's music is loud, but I think we'll hear them." She readjusted the recording equipment she'd picked up at the precinct, slowly turning up the volume. Alphonso and another voice could barely be heard. Molly assumed the voice was that of Miguel. "I told Alphonso if the music was blaring inside to suggest to Miguel they sit outside."

"Fingers crossed," Pilson said. "The music could become a problem. If recording in Spanish is a problem, we can have it interpreted at the precinct."

"Good idea. Now let's hope Alphonso follows instructions." Molly continued to raise the volume, afraid they'd miss something Miguel said. Suddenly the noise from the music faded and the voices blasted. "There we go." Molly adjusted the volume. "They must have gone out to the patio."

"Miguel," Alphonso said in Spanish, "What will happen to Jerrod's weed?"

"I don't know. I haven't heard yet from my boss. "It's bad for business—Jerrod killed."

"He was doing a good job. Why did he have to die?"

"Jerrod was warned. My boss is a tough guy. His men hurt the sister, but Jerrod still not do what they want. Jerrod not smart. He was warned. My boss has no patience."

"It is sad for me. Jerrod was my friend." Alphonso moaned. "Rodrigo works for the boss, too. He's a mean guy. Did he kill Jerrod?"

"I don't know. Nobody tell me."

Strange voices spoke in the background. Apparently, they passed by Alphonso and Miguel's table. Someone said, "Another beer?"

"Yes, two more," Alphonso answered. There was a brief pause before Alphonso continued. "Have you seen Jerrod's weed? The field is beautiful. Maybe it is yours now. Or maybe you will buy Jerrod's weed so you can cut and sell it? Maybe we be partners? Please? It is time to cut it." Alphonso paused. "Maybe your boss forget about it?"

"Maybe. I don't know. He has many fields. One is not important to him."

"In Arizona? He has many fields?" Alphonso asked.

"Yes. Three or four—five in New Mexico. Same in Colorado."

"*Caramba!* That is eight fields, maybe more. Maybe you and I buy Jerrod's?"

Miguel didn't reply.

There was a pause then Alphonso said, "It is late. I must go."

Moments later, Alphonso and another man, probably Miguel, walked out of the building's front door. Pilson raised his camera and shot several frames. The men exchanged a few words then Miguel pointed to a Ford Explorer parked two cars away from Molly's and walked away from Alphonso toward the car. Pilson snapped a close-up of Miguel's face.

"Get down," Pilson blurted as he slid under the dashboard, nearly off the seat.

Molly punched off the recording device and lay on her side.

As soon as the neighboring vehicle pulled out of its parking place, Molly sat up and started her car. Pilson slithered back into his seat. "Where're we going?"

"To follow Miguel. If we're lucky, he may be on his way to his boss' place."

Twenty minutes later, Miguel turned into a gated community and slowly drove through the residents' gate. Molly slowly followed, stopping at the guard's station. She showed the attendant her ID and badge while introducing herself and Pilson. She explained she and her partner were on official police business. The guard stepped into his office touched a button and the gate opened.

Molly drove as fast as she dared. To her left she caught the glow of brake lights and turned. She slowed her car to a crawl. Forty yards ahead on Death Valley Road, Miguel parked at the curb, got out of the car, and strode toward the stately home. Pilson, using a zoom lens, took a photo of Miguel's car's license.

The house's porch lights came on, the door slowly opened, and a large Latino man stared at Miguel. Pilson snapped three quick shots with the zoom lens fully extended. Miguel entered the home and the door closed. "Did you get a picture of the address?" Molly asked.

"Yep. Plus, a clear image of the guy who opened the door. If it's the homeowner, we have all we need to identify the guy." He turned and smiled at Molly. "Good work, Mol."

- 37 -

After the meeting with her sergeant the following day, Molly and Pilson met with Schmidt and brought him up to date on their stakeout.

"The home Miguel visited is owned by an Enrique Martínez." Pilson chuckled. "And guess what else—the car Miguel was driving is also owned by Martínez."

Schmidt grinned. "So he was drivin' a company car."

"Probably," Pilson said. "Mr. Martínez was obviously happy to provide him a car. We may have found *El Jefe*. The guy lives in a very nice and expensive house." He turned to Molly. "What do you think, Mol?"

"I know we can't be certain, but I believe there's a good chance we've located a boss—at some level—maybe not as high as *El Jefe*, but we definitely want to stay on top of this guy." Molly hesitated. "If he is a mid-level boss, he probably has more men than Miguel working for him—and maybe some women. Even if he's responsible for Jerrod's death, you can bet *he* didn't do the deed. Probably assigned one of his crew.

"I really want to see first-hand the activity taking place at that house." Molly flipped through the notes she'd prepared for their meeting. "I spoke to Sergeant Hilliard, and he agreed to arrange two surveillance vans for the next six days. I figure we can place one across the street, several doors down from the front of the house. The second one will be placed on the hill, two streets above the rear of the Martínez house. I checked it out and there's a clear view between the houses thanks to all the over-sized yards in the neighborhood. Never thought I'd see so much real grass in Phoenix."

Schmidt edged forward in his chair. "Great idea. By the way, I think it's time we crank up our effort to find Mrs. Harmon's ring. Let's call on the pawn shops at the top of our list and see what their surveillance cameras show. Some of the shops are near mini marts and they probably have security cameras. Also, I thought of checking with the university on the chance they have cameras showing the street and sidewalk on the south side of the campus. We know the guy who attacked Jill Bronson used that street to leave the scene."

"I'll help you with that," Pilson offered.

"Good." Schmidt glanced at Molly. "What's on your schedule?"

"I'm going by the hospital to see how Jill's doing, and tonight I'm having dinner at the Harmons' ranch. They're celebrating Dr. Briggs' birthday. Spelling is expected, along with his daughter. Jim Harmon spoke openly about his relationship with Julia Spelling and about the earrings he gave her. Attending the party off the clock, as simply a friend of the family, could provide something helpful to our case. I cleared it with Hilliard."

An hour after Molly's meeting with Schmidt and Pilson, she walked into Jill Bronson's hospital room. Two fresh bouquets of flowers helped lessen the austere and gloomy environment that had been Jill's home for weeks. She smiled when Molly entered the room.

"Hello, Detective. I see you found me in my new room."

"Yes, and here you can have flowers! I was happy to learn you were out of the ICU. And you're looking better each time I visit. Are you feeling better? You have fewer bandages today."

"I do." Jill placed a hand on her jaw. "And I have hardly a scar."

"I see." Molly stepped closer. "I'm very happy for you. I suspect you'll be going home soon."

Jill smiled and nodded. "Yes, Randy's going to take me home tomorrow. He has already moved in, so it will be quite a homecoming." Jill glanced away then turned back, frowning at Molly. "I've had flashes of memory since I last saw you. This morning I was thinking about the man who attacked me, and I remembered more about him. He wore a black tee shirt, and he had a scar on his neck—from below his ear to just below his Adam's apple." She ran her finger along her own neck, demonstrating the curve of the mutilation.

"Wow, that's great. Did you notice anything else?" Molly asked, taking out her phone and entering a reminder.

"Yes, he had a broken tooth." Jill tapped on her own front tooth.

Molly nodded as she added to her notes. When she finished, she took Jill's hand. "Thank you. This is good information. If you remember more, please call me. Do you still have my card?"

"Yes, it's in the little drawer of the rolling table. If you'd ever like to call me, I'll give you my cell number." Jill shared the number and Molly entered it in her phone.

"I hope you find the guy who beat me up. It's been quite an ordeal and I'm still not finished with surgery. I have one more, possibly two, to repair my shoulder. Once that's behind me, I should be able to return to work." She smiled at Molly. "My boss has been by to see me, and he assures me they're holding my job for me."

"That's wonderful. It doesn't always work out like that. I'm happy for you." Molly gave a little squeeze to Jill's hand, told her goodbye, and left. In the elevator she checked her watch. She had just enough time to get to a store and pick up something to wear to Dr. Brigg's party. There was no way she could compete with Julia Spelling, but she could at least make try.

Molly had tried on several dresses from her closet that morning, and none of them pleased her. She didn't have time to drive to Scottsdale's Fashion Square, but she could run to the Desert Ridge Mall on her way home and check out Julia Spelling's boutique. She had researched it online and liked what she saw.

When Molly arrived, Julia wasn't in the shop, but a young woman working there seemed eager to help. Together they picked out just the right dress, sophisticated enough to be admired, but casual enough to wear to an informal birthday party. Molly laid the dress on the counter. Next, she picked out a pair of costume earrings and a bracelet to match.

The clerk gushed over her selections. "Oh, the jewelry goes perfectly with the dress you've chosen."

As the salesclerk tallied her items, Molly's eyes wandered to the opposite side of the store. She pointed toward the wall and asked, "Is that an artist's worktable?"

"Yes, it is. We have a guy named Kenneth who creates, repairs, and restores jewelry for us. He's here every Thursday. You just missed him. He's been with us ever since Julia opened the shop. You'd be surprised how busy he stays. He takes rush orders home and brings them back the next Thursday, or the next day if it's necessary. Totally trustworthy."

"He must be a great draw for the store. Does he work for Julia or pay rent?"

"He doesn't work for Julia, and I've never heard whether he pays rent. Probably."

"What a convenience. Does he work on jewelry other than what you sell?"

"Yes, he fixes whatever people bring him. Does a beautiful job. Would you like his card?"

"I would. I have several pieces I inherited which need repair." Molly paid her bill and headed to her car.

- 38 -

The sun had set when Molly left Julia Spelling's boutique, and the tall overhead lights in the parking lot had come on. The dress she purchased was encased in a plastic dress bag and draped over her arm. Walking toward her car, she fumbled in her tote bag for her keys then pointed the fob at her detective car and unlocked it. She stepped sideways to avoid the neighboring truck parked over the dividing line.

As she maneuvered past the truck's side mirror, a closed fist came out of nowhere and struck her left temple. Molly fell face down between the vehicles. Her keys skittered under the truck. Her dress flew forward in front of her. Her tote bag dropped from her left arm, smashing the ground. Its contents spilled under her car.

Although dazed, Molly realized she'd been attacked. She tried to get up but was trapped between the vehicles. A sharp kick to her ribs burned. Air rushed from her lungs. Angry and in pain, she reverted to her self-defense training. A man's hand grabbed her coat from behind and yanked her to her feet. His hand covered her mouth. She bit the meaty part of his palm, drove her elbow back into his ribs and stomped on his foot.

Sucking air, she faced her attacker and threw punches at his face. His muscled arms blocked most of the flurry. She kicked him in the groin. He groaned. Then flew into a rage.

A passing car's headlights lit the area and a whitish scar, circling his throat, became visible. He was young. Powerfully built. Possibly Hispanic. She threw another punch at his face. He ducked, grabbed her hair, and yanked it hard. She stumbled and fell, pulling him down upon her.

His body pinned her arms. Then a fierce blow hit her face. She gasped. Squirmed. But it was useless. He grabbed her throat and drove the back of her head into the pavement. She kicked at him with both legs, wiggled and twisted to get out from under him. She jabbed her knee into his midsection. He grunted and slithered sideways. She reached for the gun at her waist and drove it into his gut. She pulled the trigger.

The gun didn't fire. Panic gobsmacked her brain. She screamed, "Nooo!" backed the handgun away, pulled the trigger twice, and sent two bullets into the man's torso.

He screamed and rolled over. She forced herself onto her feet, stumbled around her car, and crawled in. Using the radio, she called for assistance. Three police cars, a Fire Department ambulance, and a second firetruck arrived in minutes.

Two cops fished the contents of Molly's tote from under the truck while Molly was examined by paramedics. The cuts to both knees had stopped bleeding but burned like fire. She moved her arm and felt the blood that coated her sleeve. Her elbows and palms were scraped raw. She incurred bruises to her face and neck. The medical tech gave her a bottle of water and continued dressing her wounds.

She turned toward the police officers as they lifted her attacker into the ambulance. When he was secured, and the paramedics finished attending to her, a detective approached.

"My name's Dan Lewiston. I work Night Detectives and my squad will be investigating your officer involved shooting."

"I thought Night Dicks only worked Aggravated Assaults, suspicious death, and homicides when Homicide was too busy. I figured Homicide and Professional Standards Bureau would each complete their independent shooting investigations."

"Normally all of that is true, however, the lieutenant thought if the Night Detectives Squad did the criminal investigation along with PSB's completing the internal investigation, it would look less like a conflict of interest since you're on the job."

Detective Lewiston activated his digital recorder, read Molly the Miranda Warnings from a standard card.

Molly said, "I don't need a lawyer or my union rep present. I was in fear of my life; it was a good shoot."

Lewiston took Molly's initial statement and walked her through the events leading up to the shooting. He then took her gun as evidence, saying it would be sent to the lab for DNA, fingerprints, and a function test. He issued her another handgun. The Crime Scene Tech photographed Molly from head to toe, front to back, and took closeups of each of her injuries.

"The kid had fighting skills," Molly said. "Lucky he couldn't do much damage while stuck between the two vehicles. Did you notice the color of his shoes?"

"His shoes?"

"Yeah, I didn't have a chance to see them clearly."

Lewiston looked like he wanted to laugh then must have thought better of it.

Molly lost her patience. Rolled her eyes. "His shoes. They were multicolored with a white band around the bottom. Dirty and old."

"I did notice that. Didn't think much about it at the time."

"Hang on to him. I believe he's the offender who attacked a young woman several weeks ago. She was lucky to survive.

Name's Jill Bronson. You should be able to tie the two cases together. She's still in the hospital—at St. James."

"You know, you were lucky to survive this attack. But don't worry, that creep won't be going anywhere."

"Thank you. It will feel good to tell his victim we got him."

The detective took a step back and studied Molly's face. "I suggest we take you to the hospital, so your injuries are documented, and you receive care."

"No hospital. I've too much to do."

"You may also have a concussion, and you'll probably have a couple of shiners. Tomorrow, Professional Standards Bureau will be calling you for an interview. Make sure you're available."

The next morning at home, Molly woke with sore muscles and stiff joints. Her mom would have said she'd been yanked through a knothole. And it felt like it. She stood under a hot shower until the water turned cold then padded to the kitchen and poured a cup of hot coffee.

Around ten a.m., her doorbell rang. It wasn't much of a surprise to see Larry Pilson and Arnie Schmidt standing on her porch. She hesitated a few seconds, smiled at them and invited them in. "I just made my second pot of coffee; you got the time?"

Schmidt nodded. "You look like hell. We're glad you survived."

Pilson raised his hand shoulder high and rattled the bag of pastries he carried. "We brought something to go with the coffee."

Molly smiled. "I see that." She waved for them to follow her. "Glad to see you, I can use the company. I'm a little grumpy right now."

From behind her, Pilson said, "You know, Molly, ya gotta quit pickin' on little boys. You're going to get a reputation."

She stopped and placed her fists on her hips.

"Shut the hell up."

- 39 -

On Monday, after the mandatory three-days off following a police shooting, Molly arrived at police headquarters in time for her appointment with Detective Sergeant Greg Rinehart, one of the gang squad sergeants.

She wore her navy-blue Phoenix Police sweatpants and a sweatshirt for comfort. Every step she took was painful throughout her body. After icing her tender face, she had tried to cover her facial bruising and black eyes with makeup, but it was a waste of her time.

Detective Sergeant Rinehart was on the small side with a charming personality—a perpetual smile. He gestured to her face. "I heard about your attack, Molly. Also heard you gave as good as you got." He grinned. "I can see you still paid for it. Wear those shiners with pride; you earned them." He reached towards her. "May I take your coat?"

"No thanks. I don't expect to be here long. It's easier to leave it on. Thank you for agreeing to see me."

"Always happy to help a team member." Rinehart grinned. "We all have the same boss. How can I help you?"

"I'm working a case involving a young woman, Jill Bronson, who was violently attacked in Granite Hills Park. She's still in the hospital but was brought out of an induced coma a few days ago. She's slowly remembering more about her attacker. From witness accounts, we believe it could have been gang related." Molly paused. "Curiously, I think I was attacked by the same young man. He's in jail as we speak."

"Why do you think it's the same guy? Did you get a good look at your assailant? Would you be able to pick him out of a photo-line-up?"

"Like Jill's attack, it caught me by surprise, but my attack was after dark. A car's headlights allowed me to see the scar on his throat. The same type and size of scar Jill had described. He was also wearing the same colorful old shoes she had mentioned. To answer your question, yes, I think I could pick him out of a photo-line-up.

"Jill saw his broken front tooth, but I did not. She also described a partial tattoo which I didn't see. According to her it was on his upper arm, and it resembled the top of an animal's head—possibly a dog with one bent or broken ear."

Rinehart nodded his affirmation as Molly spoke. "Anything else?" he asked.

"Yes. Jill mentioned another tattoo on his neck, beneath his right earlobe, *AD1836*. She referred to it as a date, the year AD-1836." Molly shrugged. "I didn't see it." Suddenly, she recalled she'd seen the same numbers in the dirt near the marijuana field, but she didn't interrupt Rinehart to mention it.

"No problem. That would be Juan Soldado. He's a punk. Failed his first initiation test. Your victim is lucky because his second test required him to steal from and kill somebody in broad daylight, hence, your victim. The coward obviously went after a woman. Since he failed twice, his last chance was to kill a cop if he wanted into the gang. Since you survived, his future isn't looking so good."

Molly glared at Rinehart. "You know the guy?"

"We know all the gangs and their soldiers. The tattoo *AD* stands for Alamo Devils. The year signifies Santa Anna's conquering of the Alamo in old Texas." He rubbed his forehead. "They have been operating in Phoenix for a little more than two years. The whole bunch of them came up from Tucson. They're heavy into the drug business and they intend to control all marijuana action, from farming to distributing, in the region and beyond. Another Tucson gang tried to overtake them. It ended in a gunfight. It so happened the AD's leader was murdered by a female gang member.

"The Devils high-tailed it to Phoenix. They have a new, blood-thirsty leader, the widow of the guy they killed. Maria del Cana is her name. Tough as nails. Seeking vengeance for her loss. Blames all Caucasians, especially females, like your victim and now you."

"Do you know more about her? Have a picture of the del Cana woman?"

"Lately, she's been hanging out with her brother, Enrique Martinez. He has a home in Phoenix. There's a picture of her in the file and an address. We're watching them closely because Enrique is suspected of having a relationship with Middle Eastern terrorist families. It appears he is also into money laundering. It's logical since all his businesses are cash producers."

"Wow, I had no idea," Molly said.

"That's good. We're keepin' it close to the vest. Working on a need-to-know basis. A lot of American dollars have shown up in Yemen lately. Undoubtedly part of a money laundering scheme. Some of it has been traced to one of Phoenix's larger banks."

Rinehart stood and stepped around his desk to an ugly green, dented four-drawer, vertical file cabinet. When he pulled open the second drawer, it sounded a high-pitched squeal. He withdrew a file and held it up for Molly to see it. "Everything we have on AD1836 is here. I'll copy the contents and deliver it to you later today or tomorrow morning. Keep a tight grip on it. Remember, *it's need to know.*

"Even though Juan Soldado failed his mission three times, don't take him or AD1836 lightly. Time will pass and Juan will be sent out again to do the job right. If he fails once more, he'll be eliminated, killed. Maria del Cana is filled with hate and vengeance. Don't go near any of her gang, especially her, without backup. Stress my warning to your partners. To kill a cop would elevate the perpetrator to the highest level—immediately below Maria. That's what Juan had in mind when he attacked you."

He opened the file and highlighted a line on the inner cover. "This is her address."

Molly leaned forward. "I know that house. We did a little surveillance there the other night, but I'll compare this address with ours, just in case. We thought it was the brother's house, Enrique Martinez's."

Rinehart came around his desk and stood in front of her. "I hope I've helped. The file will give you a lot of info. I'm sure you and your people will find it of value. I can't emphasize enough, always exercise caution when getting close to these people. They're the worst we've dealt with. I know I don't have to tell you that now, but it is easy to become over-confident. Remember, these people are pure evil."

Molly stood, offered him her hand which he shook with another friendly smile. "Thank you, Detective Rinehart. My partners and I will read the file cover to cover. It's a relief to have the name of Jill Bronson's attacker. It's an important step forward. Jill Bronson's brother was murdered a couple days after her attack. Next step, besides finding the killer, is to make a connection if there is one."

Rinehart tipped his head. "I'd like to monitor your efforts—see how it turns out. If you need assistance with the gangs, call me. We've infiltrated all the gangs in the area with our CIs. Believe me, you've got your work cut out for you. We have a lot of experience, and we're happy to give you a hand—just say the word."

Molly thought about the danger for a confidential informer, and the work ahead as she returned to her cubicle. A murder case was never simple, but international gang involvement added another unwelcome layer. The Bronson murder case was like an octopus with five of its eight tentacles constantly grasping, twisting, and threatening. Along with the Bronson murder and its possible connection to the marijuana field, there was Jill Bronson's near-deadly attack. It appeared to be a warning to Alphonso to do as he was told and grow more marijuana for the AD1836 gang. Plus Mrs. Harmon's stolen ring, and the suspicious activity involving the theft of Harmons' stallions' semen. Molly shook her head, hoping she'd seen the last of the crimes connected to her investigation.

Molly gnawed at her lip. At last count, it appeared three vials of Rothman's semen had gone missing, possibly more. So far none of the semen of the other stallions standing at Harmony appeared to be black-marketed. Molly couldn't imagine the total financial detriment to the ranch over time, but it had to be enormous.

- 40 -

Early Friday evening, Molly was the first to arrive at the Harmons' home carrying a dozen roses in a vase she'd picked up on the way. Jimmy met her at the door smiling broadly. "You brought me roses; how sweet!" He reached for the flowers, curling a hand around the neck of the vase. "You needn't try so hard to win me over. You know I've always been yours for the taking."

Molly chuckled. "Oh, really? You assume way too much. Obviously, they're for your mother."

"I'm crushed. I thought for sure they were mine."

"Wrong again." She brushed by him and walked inside.

He caught up to her and immediately dropped his voice. "Your face is bruised. What happened?"

Her hand floated up to her face and she touched her cheek. "It's nothing. I tripped."

He tenderly cupped her jaw. "You have more than one. Will you tell me about it sometime?"

She nodded. "Sometime. I tried to cover the bruises with makeup. Guess I didn't do a thorough job."

He gave her a small smile. "You tripped? Right. Just don't stand near a lighted lamp." He raised the vase higher. "I'll give the flowers to Mom then I'll get the paperwork I promised you. I think you'll find it interesting."

Jim headed into the kitchen and moments later he and his mom returned. "Molly, dear, thank you for the beautiful roses—and thank you for coming." She gestured to the family room. "Please make yourself comfortable. I have just a few more details in the kitchen then I'll join you."

"Thank you," Molly said as she started to walk away.

"Hang on, Molly." Jim turned to his mom. "I have something for Molly in my car." He reached for Molly's hand. "I'll check the grill on our way; we'll be back in a couple minutes."

Once outside, Jimmy led the way. "I'm glad we can do this before everyone gets here. I think you'll find the paperwork on the earrings fascinating. I never bothered to read them before today. Guess I'm not much of a shopper."

Molly leaned against Jim's car's front fender as he retrieved the printed forms he'd received in Hawaii, including the receipt of purchase. He handed her the few pages and she flipped through them.

Her first surprise was the small amount he'd paid for the emeralds, as written on the receipt, then recalled he'd mentioned a store-wide sale. Although the gift shop was in Honolulu on Oahu, Hawaii's most commercial island, a laboratory located on the big island provided the description of the stones. Her second surprise was the gems were created using the ash collected after Mt. Kīlauea's last big eruption. The process they used, plus a short list of chemicals, was included, but Molly stopped reading after she understood the stones were lab-created.

"Why didn't you tell me?" she asked Jimmy as she tucked the papers into her handbag.

His eyebrows shot to his hairline. "I hadn't read the information that came with the earrings, and I couldn't remember exactly where the stones came from—which island. I was so pleased to receive a great sales price, I didn't think more about it."

Molly smirked. "Okay, wise guy." She gave a small shake of her head. "You were never one for detail, except where the horses were concerned."

"I was so uncomfortable when you first asked me about the gemstones. I got flustered over your suspecting me of taking Mom's ring. Then when we were at your car and you asked for a receipt, I figured we'd settle it soon enough. I knew I hadn't done anything wrong. No harm, no foul."

Molly's heart filled with regret. Instead of her talking to Jimmy about the emeralds, she should have sent Pilson or Schmidt. She realized she had been happy for a reason to see Jimmy again. She sighed. "I'm sorry. I should have handled this better from the start."

He shrugged. "Nah, you handled it fine. Although I did wonder if I was about to go to jail." He laughed as he reached out to hug her. "It's all good—we're all good. Right?"

She smiled. "Like always."

"Right. One other thing, will you go out to dinner with me Saturday night?"

"Like a real date?"

"Hell, yeah. A real date."

She gave him a small, confounded shake of her head. "I would love to, but I can't." She cleared her throat. "As long as I'm working Jerrod's murder case that involves everyone on the ranch, I simply can't. It would be a conflict of interest."

He nodded. "I understand. I should have thought of that."

"It's all right. A common error."

He tipped his head. "Well, as acquaintances from way back, let's check the grill before Mom comes to check on us." He led her around the corner to the back patio.

Molly laughed, hurrying to keep up. "Like the teenagers we once were?"

He grinned down at her. "We'll make up for lost time one of these days." He opened the grill, dumped in the last of the coals from the bag, grabbed a bar-b-cue tool and pushed them around. Standing off to the side and a step behind him, Molly realized he was still the attractive man she had once crushed on.

- 41 -

As Molly and Jim entered the house, Doris came from the kitchen carrying a platter of appetizers. She asked Jim, "How much time on the grill?"

"The coals should be just right in a half hour. Where's Dad?"

"Holding court with our guests in the great room. Let's join the party."

They followed Doris into the large living area where a fire burned invitingly in the big rock fireplace. Dr. Briggs and two couples Molly suspected were related to him, along with Dr. Spelling and Julia, turned and stared as they entered the room. Molly greeted George Harmon with a hug then wished Dr. Briggs happy birthday. Standing near him, she was reminded how large a man he was. He introduced his family to Molly, and an easy conversation developed as Doris moved through the room offering appetizers.

The women were dressed in casual attire, including Julia who wore a simple black dress with silver high-heeled sandals. The only jewelry she wore was a small pair of black Tahitian pearl earrings and an intricate scrimshaw brooch.

Julia smiled at Molly. "Nice to see you again, Detective. I thought you'd be wearing your new dress I heard about."

"Please, call me Molly," she said. "I had a bit of an accident with it; it's in the dry cleaners." Molly was thankful no one asked what had happened.

Julia nodded. "I understand your family and Jimmy's are long time friends.

Molly said, "Jimmy and I competed against each other when we were kids. His horse usually outshone mine." Molly quickly changed the subject from her and Jim. "Your pin is lovely. Did you find it while traveling in Alaska?"

"My dad bought it for me on one of his many trips. He's a collector so he always comes home with something. He has a nice exhibit in the AI facility office, but the collection on display at our house is amazing." She turned to her father. "Dad, you should invite Molly over to the house to see your scrimshaw display."

Dr. Spelling smiled at Molly. "Anytime Detective. I would be happy to share the assortment with you. Perhaps one evening next week."

"Thank you, I'd like that. I'll get in touch with you after the weekend. Have you been collecting for a long time?"

"Not too long. Mitch... Dr. Briggs was the one who introduced me to the ivory arts." He turned and smiled at Briggs, who appeared to be listening to the conversation. "His collection is more diverse than mine, whereas I've been interested in the antique Alaskan scrimshaw pieces. I've always had a curiosity about history and the allure of the sea."

Molly listened closely then quietly excused herself to help Doris Harmon with last minute dinner details. When she walked into the kitchen, Doris headed toward the dining room with a large basket of golden-baked dinner rolls fresh from the oven. Before Molly could offer to take the rolls to the table, someone knocked on the back door.

"Oh," Doris muttered. "That's probably Billy Fenton with the ice. I called him when I realized I'd forgotten to pick it up at the market this morning. Will you answer the door?"

"Happy to." Molly hurried through the kitchen as Doris continued to the dining room. When Molly opened the door, Billy, one of the trainers, stood beneath the porch light, arms cradling two large bags of ice.

"Evening, Detective, I have the ice Mrs. Harmon asked me to get for her."

"So I see." She stepped back. "I'll hold the freezer door open so you can stack the bags inside."

When Billy raised his arms to put the ice on the top shelf of the tall freezer, its light shown on the unusual buckle on his belt.

"What an interesting belt buckle. I've never seen one quite like it." Molly closed the freezer door, still staring at the buckle.

Billy chuckled. "Yeah, I got it from Doc Spelling. He bet me I couldn't make one of the old, ornery mares behave when it was time for her to be bred to Rothman. That mare has always produced gorgeous Rothman foals. But she was known for getting mean when she's fully in season and taken to the stallion." Billy chuckled.

"I took Spelling's bet right away. I told him I'd clean stalls for a week in the AI facility if I lost. But if I won, I wanted the belt buckle he was wearing. Of course, I didn't tell him the mare liked me special. We had a good understanding—that old mare and me." Billy laughed. "As usual, after a little encouragement, Silver Coin behaved like a lady while being bred, and I won the bet." He rubbed his hand across the buckle. "Love the feel of it. I practically never take it off."

"It looks new. How long have you had it?"

"I won it right after Halloween."

"Wow," Molly muttered. "Time has flown. Before we know it, the Scottsdale All Arabian horse show will have come and gone."

"You're right about that. We're already gearin' up in the barns for the big event. Next week we'll be shavin' off the show horses' winter hair. They should be all slicked out by Scottsdale time. Too much to do and too little time to do it." Billy waved goodbye and headed into the night.

When the evening ended, Jimmy walked Molly to her car. "You seemed to be quite interested in the doctors' ivory collections."

"Yes, I am. I guess because I've lived in the desert all my life, I'm curious about ocean-related topics. I once wrote a paper for a college class pertaining to the discovery of Noah's ark. I loved doing the research. All those years ago, a diver, Ron Wyatt, wrote he'd found the ark in the Black Sea near Turkey. Claimed he had also found numerous artifacts to corroborate his tale. I was attracted to the story because his name reminded me of Wyatt Earp. Another one of my quirks."

"I've always loved your quirks." Jimmy stared at her as a slow smile crossed his face. "You know you're really quite special."

Molly chuckled. "Yeah, all the boys say that."

"You are. I mean it."

Molly's spoke sternly. "When I solve this damn murder case with all its subcases then you can tell me I'm special. I hoped to learn something useful tonight but found nothing further."

"You have the paperwork on Julia's earrings; it has to be worth something."

"True." She studied him. "I'm sorry we had to have that difficult conversation."

"Not to worry. It's all in the past, so let's forget it." He slipped his arms around her, hugged her, and bid her good night.

She slid into her car, jockeyed it around on the driveway, and waved goodbye. He cautioned her to drive safely before she headed for the ranch's gate. While driving home, she thought about Jimmy's last words. Did he think she wouldn't drive carefully? Doesn't everyone think they'll drive safely when they turn their keys in the ignition? Her mood drifted to an unpleasant, darker place. Although she tried to shake it off with happy thoughts of her younger years, she couldn't. Each attempt was interrupted with the grim truths of her life as a Phoenix homicide detective. Maybe her mom had been right... *police work is best left to hard-hearted men.*

Nah.

- 42 -

On Monday morning, Molly woke with minor aches and pains from her attack and her spirits rose. Hopefully, the worst was behind her. In the bathroom she examined the bruises on her face. A double layer of makeup was still necessary if she went anywhere, but leaving the house wasn't on her schedule, except for a morning jog.

She dressed in sweats, grabbed her Diamondback's cap and sunglasses, and headed out for her run. She did her usual three-mile loop, and when she returned to her driveway, checked her time. The results weren't as good as she wanted, but they were what she expected given her aching body. They say you have to run through the pain—right. Easy for them to say. Who is *they*, anyway?

She picked up her newspaper and headed inside for a shower. She flipped on the coffeemaker as she entered her kitchen.

An hour later, she contacted Dr. Spelling and asked if she could come by to see his scrimshaw collection as they'd discussed the previous evening.

"Absolutely," he said. "I enjoy showing it off." He paused. "Let's see, could you make it around six o'clock? We'll all be home from work about that time."

"Sounds perfect. I'll see you at your house."

Molly arrived at the Spelling home a few minutes past six and was greeted happily by Dr. Spelling. "Nice to see you, Detective." He guided her down a short hallway to the door to his office.

"Please call me Molly. We're both off the clock."

"Thank you. My name's, David, but everybody calls me Dave."

As they entered the room, he flipped a switch and to her right the lights in a display cabinet came on, casting a glow over the entire room. The large breakfront took up the entire wall and contained four glass shelves with too many objects to count. Molly walked to the far end and stared at the scrimshaw. "Wow, this display cabinet is beautiful, and the size of your collection is very impressive. How long did it take to acquire all of this?" She gestured with her hand to the entire display.

"About five years, I'd guess. Mitch... Dr. Briggs introduced me to the artform a couple years after we started working together. I was fascinated by it immediately. He gave me the drawings of his cabinet and I had the same guy he used build mine." He turned and seemed to study his collection. "It's rather romantic, don't you think, when you imagine some lonely sailor carving by candlelight, hoping the calm will soon pass and the wind will finally fill the sails to push them closer to port?"

Molly grinned. "I suppose. When you imagine it that way." Her eyes settled on the huge tusk that appeared to be the centerpiece of his collection. She pointed to it. "Is that an elephant's tusk?"

"No, that comes from a very old walrus. It's circa 1900. Mitch has a piece in his collection dating back to Columbus and one of his voyages." He chuckled. "Mitch could easily handle the cost; I was lucky to afford this one."

"Where did you find it?"

"I found it in a shop in Juneau two years ago. As the story goes, they had it stored in an old barrel in their backroom for nearly twenty years, before they happened upon it and put it on display. The shop owner said his grandfather acquired it when he owned the business. I was impressed with the extent of the detail in the carving. Notice the number of sails on the three masts of that Portuguese caravel and the intricate shading to create dimension."

Molly leaned closer to the glass door. "It must have taken months to complete. The way the sails appear to billow is amazing." She turned to face Spelling. "I can see how your interest was piqued. The artwork is beautiful." Molly bent over to study a small pin on the self below.

"I like this brooch. Does it have a story?"

Spelling was slow to answer. "I believe it was found among the ruins of a ship that was sunk during some war. I can't quite remember the details. I think the woman's image is of a Spanish princess. I bought it when I first started collecting. I've always believed the story was a bunch of BS told by the salesman. But I liked it, so I bought it anyway. Mitch tells me the piece probably goes back to the late eighteenth century, but who knows?"

"If it was found in a sunken ship, I would think the ink or dye they used to color or highlight the carvings would have been washed away."

Spelling glanced at Molly momentarily. "I never thought of that. That's a good observation. I'll ask Briggs... see what he says."

A woman's voice called out from somewhere in the house. "Hellooo! Where are you?"

Spelling smiled. "That's Lisa." He stepped closer to the door. "We're in the office!"

Footsteps sounded nearby in the hall outside the office door. An attractive woman, possibly in her forties, carrying a briefcase, walked to Spelling's side and kissed the side of his face. He smiled and returned the kiss. He introduced the women to each other, and Lisa offered Molly her hand.

As Molly shook Lisa's hand, she said, "It's very nice to meet you. Dr. Spelling was just showing me his fabulous scrimshaw collection."

Lisa stepped closer to the display cabinet and pointed to a cameo brooch with matching earrings. "This is one of my favorites, especially the earrings. They are so delicate."

Molly studied the jewelry then turned to Lisa to comment. The light from the cabinet shown on the side of Lisa's face, causing the emerald studs she wore on her earlobes to glisten. "I love jewelry, don't you?" Molly asked.

Lisa chuckled. "I think every woman loves jewelry; I definitely do."

"I noticed the earrings you're wearing. They're beautiful."

"Thank you." Lisa's hand rose to her ear, and she stroked the stone. "Julia gave them to me. I've been wearing them ever since."

- 43 -

On Tuesday morning, Molly headed into police headquarters, dropped off a box of pastries in the break room, and headed for Pilson and Schmidt's cubicles. Both had arrived before her.

"Good morning, gentlemen," she called to them as she hurried by, heading to her workspace to drop off her coat and scarf. "Can we get together in the next few minutes? I'd like to bring everyone up to date."

Schmidt and Pilson agreed. "I'll get us the conference room," Pilson said.

"Stop for coffee on your way. I brought goodies." Molly spoke loud enough for three other detectives to immediately stand and head for the break room.

Minutes later she and her partners were gathered around the large table in the conference room, coffee and pastries in hand.

"How'd the birthday party go?" Schmidt asked Molly.

"It was interesting." Molly went on to explain about Julia's earrings being man-made.

Pilson looked up from his notes. "That's interesting. You know my sister lives in Seattle, and years ago she bought a ring with what I'd swear was an expensive emerald. Turned out, just like Julia's earrings, my sis's ring was made from Mt. St. Helens' ash. Remember when that big ole mountain in southwest Washington blew its top? Month of May of nineteen eighty, I think it was. I've seen before-and-after pictures of Mt. St. Helens. It was gorgeous at one time, but not anymore. On the positive side, one of their long-serving County Commissioners, a talented guy named Van Youngquist, took on the job of restoring the area. A lot of tree-planting was done. They created a beautiful visitor center that contains the story of the mountain and the volcano that ripped it apart—plus a beautiful new highway leading up to it. No committee needed—just Youngquist."

Schmidt laughed. "Larry, you sound like an encyclopedia." He grinned. "But some day, I'll go there. I can only imagine the photographs they must have on display."

Molly chuckled. "Me, too. Here's another strange thing. When I visited Spelling's to see his scrimshaw, his girlfriend, Lisa, came in wearing emerald earrings Julia had given her."

"Did she say anything more about them?" Schmidt asked.

"No, it was strange." Molly raised a palm. "It sounded like Lisa simply admired them, and Julia gave them to her." Molly tipped her head. "Why would Julia give them away after telling us how much she liked them?"

Pilson said, "Maybe she found out they weren't genuine, and it made her angry. So she didn't want them anymore."

Molly shrugged. "Yeah, maybe."

Schmidt yawned and faced Molly. "Did ya learn anything else from the party?"

"Well one thing, but it's probably too soon to talk about," Molly answered.

"Like what?" Pilson asked.

"Do you remember talking with a kid by the name of Billy? Billy Fenton?"

Both men shook their heads.

"He was my first interview. I didn't learn anything from him either. Anyway, keep an eye out for him if or when you go back out to the ranch. He's a junior trainer and apparently well-liked by the family. Mrs. Harmon depends on him when she needs a little extra help."

"What about him?" Schmidt asked.

Molly regretted she didn't have a picture to show them. "He was wearing a belt buckle with a piece of ivory scrimshaw on it. I've got this nagging gut-feeling we should pay attention to it, could be something we're over-looking. It might lead to clues worth following." She shook her head. "I don't know. Get a look at it so we can talk about it. It's probably nothing. Now, let's talk about your accomplishments from yesterday afternoon."

Pilson was the first to respond. "After I left here, I went to the pawn shops that were top of our list, mostly to let them know we were still working on Mrs. Harmon's ring. So far, none of the shop owners had seen it. They assured me they were watching for it. I mean, who could forget a four-carat diamond? I looked at their security camera recordings but came up cold."

Schmidt nodded. "Same here. I went by the university and found they do maintain cameras on the property around the campus perimeter, as well as the sidewalks and parking areas. I spent the rest of the day looking at footage but got nothing. Still, I think I'll give the college another try." He glanced at Molly. "Did you get anything from Jill? You did see her, right?"

"Yep. Randy has moved back in with her. She remembered more about her assailant. One thing stood out. Jill told me the guy had a scar on his neck that runs from his ear to nearly his Adam's apple, and he's young. Plus, she recalled seeing a broken tooth in the front of his mouth."

"Whoa!" Pilson burst. "That sounds like the guy who attacked you out at Desert Ridge Mall, except for the broken tooth. You didn't mention that."

"That's right. I made a note to check with our gang squad because we know she saw a partial tattoo that was like the design in the dirt we saw at Jerrod Bronson's weed field. The kid who attacked Jill and me was going through a gang initiation according to Detective Rinehart. We may be close to a definite connection between Jill's attack and her brother's marijuana field."

"He may be nothing but a grunt-soldier," Pilson muttered. "I heard somebody bailed him out already."

"Not surprising. The revolving door treatment." Molly stood. "Any chance you guys could swing by the ranch and poke around a bit. Maybe have a conversation with Billy Fenton and get a good look at his belt buckle."

"Sure," Schmidt said. "I can do that." He turned and looked inquiringly at Pilson.

"Right, me too." Pilson grinned at Molly. "Where're you going?"

"I think I'll swing by the hospital and visit with Jill Bronson. Each time I visit with her and see the damage she suffered, I've really want to get the guy. I hope we have."

Molly slid into her official car and pushed her key into the ignition. Before she could start it, her phone rang. She checked caller ID and answered, "Detective Raines."

"This is **Sergeant** Hancock. I'm calling about the diamond and emerald ring you were looking for a while back. I may have some information on it. Although I put it in the computer to automatically do a weekly search, I've been manually checking every couple of weeks just in case. Sometimes the automatic search can miss things if we don't use the right key words."

"Thank you very much for the call. What do you have?"

"We received a report from a pawn shop located on West Daily and Glendale Avenue. I think they may have the big diamond ring you're looking for. I doubt you would have gone there because it's way down on the list I gave you of shops who might buy such an expensive item. It's kind of a surprise. This outfit specializes in firearms, old ones, in particular. But not diamonds. Still, stranger things have happened."

"Can you give me a name and address?"

"Of course. It's called Best Price."

Molly wrote down the address Hancock gave her, thanked him again, and headed for the ranch for a visit with Mrs. Harmon. From the collection of ranch hands' photos, Mrs. Harmon had put together, Molly hadn't received one of Billy Fenton who had risen sharply on her list of suspects. Although unlikely he was the thief, she was determined not to make an avoidable mistake.

- 44 -

Before Molly left the parking lot, she texted Pilson and Schmidt: *I assume you're at the ranch. Wait for me there. On my way. May have caught a break.*

Thirty minutes later, Molly parked behind Schmidt's car, along the fence of the outdoor training arena. Schmidt stepped from his car, walked to Molly's side door, and opened it. He grinned down at her. "Whatcha got, Skipper?"

"Where's Pilson? I don't want to have to tell it twice."

"He'll be right along. He was talking to that Big Bev girl in the second barn over."

"Okay," Molly said. "Stay right here. I'm going to run down to the house and pick up a photo of Billy Fenton." She hesitated. "Did you talk with him?"

Schmidt grinned widely. "Sure did."

"Okay, hold that thought. I'll be right back." Molly ran a few strides then slowed to a fast walk. Her ribs still bothered her, but she'd adjusted to it.

Mrs. Harmon answered Molly's knock and hugged her hello. Molly spoke rapidly in a whisper in case Cindy was nearby. "I need a photo of Billy Fenton. Do you have one?"

Mrs. Harmon nodded, raised her index finger, signaling she'd be right back and hustled off in the direction of the offices. She returned promptly. "Here you go," she whispered and held the picture out to Molly. "Do you have news?"

Molly whispered back, "Possibly a lead on your ring. I'll keep you informed." She hugged Doris then hurried to her car where Pilson now stood next to Schmidt.

Molly tucked Billy's photo in her jacket pocket, grabbed her phone and texted the address for the Best Price pawn shop to Schmidt's phone. "I sent you the address for the pawn shop that may have taken in Harmon's ring, in case we get separated." She opened her car door and slid behind the wheel. "I'm heading there now. I'll meet you there."

Outside Best Price Pawn Shop's front entry, the door was flanked on both sides by large display windows showing a range of firearms, handguns, shot guns and rifles. Molly studied the collection. Her eyes settled on an antique 1894 Winchester, single-shot, shotgun. It was identical to the gun her grandfather had used when he took her bird hunting. Grandpa Stonehill was always a hero to Molly, and she still treasured the memories of sitting in a cold duck blind or walking through a corn field, hunting pheasants.

"Whatcha lookin' at Molly?" Pilson asked.

She glanced his way with a smile and pointed at the shotgun standing upright in the corner of a line of newer long guns. "That old Winchester. My gramps had one just like it." She smiled. "He never missed with the old thing."

She looked from Pilson to Schmidt. "Let's go," she said as Pilson pulled the door open. The old shop was the size of a Mini Mart with merchandise displayed in cabinets along the walls and various items hanging on the walls above. In the center of the room was a waist-high rectangular mahogany and glass display case holding Native Indian silver and turquoise jewelry.

They approached the overweight, middle-aged, bearded clerk who greeted them from behind the display case at the back of the store. Molly introduced herself and produced her ID then introduced her fellow detectives. Schmidt and Pilson stood on either side of her as she laid out the photos for the clerk to study.

"We're searching for a four-carat diamond ring. Has anyone tried to pawn or sell such an item in your store?"

"Always possible." The clerk said. "If so, they had to produce a driver's license and we should have made a copy of it."

"Would you mind looking at these photos and let me know if you recognize anyone?"

"Maybe." The clerk's hand quivered as he positioned his black-framed gasses near the end of his nose and bent closer to the pictures. "I'm sorry. I don't recognize anyone in these pictures. Of course I wouldn't, cause I didn't handle the transaction. My clerk did."

"On a chance, take a second look. Take your time."

The man studied the photos briefly. "I've never seen any of these people."

"You're sure?" Schmidt asked.

"Yep. We did take in a ring with a large diamond but can't say for certain it's the one you're looking for. The customer was a girl."

Stunned, Molly stared at the man. "And she's not in any of these photos?"

"Nope. Like I said, my man bought it. He said she was a good-lookin' blonde, mid to late twenties, medium height with a nice build if you get my drift."

"Loud and clear," Schmidt said.

"Grady, my clerk, said the woman didn't seem to know much about pricey jewelry. He low-balled her and she didn't argue; took the money and ran.

"I have the ring in my safe. Big ole diamond with large settings on either side. Could be the one you're lookin' for."

Molly's heart pounded in her chest. "I suppose it could be. Sounds like it. Could you also show me the copy of the young woman's driver's license?" She did her best to keep a calm demeanor, while crossing her fingers and imagining Mrs. Harmon's face when she told her they'd found her ring. Maybe she'd shed tears. Big, beautiful happy tears. "Owner's name is engraved inside the shank?"

The clerk raised his chin, looking down his nose at Molly. "Well, hot damn, Detective! I do believe you've found what your lookin' for." He turned toward the curtained doorway behind him. "It'll just take me a minute."

He disappeared, and Schmidt patted Molly on the arm. "Things are looking up, Skipper."

Pilson said softly, "Sometimes we get lucky, sometimes the Lord lends a hand."

Molly nodded without looking away from the shabby black curtain. In a matter of minutes, the clerk strode back to the counter and laid the ring on a spongy pad.

Anger suffused Molly's face the minute she saw the ring, but she remained silent.

The clerk reached into a nearby drawer for a jeweler's loupe, picked up the ring and studied the shank. "Is the owner's name Doris H, by any chance?" He handed Molly the ring.

Molly stared at it, taking a deep breath. "Did you remove the emeralds?" She slid a finger over the bent and empty prongs that once held the most beautiful emeralds she'd ever seen.

"Hell, no! That's how Grady bought it. There weren't no emeralds that I saw. I was happy just to get the diamond. It's a beaut, ain't it? And damn, it's big."

Molly tapped her finger against the glass cabinet's surface as she spoke each word. "You're telling us the woman brought in this ring without stones on either side of the diamond?"

"That's what I'm tellin' ya. Whoever yanked 'em out didn't plan to replace 'em. Broke one of the points. At the time, I figured it was the reason she didn't try to negotiate. I can't sell it as a ring, but that don't matter; the diamond is what counts."

"Can we see the driver's license?"

"That's a problem. Grady forgot to get a photo. Hope we're not in trouble. It was just a stupid beginner's mistake."

Telling Mrs. Harmon just became more difficult. Molly grabbed the digital camera from her jacket pocket and took pictures of the ring, glanced up at the clerk, and cleared her throat. "I'll file paperwork today letting Phoenix Police know the ring's been found. An Official Hold, according to Phoenix City Code (PCC)19-80, will be placed on the ring."

"How does that work as far as I'm concerned?"

Molly took a deep breath. "An email will be sent to our Pawnshop Detail with the officer's serial number—that would be mine—and store number, plus the ticket number, Incident Report number, and a description of the property. The Pawn Shop Detail will be responsible for entering the property in the records management system and mailing a written Notice of Hold to you."

She raised her hand. "Understand this. You are not permitted to sell it to anyone, other than the legal owner, until the hold is released." She paused. "Is that clear?"

The clerk frowned. "Yeah, yeah. I know how it works. The city always get its cut." He paused and glanced at her from beneath his brow. "You got that spiel memorized?"

Schmidt chuckled. "Yep. She has a mind like a steel trap. You should hear her quote Bible verses."

Molly licked her lips instead of slugging Schmidt. "I'll let the owner know you have the damaged ring and are holding it according to the law. Phoenix Police thanks you for your cooperation."

Molly and her two partners headed for the door. She glanced up at Schmidt and clenched her jaw. "Isn't this just dandy? I am so pissed over the damage to that ring and the screwup over the driver's license, I could scream. But at least now we can concentrate fully on solving a murder."

Pilson chuckled. "Not exactly; there's still the ring thief and semen thief."

- 45 -

Molly slid into her unmarked car, regretting she had to tell Doris Harmon about her stolen ring. For days, she'd anticipated bringing great news to Doris by returning the beautiful ring. She gnawed at her lower lip. Detective work, it seemed, *always* came with a downer. Solving a crime provided only a momentary high for the detective involved, but it never lasted long enough... only as long as it took to be assigned another case. Molly turned left out of the parking lot and headed for the freeway.

Forty minutes later, Doris came out her back door carrying a large basket of carrots. Molly stepped from her car, called her name, and Doris waved her over.

"Where are you going with all those carrots?" Molly asked, jogging toward Doris.

"They're for the horses in the stallion barn. Today, it's their turn. Let's walk over there while we talk." She raised the basket. Take a big handful; you can help me hand them out."

Molly fell in step next to Doris and matched her stride. "I have news for you."

"What's that?"

"We found your ring."

Doris stopped walking. "You did? Where?" She didn't wait for an answer. She wrapped Molly in a one-armed hug. "Oh, my goodness, I'm thrilled."

"Hang on, Mrs. Harmon. It's not very good news."

"Oh, no, tell me all about it, Molly."

"Somebody, a young woman I understand, pawned it. I got word of it and my two partners, and I went directly to the pawn shop. The owner showed it to us. I saw your name engraved inside the shank. So there's no doubt. Trouble is, whoever stole it removed the emeralds. I put a police-hold on it so they can't sell the diamond before the matter is resolved."

"Well, at least that's something," Doris said. "When can we go get it?"

"I suggest you talk with your attorney about the process involved. The police-hold will have to be dealt with properly. The pawn broker now has a vested interest—because he bought the ring—and that must be resolved. Your attorney can explain it in full."

"Oh, Molly, thank you. Despite it all, I'm grateful. I'll call our lawyer as soon as I return to the house. Does Jimmy know?"

Molly smiled. "Why don't you tell him? He'll be very relieved... George, too."

"Yes, of course, George. He and Dr. Briggs are at the teasing shoot re-teasing a few mares to determine if they can be bred today. I'll go that way when I leave the stallion barn." Doris gestured to Molly's handful of carrots. "Would you drop a few carrots in Jason's Gold's feeding crib. He's having his morning swim with Big Bev. I'll leave the basket by the barn door, so he doesn't see or smell them until he finishes his workout. Do you want to come along and say hello to George?"

"I wish I could, but I'm expected downtown in about thirty minutes. I need to get going." Molly hugged Doris once more and hurried toward her car.

- 46 -

In the tower above Mesa's Gateway Airport in Arizona, air controller Don Stapleton reached for his thermos. The clock above the door read two-thirty a.m. Don poured steaming coffee into his favorite mug, replaced the thermos's lid, and stowed it in the deep bottom drawer of his workstation. He glanced at the night sky, thankful planes seldom arrived this early in the morning.

He sipped his coffee and gazed into the star-studded distance, squinted, blinked several times then reached for his field glasses. Sure enough, headlights on a small plane appeared headed for the airport.

Two minutes later, Don received a request from the Cessna Citation XLS to land. He grabbed his mic and directed the pilot to approach from the north, to use the main runway, and mentioned the velocity of the gusting breeze. Don followed the small jet's approach and sighed with relief when it landed safely.

Instead of taxiing toward the airport, the pilot traveled past the tower to the south end of the runway, farther than Don expected. The plane's red taillights glimmered as it turned onto a crossing lane to a temporary runway seldom used these days. The plane turned left onto the old runway and rolled fifty yards to the south before it stopped and killed its engines.

Don turned to his colleague. "Hey, Leo, did you see where that Cessna parked? Any idea what he's up to? Is that permitted? The pilot didn't ask permission to use the old landing strip."

Leo shook his head. "Nope, but about three months ago—I think you were on vacation, a Cessna arrived in the middle of the night, followed by a Gulfstream. I asked our boss about it, and he said he didn't know anything. They didn't stay long, so we agreed to forget about it. No harm, no foul."

Ten minutes later, static emitted from the radio attached to Don's earpiece followed by another voice indicating he was piloting a Gulfstream 280 and wanted landing instructions.

As before, Don directed the Gulfstream to approach from the north and provided all necessary information for a safe landing. He continued using his field glasses to follow the plane as it set down on the main runway, taxied southward to the crossing lane, turned right then left onto the old original runway. The Gulfstream slowly approached the Cessna, made a 180-degree turn, and stopped. After positioning his plane for takeoff, the pilot killed its engines.

Pilots and co-pilots from both planes exited their craft, clamping a hand to their hats, fighting the wind that threatened to whisk them away. The men greeted each other, appeared to exchange a few words then returned to their planes. Each plane's crew opened their cargo door and lowered a ramp from the doorway down to the tarmac.

Don's limited view of the commuter planes' interiors surprised him. Neither plane had passenger seats, only cargo space.

With the help of a winch, installed in the cargo hold and a ramp, the Cessna's crew unloaded a blue tarp-covered, pallet of merchandise onto a wheeled dolly, sitting close to the plane, and pushed it toward the ramp of the Gulfstream.

One corner of the tarp flapped in the relentless wind. Don gasped, lowered his glasses, and turned to Leo. "Those guys are moving a shitload of cash from the Cessna to the Gulfstream. What the hell are they up to?"

"I don't know," Leo said. He stared at Don for a couple of seconds. "And I don't want to know."

Don picked up his field glasses and focused on the two planes. "My mom used to say, 'nothing good happens after midnight.' By the looks of it, she was right. Should we report this?"

Leo rubbed his jaw. "Just enter the landings and takeoffs into the log. If somebody comes around asking questions, tell 'em what you saw... or not." A Gulfstream crew member stood in the wide-open doorway of their craft and tossed a length of rope down to a man who attached it between the wheels of their pallet then signaled using a thumbs up. The Cessna's crew shoved the pallet to the base of the ramp, and the three men hauled the cargo into the Gulfstream. They repeated the procedure two more times.

Each crew stowed their ramps and started their engines. The Gulfstream's pilot asked the tower for permission to take off after providing the necessary flight plan. Permission was granted and the Gulfstream took off without incident.

Ten minutes later, The Cessna rolled onto the main runway, paused, and asked for permission to take off.

Five minutes later, all was quiet in the Gateway tower. The clock read three-fifteen.

Don glanced at the clock as he lifted his thermos out of its drawer. "Those guys transferred three pallets of cash and were here and gone in only forty-five minutes, Leo. Witnessing what we both saw, my nerves are shot. This could mean trouble;

trouble we don't want. It seems like we should be alerting somebody. Our boss. The Feds. Somebody?"

"Forget about it."

- 47 -

Two days after her last visit to the ranch, Molly rang Doris Harmon's cell phone and reached her on the first try. She asked for Billy Fenton's home address. After texting it to Pilson and Schmidt, she pulled the jeweler's card from her tote bag, given to her at Julia's Boutique, and called Kenneth at the number shown. When he answered, Molly introduced herself and arranged to meet him at a fast-food joint in his neighborhood.

Twenty minutes later, she sat across the table from Kenneth in Murphy's Hamburger Haven. He was guarded at first then relaxed when Molly assured him he was not under investigation. "I'm here because I'd like to have your help with something. At this point, it doesn't concern you, but it might in the future."

"I'm happy to help if I can," Kenneth said.

"I'd like you to do a little undercover work for me. I'm looking for two stolen emeralds, one carat each, give or take. It's possible an innocent person, unaware a crime has been committed, may have received them, and wants to have them placed in a setting of some kind. Possibly in a ring, a pendent, or maybe earrings. All I would like you to do is call me if anybody brings you an emerald or two and asks you to do the job." She smiled encouragingly. "Treat it as you would any other custom order but call me as soon as you have privacy."

He nodded. "I can do that." A smile tugged at his lips. "It sounds very mysterious—and important. Not quite James Bond I guess, but serious enough."

She didn't return his smile. "It is serious. Remember, whatever you do, don't talk about this with anyone, especially Julia and the women who work at the boutique. There is a chance you will recognize the person who comes to you. If someone should bring you the emeralds, don't assume they're guilty of anything. Keep your cool and agree to do whatever they ask." She leaned back, relaxed, and smiled. "That's all there is to it."

He rolled his eyes and grinned. "That's all? *Really?*" He sounded curious. "No prob. I do all my custom work at my home. Only Fort Knox has more security than I do at the house. When I'm in Julia's boutique, I only work on costume jewelry—no real stones. The fine jewelry pieces my customers bring into the store for repair are immediately secured until I take them home at the end of the day. Customers who bring real gemstones to me are usually worried about theft. They've heard the stories of jewelers replacing highly valuable stones with gems of lesser quality."

Molly nodded. "I see. There is a good chance none of this will happen, but I know you've built a good business and developed a strong customer base, so there is a chance the emeralds might make their way to you." She handed Kenneth her card, thanked him for his time, and asked him to call her day or night if one or two emeralds showed up. They shook hands and Molly headed for her car.

As Molly walked from the hamburger shop, her phone rang. Caller ID showed Pilson.

"What's up, Larry?"

"Arnie and I have scouted Billy Fenton's neighborhood and his house. Didn't spot anything noteworthy regarding the house. It's a nice home and he keeps it up. We peeked in some windows... nothing out of the ordinary. Tried the doors. None were unlocked. The neighborhood is upwardly mobile middle class. Nice mid-priced homes, well-kept yards. We rang a few doorbells. Nobody home, except for the next-door neighbor and the woman living across the street. Both were stay-at-home moms, one with small children, the other with a teenager. If we want to go into Billy's house, we'll need a warrant. But get this, we're not so sure Billy-Boy was out of town at the time of Jerrod's murder, like he told us."

"Really? Why is that?"

"The murder occurred three or four weeks ago, right?"

"Yes, right before Halloween. I don't recall the exact date, but it's in the murder book. Easy to check." Molly hesitated. "Do you think a junior horse trainer, probably paid not much more than minimum wage, could afford the rent on that place—in that neighborhood?"

"I kinda doubt it, but who knows?" Pilson said. "Billy could be a trust fund baby. We talked to both neighbor ladies and each of them remembered Billy being at home for about a week around Halloween. One of the women said they thought Billy might have been ill with some bug going around because his car remained parked in his driveway for three or four days. She was concerned so she went to check on him, but no one responded when she rang the doorbell.

"The other woman said she thought he was taking a staycation. She commented on how nice his car was. Said it's been in his driveway every weekday morning when her teenage daughter left to catch the school bus. The mom says she always walks her daughter to and from the bus stop because she's fearful of the illegal gangs coming across our southern border and making their way north. She complained a few blocks to the west some privacy block walls had been tagged with gang symbols and logos. She added there's been some gossip of a possible human smuggling stash house one street over.

"Because of his parked car, she believed Billy was still home when they left their house to go to the bus stop, which was unusual. Later, around mid-morning, while she was outside watering her flower beds, Billy drove away. She saw him return home in the afternoon as she walked to the mailbox. They made eye contact and he waved to her. He wasn't wearing work clothes, so she thought he must have taken the week off."

"How could she tell?" Molly wondered out loud.

"I asked. She said when he went to and from work, he usually wore a cowboy hat. Otherwise, he typically wore a baseball cap. But that week, he wore no hat at all, but had a nice-looking leather jacket—not something he'd wear to work at the ranch." Pilson paused. "She also mentioned Billy often entertained ladies at his house on the weekends. Not wild parties... one girl at a time... two or three different girls based on the cars they drove. Like there was no one special."

Molly rubbed the back of her neck. "He looks like an attractive guy in his photo. Maybe that's another reason she meets the school bus with her teenage daughter; doesn't want her daughter to develop a crush on the handsome neighbor."

Pilson chuckled. "That squares with what I learned from Big Bev; the girls at the ranch like him. How old do you think he is?"

Molly said, "Late twenties. Not yet thirty."

"And he still goes by Billy?" Pilson sounded surprised.

"He's from the South; names like that are common there."

"I suppose. I know it doesn't sound like much, but we were told in definite terms he was out of town the entire week of the murder. I doubt he was just hangin' out at home."

"Who told us he was out of town?" Molly asked.

"I was afraid you would ask me that. I'm sorry, Molly. It's slipped my mind."

"No worries. You've uncovered quite a lot. We need to know more about him. I'll call Doris Harmon and ask her about his time off. He's definitely risen on my list of suspects. "Let's get together Friday afternoon with Schmidt and review what we've got so far. There's obviously some bad stuff going on out there at that ranch."

"I agree. It's beginning to feel like The Liars' Club."

- 48 -

The following day around three o'clock in the afternoon, Molly took a call at the precinct on her desk phone from a man who refused to give his name. "How can I help you if you won't give me your name?"

"I don't need help. I'm calling to give you some information. It could be important. What you do with it is up to you."

"What do you have for me?" Molly asked.

"A couple of nights ago at the Gateway airport two planes flew in during the early morning hours and transferred a large load of American cash from one plane to the other. I don't know where they came from, but one of them, a Gulfstream 280 received the cargo and gave a flight plan going to a small airport located in the Dallas/Fort Worth area."

"Is that all you can tell me?"

"Yes, ma'am, that's it."

"Well, it's way out of my jurisdiction. I suggest you reach out to FFA, or possibly the FBI with that information."

There was a click as the caller hung up. Molly sat, pondering the call, and staring at the phone. It was the first time she could recall, a person making a police report, or so he thought, refused to give his or her name. After a few minutes of self-debate, Molly inhaled a deep breath, stood, and headed for the coffee room.

A little after five p.m. she received a call from Kenneth. "I'm alone in Julia's shop. She and the girl who clerks here have both gone. I promised them I'd lock up. Nothing unusual about that. I'm calling to say the emeralds you thought might come my way—just did. I didn't think it would happen this fast, if at all."

"I'm also surprised," Molly said.

"Right. A guy by the name of Richard Franklin brought them in and asked me to make a pair of stud earrings."

Who the hell is Richard Franklin?

"They're high quality, one carat emeralds," Kenneth continued. "Round, brilliant cut. A beautiful pair. Surprisingly clear." I don't have the equipment in the store to properly appraise them, but I can tell you more after I take them home to my workshop."

She listened to Kenneth while racking her brain to remember some guy by the name Richard Franklin. Nothing came to her. "You're sure about the name? What did he look like?"

"Yep, I got the name right. I wrote it on his work order. Not quite six feet tall, muscular build, mousy brown hair showed under his dirty ball cap. What really stood out was the dirt under his fingernails. What's a workin' guy like that doing with two costly gems?"

Molly chuckled. "That's what we all want to know. How was he dressed?"

"I didn't pay much attention. Jeans and a long-sleeved gray plaid flannel shirt, rolled up to his elbow. Nothin' stood out. Except, I did notice an old scar cutting through his right eyebrow. Probably from an injury when he was a kid."

"Good catch." Molly did a quick review of what Kenneth had said. Nothing out of order except for the guy's name. "What was his cap like? What color?"

"Black. Dirty. Kinda wrinkled. I figured he stuffed it into his back pocket a half dozen times a day. At first, I took it to be an Arizona Diamondbacks' cap. There was a coiled snake above the brim. Head erect and its mouth open. But no team lettering... just the snake."

"When is he going to pick up the finished earrings?"

"I figured I'd make them up over the weekend at home. Told him to come in at five next Thursday to take delivery; that's the only day I'm in the store for sure. I tried to talk him into adding four or five little one-point diamonds in a half circle at the base of each emerald, but he wouldn't go for it. He was adamant. He wanted them plain. Too bad really, the emeralds would have looked great sitting above the diamonds. The diamonds would create a larger appearance on the wearer's ear lobe, for a much more impressive look. He probably was worried about the additional cost—although he didn't flinch when I told him the price of the stones. One-pointers aren't that expensive. Of course, we were talking a total of six, eight, or ten stones."

"Thanks, Kenneth. You've been very helpful. I have another favor to ask. Will you meet me at Hamburger Haven on your way home from work this afternoon? I'd like you to look at a few photos—not many. Maybe you'll recognize the emerald guy."

"Not a problem. I can be there by six-thirty."

"Great," Molly replied. "I'll see you then."

When Molly walked into the hamburger joint, Kenneth was seated in a back corner, a soft drink in his hand. She stopped at the counter, ordered a Coke, and carried it to Kenneth's table. "Thanks for meeting me." Molly smiled.

She removed her packet of headshots, including Billy Fenton's, from her tote. Before she had laid out all the photos across the table, Kenneth said quietly, "That guy." He tapped the photo of Billy. "That's Richard Franklin. He picked up the picture and studied it then laid it in front of Molly. He pointed to Billy's eyebrow. "There's the scar I mentioned." He glanced at her and smiled. "When somebody brings me gems as nice as those emeralds, I don't forget their names or their faces."

Molly pushed the photos together, creating a small stack, and slid them into her bag. "Thank you, Kenneth, that's very helpful."

He leaned toward her and spoke softly. "What kind of a crime are you trying to solve?"

"I'm working on a jewelry theft case. That's about all I can tell you."

Molly stood, and he did the same. "Well, Detective, if I can do anything more to help out, let me know." He followed Molly out to her car. "Are you thinking of being at the boutique when Franklin picks up the earrings?"

She unlocked her car. "You read my mind. I'll be there. Five o'clock, next Thursday. Right?"

He nodded. "See you then."

Molly slid into her car, gave him a wave, and headed home.

- 49 -

On Friday afternoon, Molly and her two partners each carried a coffee and a handful of oatmeal raisin cookies from the break area to a table in an interview room.

As soon as they were settled in their chairs, Molly said, "I'll start." Both men nodded. She took her time spelling out her encounters with Kenneth, the jewelry repairman working out of Julia's boutique. "According to Kenneth, the emeralds Billy brought him to create a pair of emerald stud earrings were genuine and high quality." She explained how Kenneth tried to convince Billy to add small diamonds across the bottom of each emerald, but Billy was adamant he wanted only the emeralds mounted. Kenneth described it as though adding diamonds was totally out of the question for Billy."

Pilson said, "Although we don't know how Billy got hold of the emeralds, it's possible he may have delivered the stones to Kenneth on behalf of a friend who gave him specific instructions on how they were to be set. I wouldn't be surprised someone paid him to make the delivery." Pilson pressed his tongue against his cheek. "How would Billy know to take the stones to Kenneth who just happens to work one day a week at

Julia's boutique? He'd have no reason to go into a women's boutique." He paused. "He must have been instructed. I suppose he might have a reason, but it's highly unlikely. Anyway, somebody knew about Kenneth and his routine; I doubt Billy did."

"Right, my good man. Excellent point." Schmidt chuckled then his expression turned serious. "Perhaps I'm taking a leap too far, but maybe there was a reason the earrings Kenneth was to make should look exactly like Julia's."

"That's what I'm thinking," Molly said. "What if somehow Julia got hold of the emeralds from Mrs. Harmon's diamond ring?" Both men smiled. Molly sighed. "I know, I know. Hear me out. What if Julia discovered Jimmy Harmon's gift of emerald earrings were man-made, and suddenly, she had a chance to have real gems? She is the well-educated daughter of an admired veterinarian and a respected businesswoman in the Phoenix Valley. When it comes to women's clothes—I mean, her store's doing great. She sells some very high-end labels, and she's successful. Who would suspect her of any wrongdoing?"

"Right," Schmidt said again. "Maybe Harmon's beautiful diamond ring unexpectedly, or not so unexpectedly, fell into Julia's lap after the theft occurred. She couldn't keep it. Everybody knew it belonged to Mrs. H. So, Julia would want to get rid of it as fast as she could—you know, like pawn it."

"Logical but we can't be certain—not yet," Molly said. "The pawnbroker told us the woman who brought it to him was blonde. Julia's hair is dark, almost black."

"She could have had help with that," Pilson said. "Sometime back, I can't remember exactly when, Cindy, the ranch's secretary told Big Bev *Julia had dyed her light brown hair to black*. Plus, it's easy to imagine whoever stole the ring and removed the emeralds, believed they could be reset and sold, and still sell the diamond—or maybe the diamond was already sold. I might point out the pawnbroker didn't hesitate to buy the diamond ring—minus the emeralds."

"True," Molly said. "Julia still lives with her dad. Do you think we have enough information to gain a warrant to search Spelling's home, Billy's home, and their bank records?"

Molly counted on her fingers. "We know there has been fraudulent activity concerning the theft of stallion semen. That points to one or both vets. We have the forensic accountant to back us up with that. We have the theft of an expensive diamond ring. Cindy is blonde and known to date Dr. Briggs, Alphonso, and Jerrod, the deceased. She could be involved. Somewhere in the larger scheme, it may have been necessary to murder Jerrod. Billy's scrimshaw belt buckle is still a potential clue worth consideration, plus now we know he had the emeralds in his possession. It's odd how often Billy shows up in our investigation." Molly searched their faces, wondering if she was presenting a convincing argument.

She stood and paced across the room, returned to her chair but didn't sit down. "Our attention has been solely on the murder and the theft of the diamond ring. We've given too little attention to the repeated thefts of the stallion semen. We know of three recent thefts of semen, but how many vials of semen have been stolen in the past? These crimes may be connected in some bigger scheme. We don't know how long the semen theft has been going on—the total loss of income could be huge. Perhaps that is where we've missed the proverbial boat."

She picked up her mug and swallowed the last of her coffee. "Everybody knows we should follow the money, but in this case, we've been following the shiny things—literally. I say it's time to dig into the money trail."

Pilson turned to Schmidt, raised his eyebrows and Schmidt nodded. Pilson grinned. "I agree, Molly. We need a deep dive into the financial affairs of all parties involved. But sadly, I don't think we have enough to get a judge to agree."

Molly nodded. "You could be right. I have a thought how we might get that done."

Schmidt jerked his head up and stared at her. "And? What miracle do you plan to pull out of your hat?"

"Give me the weekend to think about it. If I'm right, I may be able to lay out a workable plan come Monday morning."

- 50 -

Molly's cell phone interrupted her sleep. Eyes closed; she patted the bedding until she felt her phone.

"Detective Raines? Is this you? This is Tillie Gull. I own the motel on the highway outside Payson. I met you a while back when you were investigatin' that fella who owns land up near Strawberry. You know, somewhere around the National Park."

"Of course, Mrs. Gull, I remember. How are you?"

"I'm right fine, but I thought you should know we got a terrible fire a-burnin' north of us. That sucker's going through the National Forest like wild horses racin'. We're thinkin' it spells trouble for your friend's property. Thought you'd want to know."

"Oh my gosh! It's the first I've heard of it. I really appreciate your call. I'll look into it."

Molly ended the conversation, reached for her robe, quickly slipped into it, and headed for the kitchen. After switching on her coffeemaker, she paused long enough to turn up the furnace's thermostat then hurried out to the driveway to pick up the morning paper. Molly read the headlines as she walked inside. *Wildfire Near Strawberry.* The lead article began: *Six-*

alarm inferno! Raging out of control. All area fire departments have sent their people to fight the unrelenting blaze.

Molly sipped her coffee and sat down at the breakfast table to read every article covering the fire. She started with the news reports on her phone then opened the newspaper. When she finished, she dialed Tillie Gull's phone number. Tillie picked up immediately, and Molly reintroduced herself. "Mrs. Gull, what are you hearing now about the fire?"

"Oh, dearie, it's a bad one. Big and bad. It went through the forest fast as a rabid dog runnin' for his life, eatin' ever tree as if it was day-old fish. I'm afeared your friend's forest land is part of a big black scar on our land. Nothin' left but charred ash and tree stumps."

"Thank you for telling me, Mrs. Gull. Are you safe where you are?"

"Yes, ma'am. We ain't got a worry. They say they can keep it on the other side of the highway runnin' up to Strawberry. Wind is movin' it west, so we're good. I sure feel sorry for the folks out thata way. If you come up to have a look, we've got a room for ya."

"Thank you, Mrs. Gull."

Molly ended the call, wishing there was someone of authority, whose professional confidentiality could be trusted, somebody she could speak to who would know what happened to Jerrod's property and the marijuana field. But it was Saturday. Nobody would be working in a government office.

She thought of Lar, wondering if she had lost him as a helpful professional source. *Might as well find out.* She tapped Lar's number into her phone. If he refused her call, she'd know.

"Hello Molly."

He sounded a little too happy. "Hey Lar. Have you heard about the fire near Strawberry?"

"Just reading about it. It's close to the area of your investigation, isn't it?"

"Definitely. It could impact my murder case. Jerrod Bronson owned a marijuana field within the Coconino Forest and I'm trying to find out if it burned in the fire. Any chance you could contact someone who could tell you?"

"Always possible. Let me call you back."

In less than an hour, Lar returned Molly's call. He didn't bother saying hello. "It's gone, Molly. The marijuana's gone... up in smoke. Pardon the pun." She could hear in the way he spoke he was smiling. "I talked to one of the fire chiefs. Six of his men saw it burn. Said the stink from those plants filled the air for miles."

Molly sighed. "I'm not sure if it's good news or bad... for my purposes anyway." She ran a hand through her hair, intending to sign off. "Thanks, Lar. You saved me a trip up there."

"Don't hang up." He paused. "Any chance we could get together—just to talk?"

"Not right now, Lar." She cleared her throat. "Thanks for the help. Gotta go." She clicked off.

- 51 -

Over the weekend, Molly worked at home, updating the murder book, and typing on a fresh sheet of paper the high points of each workable offense within the framework of the multi-pronged criminal case. She included a timeline of events for convenience then slipped it under the book's cover. On Monday morning, she drove straight to headquarters without stopping for her Monday morning breakroom donation of donuts. She arrived thirty minutes ahead of schedule, hung up her coat, and shoved her tote bag into a desk drawer. She hesitated then took a deep steadying breath, grabbed the murder book, and headed for Lar's office. Of all the "higher-up" people in the department, Lar was the most likely to have a lengthy list of reliable connections.

Two floors above, she stepped from the elevator and headed down the hall, mindlessly counting the doors as she passed them. When she reached Lar's door, she paused and smoothed her clothes. She raised her fist and tapped on the frosted window below Lar's gold-lettered name and title.

"It's open," Lar's all-business voice called out.

Molly squeezed the murder book a little tighter to her chest, turned the doorknob, and walked in... just as she used to, once upon a time. Strange how long ago it seemed.

"Good morning, boss." She forced a tight smile.

He stared at her from his desk chair, not bothering to stand or trying to conceal his surprise. He glanced at his watch. "You're here early. It must be important." He tentatively smiled while his eyes shown with curiosity. He gestured to a pair of chairs in front of his desk. "To what do I owe the pleasure? I see you're carrying a murder book, so I'm regretfully assuming it's a work matter."

Molly sat and opened the murder book across her lap. "It is. Do you have time to discuss the Jerrod Bronson murder case?"

"I have a meeting in the chief's office in thirty minutes, but I'm all yours until then." He flashed a flirty smile; one she'd seen *sooo* many times.

Molly didn't respond to his comment. "Thank you. I assumed you would have a busy day ahead of you." She flipped a page in the book and removed her notes. "I made a few bullet points to walk you through what we've uncovered."

"Go ahead."

Molly named the victims and the crimes each had suffered. She explained in detail the turn of events along with the timeline, from the days of Bronson's sisters attack and his murder to the present. She closed the murder book and breathed deeply. "The reason I've come to see you is to ask if you'll assist us in acquiring warrants to search the residences and workplaces of each of the suspects involved, along with their bank accounts. Based on the forensic accountant the Document Crimes Unit sent to the ranch to investigate, we know a great deal of money has changed hands under the table. We have discovered the theft of stallion semen along with the Harmon diamond ring. I believe you have enough gravitas with at least one judge, or more, who will understand the seriousness of this case and the necessity to enable us to follow the money."

Lar raised his chin and studied her. "Why do you think you're not persuasive enough to get your own warrant?"

"I'm concerned I don't have enough experience with the appropriate judge, whomever that may be, to gain his or her cooperation when we still have a few, possibly too many, loose ends. I believe the way to tie up those ends is via the money trail. I can't do that without getting a look at the various bank accounts."

He nodded. "I've followed this case enough to know its challenges. Let me think about your request and I'll get back to you."

Molly stood. "Thank you, Lar. I appreciate any help you can give us. The Harmons are hard-working people. They've suffered a lot. I'm trying my best, for their peace of mind, to bring the perpetrators to justice. The Harmons deserve it.

"The murder of Jerrod Bronson has cast a long shadow over the ranch and threatened their future business success. The dollar figure of the lost ranch income due to the theft of stallion semen is enormous, creating a terrible financial strain on the continuance of their breeding activity. Somehow they've managed to pay every ranch hand's salary, but it hasn't been easy." She reached for the door and paused. "Obviously, Mrs. Harmon's loss of her gorgeous anniversary ring, a gift from her husband is heartbreaking."

He stared up at her. "Molly, Molly." He sighed. "Your heart still bleeds."

"Probably always will." She straightened her shoulders. "I hope you'll help my partners and me solve this case." She opened the door and looked back at Lar.

"Thank you for seeing me." She didn't smile.

- 52 -

On Tuesday morning, when Molly arrived at work, the message light on her desk phone flashed steadily. It had to be from Lar. He was the only cop she knew who refused to use texting or emails. She pushed the speaker phone and listened to Lar's message.

"Molly, give Judge Mildred Carry a call and provide her with a list of names and causes for the warrants you're seeking. Her number's in the manual. She'll probably have a few questions for you, but none you can't handle. Ms. Carry is a savvy judge, one who won't stand in your way unreasonably. When you share the details of the crimes committed, I'm quite sure she'll sign your warrants."

An hour later, Molly hurried to Pilson and Schmidt's desks to show them the hard copies of the warrants she'd just printed with Judge Mildred Carry's signature at the bottom. "They include not only the person's residence, but also their place of employment."

"For which suspects?" Schmidt asked.

"So far, we've got one for Billy Fenton, Julia Spelling, Dr. Spelling, and Dr. Briggs. Just in case, I also asked for one on the deceased, Jerrod Bronson, and Cindy Harper, the ranch secretary."

"What did you think of Judge Carry?" Schmidt asked. "I've heard she's a stickler for the rules."

"Our conversation went well. I found her to be fair-minded. She was willing to listen—even told me she would issue subpoenas for the financial institutions when we can provide names and addresses for the banks' they do business with. Keep an eye out for any documents that bear the names and addresses of banks or other financial institutions when you do your searches. We need that to establish a credible money trail."

"Okay," Larry Pilson began, "how about I take Fenton, and Schmidt takes Briggs. That leaves you, Molly, to investigate Spelling and Julia. Since they share the same residence, you may be able to kill two birds with one stone."

"What about Cindy?" Molly asked.

"I'll take her," Schmidt said. "I'm expecting to finish with Briggs in short order. He doesn't strike me as the kind of guy who'd risk his career. He has a very sweet deal working as lead vet at Harmony."

"Sounds good to me," Molly said. She glanced at Schmidt then Pilson. "Be sure each of you notify the precinct commander and chain of command where the warrants will be served. We'll have patrol officers secure the locations and assist with any unlikely arrests. I'll text you the addresses you'll need." Schmidt nodded he understood. Pilson did the same.

Next, she said to Pilson, "I'll get the home addresses from Doris Harmon. I doubt that info is in the murder book, but I'll record it as soon as I have it." She stood. "See you both back here at four o'clock." Pilson and Schmidt stood and followed her out.

It was mid-morning when Molly drove by the Spelling home. A patrol car sat behind a small SUV with a business name painted on it sides. It read Efficiency Cleaning. Both vehicles were parked in front of the house. Molly pulled in behind Patrol's car as three women, carrying a variety of cleaning equipment, came out of the home's front entrance.

Molly scrambled out of her car, waved to the women, and shouted, "Wait a minute!" She waved again. "Don't close the door!" Molly dashed up the steps to the porch, followed by two patrolmen. She showed the women her badge, and said, "I'm from the police. I must go inside. It's okay. I have a warrant." She waved the legal paper but did not bother to show it to them.

The women stared at her badge and moved several steps back. It appeared they didn't speak English. One pointed to the document and said something in Spanish as she pushed the door back open.

"Is there anyone in the house?" When nobody responded, Molly tried her rusty Spanish. "Los persones en la casa?"

They all shook their heads then hurried down the steps to their car as if they were running from a ghost.

Molly turned and spoke to the patrol officers. "Sarge, here's my digital recorder. I haven't yet turned it on; button is on the side. Would you mind making the Knock and Announce for our entry?"

"Not at all." The sergeant took the recorder and said, "Hang on a second. I'll have one of my officers go in with you in case there are more people inside than what the cleaners indicated. My other officers will secure the scene—inside and out."

After the knock and announce, Molly thanked the sergeant, retrieved her recorder, and entered the home. She went directly to Dr. Spelling's home office, carrying with her a duffle bag containing evidence collection items, complete with booties, gloves, bags, and property impound forms. She was mildly surprised she hadn't noticed the elk's head mounted above the window when she was there before. She placed her coat and bag on one of the chairs and donned a pair of latex gloves then searched the desk drawers. She anticipated finding something with names and addresses of the financial houses where Spelling did business. She was disappointed.

She hoped she hadn't wasted a trip. In the desk's file drawer, she rifled the folder's tabs. When she discovered one titled *Financials,* she exhaled the breath she'd been holding. She placed the file on the desktop and opened it. Among the various documents was a copy of a Wire Transfer Receipt for $20,000.00 going to Dr. David Spelling from Cincinnati First Savings Bank, and from Charles Everett's account, showing full name and account numbers. Molly took a picture of the receipt with her digital camera. She noted the needed information and after scanning the rest of the file's contents, closed the folder.

On a side wall, a gun cabinet held two hunting rifles and a shot gun, visible through its glass door. The doorframe's brass keyhole had no key in it, so Molly assumed it was locked. But she tried the door anyway. It opened. Molly frowned at the careless way Spelling stored his firearms. She stared momentarily, appreciating the wood stocks on the long guns which gleamed from many coats of polish.

There were two handguns and several boxes of ammunition. She assessed the small arsenal. Obviously, Dr. Spelling was an avid hunter, as well as a collector of scrimshaw.

Moving on, she opened the closet door and studied the contents. Finding only boxed office supplies and a container labeled Veterinary Supplies, she did a quick search, closed the closet door, and headed out of the room. She stopped to admire once more the wide variety of pieces in Spelling's scrimshaw collection.

From the office, she ambled into what appeared to be Spelling's untidy bedroom with an unmade bed. Next to the bed a nightstand held a half empty glass of water positioned dangerously close to the table's edge. The messy assortment of worn clothing draped over a slipper chair, included two or more days of underwear and casual slacks with the belt still in the loops. *Someone should introduce him to a dirty clothes bin.* She quickly searched the six dresser drawers. In drawer number three from the top, she found a stash of women's lingerie and a small jewelry box. She checked the box's contents and found a pair of emerald stud earrings... probably his girlfriend's. She placed them in an evidence envelope and tucked it into a side pocket of her bag. She spent a few minutes looking through the rest of the costume pieces—rings, necklaces, and several more pairs of earrings.

Molly moved on to Spelling's closet and found several dresses, slacks, and blouses hanging beside Spelling's clothes. She did a quick search of the rest of the room and found nothing more of interest. From there, she headed down the hallway to what she assumed was Julia's bedroom.

First, Molly checked Julia's closet. Half the hanging rod held the clothes she expected to see. The other half of the rod contained clothing bearing price tags, stored in garment bags. Some of the bags held off season clothing or possibly overflow merchandise from Julia's store.

Searching the nightstands, she found nothing of interest. The nine-drawer dresser's top center drawer contained Julia's jewelry collection. Molly carefully pushed the pieces around, examining each one with her phone's flashlight. The emerald earrings were not there, but a pair of pearl button studs were, along with a pair of tiny ruby studs. She ignored the rest of the jewelry then opened the side drawer.

An application for a business loan was folded in half and lay beneath the clothes in the bottom of the drawer. According to its date, Molly guessed it was long forgotten. She entered the bank's name and address into her phone. She checked the rest of the drawer carefully, hoping to find something more. Molly rummaged through each of the remaining six drawers, finding nothing out of the ordinary. She searched the rest of the house, opening closet doors and all the various drawers in the kitchen and dining room.

She removed a copy of the search warrant from her bag and listed the jewelry she had taken as evidence. She placed the copy of the search warrant and the brief list of items removed on the dining room table. She slipped into her coat, grabbed her bag, and left the house, locking the door behind her. She thanked the patrol officers and headed for her car.

As she drove away, she thought about Lisa, Spelling's girlfriend, who kept her emerald earrings, along with her few clothes, at Spelling's house. Did she love the earrings as much as she'd indicated? Her mind zigged to Julia. Had she given Jimmy's gift of earrings to Lisa just because Lisa admired them? Maybe manmade emerald earrings were common? Sold in all the department stores? For Julia to give her earrings to Lisa wasn't a big deal. But somehow it didn't feel right. Perhaps she and Jimmy Harmon had had a falling out.

Molly drove up the ramp onto the 101-freeway heading for the ranch to speak with Doris Harmon. She suddenly changed her mind. Instead of driving past Desert Ridge Mall, she abruptly turned in and parked in an out-of-view spot around the corner from Julia's boutique. When she entered the store, the chime rang, and Julia came from the backroom wearing a smile.

"Oh, hello, Molly," Julia said. "Can I help you with something?"

"The last time I was here, I admired a bracelet." Molly walked to the costume jewelry display case and pointed down, tapping the glass top. "There it is. I'd like to buy the pearl bracelet with the lavender stones." She handed Julia her charge card. "My niece will love it."

They spoke little as Julia rang up the purchase and returned Molly's card. She wrapped the bracelet in tissue, placed it in an appropriate box, and slipped it into a dainty bag. She handed the bag to Molly. "Thank you for coming in. It was a nice surprise to see you again."

Molly smiled. It was a nice surprise. Julia was not wearing her emerald earrings, and they weren't at home in her drawer. Perhaps they were with Kenneth being reset.

- 53 -

That afternoon, Molly and her two partners gathered in the conference room to update each other on the results of the day. Molly sipped her soft drink then set it aside. "Larry, why don't you start."

Pilson nodded. "Patrol met me like always and I entered Billy Fenton's residence. I started in his bedroom. Found nothing unusual. A bunch of grooming stuff in his bathroom. I came across bottles of ibuprofen, plus a prescription. I wrote it down. An antibiotic. There was a box of condoms in the bedside table's drawer.

"He had a fancy entertainment setup in the living room with a large collection of albums and CDs. He's obviously into music. Music and horses. He had framed pictures of himself showing various horses, all Arabians, and receiving ribbons for winning. I couldn't tell if they were taken around here at the local horse shows or from back home—wherever that is.

"I thought I was going to come up dry with his banking info, but I found two ATM receipts from Phoenix Savings and Loan, each one for three thousand dollars. The receipts provided the bank's name." He grinned at Molly. "You might really like this: I also found a receipt from that guy's jewelry repair shop showing Fenton dropped off two, one-carat emeralds to be set as earrings. He had tucked it in the back of his address book."

Molly stared at Pilson. "It confirms Billy Fenton's involved somehow with the theft of Doris Harmon's ring." Molly gave a slight shake of her. "Good work, Larry. Did you take a picture of the receipts?"

"I did."

Molly turned to Schmidt. "Arnie, what do you have for us?"

"I may have some good news. I went to Cindy's apartment first. Patrol arrived before I did and had the manager with them waiting for me. So entry was simple. Her place is sparsely decorated but terribly messy. She could stuff it all in a single box, move out in the morning, and be resettled in the next place in time to cook dinner.

"Like Billy Fenton, Cindy had four ATM receipts from Scottsdale's Riverside Bank and Trust dated over a fourteen-month span of time. Each receipt was for three thousand dollars. They were stuffed in a side pocket inside a piece of carry-on luggage. I took pictures of each one and returned them to their luggage pocket." He smiled at Molly. "That's all I got regarding Cindy."

"How about Dr. Briggs?" Molly asked.

Schmidt chuckled. "The doc lives well. Lotta expensive clothes in the big boy's closet. He has three tuxedoes. Who the hell needs three tuxedoes? Most guys don't own even one in their whole lifetime. He has a huge collection of that scrimshaw crap in an elaborate display case that covers an entire wall in his family room. In a number ten envelope, taped to the bottom of one of his desk drawers, were two copies of wire transactions from the Banc d' Madrid, initiated by a Dr. Gustav Herzog wired to Dr. Mitchel Briggs. Each were in the amount of twenty thousand American dollars. One dated earlier this year and one dated the end of September.

"On a high shelf in the kitchen pantry, I found a Journal of Accounts and I flipped through it. I had no idea vets made such big money. One other thing, I took a picture of his jewelry collection. Here," he reached for his digital camera. "Take a gander at this. It screams expensive." He looked from Molly to Pilson and back to Molly. "This guy is rollin' in dough... I mean, what the hell? He's a *damn veterinarian*."

"Large animal vet," Molly quietly corrected. "He's not treating dogs or cats."

"Yeah but wait 'till you see the pictures of the pages in his journal. You won't believe your eyes." He laughed. "I have one more thing to share. Get this—I found nothing of value in his office at the ranch, but when I was leaving the ranch, I bumped into that Big Bev girl. I struck up a conversation and she told me she'd learned Cindy was pissed at Jerrod, the deceased, and Julia Spelling, because they had a thing going on." Bev said Cindy spilled the beans at a get together several nights ago at some restaurant."

Pilson raised a question. "What'd she do? Blurt it out for all to hear?"

"According to Bev, Cindy was sitting next to her and drank more than she could handle and got to grieving over Jerrod. Went so far as to say Jerrod asked her to marry him. She accepted then a few nights later, Cindy caught him and Julia cuddled in a booth at one of the restaurants... Danger Zone. I think that's what the restaurant is called. Never mind. It doesn't matter.

"But that's not all. Cindy said Julia made comments that Cindy had stolen Mrs. Harmon's ring. Cindy denied it, of course. She said Mrs. H would take it off while working in the kitchen and one day, when the house cleaners were there, one of the women must have taken it from the window ledge."

"Is the information reliable enough to dig into it?" Molly asked.

"Julia told Cindy to tell Mrs. H so they could follow up. Mr. Harmon called the cleaning outfit and was told the women on that crew had all been fired and had returned to Juarez, south of the border."

Molly shook her head in dismay. "Wow, Cindy is a piece of work. Good job, you guys." She stared at the men. "Somedays, it's too much to be believed. I'm looking forward all the more to analyzing whatever the banks provide to see where the money leads us."

Pilson slapped Schmidt on the back. "Good job, *Scoop*." He turned to Molly. "Okay, Mol, whatcha got?"

Molly updated her partners and concluded by emphasizing the fact she found Lisa's emerald earrings at Spelling's home among Lisa's clothes. "I took the earrings from the home as evidence, and they're now stored in our evidence storage locker." She pointedly explained the importance of Lisa having earrings in her possession, whereas Julia did not have emerald earrings in her jewelry box at her home nor was she wearing them when Molly dropped into Julia's boutique. "It begs the question, is Kenneth resetting Mrs. Harmon's stolen emeralds as we speak? Obviously, we now have two pairs of emerald studs, one pair in our evidence locker, and one pair possibly in Kenneth's hands. It will be interesting to find out who picks up the earrings Kenneth is making."

"What about her banking activity?" Larry Pilson asked. "Did you find anything we can use there?"

"I did," Molly answered. "She had a receipt for a Western Union MoneyGram for less than a hundred dollars. It contained information regarding her account at First Scottsdale National Bank. The money was sent to a woman in San Francisco. I followed up and found it was payment to settle a bet of some kind."

Schmidt stared at Molly. "Do you think she may have gambling issues?"

"I don't think so," Molly said with a chuckle. "At least I didn't find anything that would suggest it. When we get our results from the financial subpoenas, I'll watch for activity on Julia's records that point that way. However, I'd be surprised if she had such a problem."

"We should pay close attention to her dad's spending habits, too. He could cover her gambling debts."

Molly smiled. "Good point, Larry." She gave a small shake of her head. "Oh what a tangled web we weave..."

- 54 -

Molly called Judge Carry's office to request the subpoenas she would need to obtain each suspect's bank or financial accounts.

"Good morning, Detective. How can I help you?"

Molly smiled into the phone. "We served each of the warrants you signed with good results, your Honor. Within five days, I'll bring to your office the Return of Search Warrant documents. Now, it appears I need to subpoena several financial institutions, as you mentioned I might when we last spoke. I will email you the copies of receipts and other documents we discovered in several suspect's residences. I think you may be shocked when you open my email attachments. I'm not sure what to ask for in this case. It's becoming quite confusing, and I don't want to overlook anything."

"Not to worry," Judge Carry said. "From what you told me when we spoke before, it's probable you have a money laundering case along with the other felonies. We'll request any and all Suspicious Activity Reports the banks may have. The banks refer to them as *SARS*. I'll use my legal connections and we'll find out everything we need to know about the people you've named as suspects. We'll cover everything, starting with a request for all domestic outgoing and incoming bank activity with all supporting documentation. We'll request all accounts the suspects have in their own name and/or accounts or documents on which they are a signer." The judge paused. "Given the harmed party is in an Arabian horse breeding business, I'll demand the same documents going to and from the Bahamas, Grand Cayman Island, Switzerland, Spain, Australia, Germany, England, Egypt, Russia, Brussels, Saudi Arabia, Dubai, Brazil, Poland, and Argentina. And the United States, of course. Have I overlooked anything? Aren't those the countries where the Arabian horse business is popular?"

Molly chuckled. "Wow! I don't think you've missed anything at all, and yes I'd say you have the right countries in mind."

"Good. I'll also include all bank restricted accounts including Office of Foreign Assets Control alerts and holds. We'll also want to see any OFAC alerts or holds that pair with the Bank Secrecy Act or Anti Money Laundering." The judge paused. "You should be aware if the OFAC boys get involved, the Feds will follow on their heels."

"Oh great," Molly muttered. "That's all I need."

"I know," the judge said. "It sucks, but what else can we to do?" She sighed then cleared her throat. "Continuing: we'll want any applications for credit or requested Credit Reports starting today and going back one-hundred and eighty days along with all supporting docs including those granting or denying credit, and for what reason.

"Besides the damage done to our local rancher, if there is money laundering going on, I think we should be able to root it out with all the crap we're asking for, don't you?"

Molly laughed. "Goodness, Judge, I think we'll not only root that out, but we'll discover when the SOBs went to their last Catholic confession."

"Amen!" Judge Carry pronounced then laughed, suggesting to Molly the judge loved her job.

"What's next?" Molly asked.

"Come by my office and drop off the Return of Search Warrants, pick up the subpoenas, and hand deliver them to the bank employees in charge. They'll send them to their legal division where they'll sign off and you'll get your results in two to three days."

"Wow, I never dreamed the process is so lengthy."

The judge chuckled. "Ain't government grand?"

That same afternoon, Molly walked into Arizona's Bank of Commerce and was welcomed by one of the greeters seated behind a desk near the entry. Molly approached the woman and identified herself then asked to speak with the branch manager.

A few minutes later, Molly handed the gentleman his copy of the subpoena and asked if he would please process the requirement as soon as possible. "We are eager to solve a particularly nasty murder case and this information should be very helpful."

"I see." He gave her a tight little smile. "We'll do our best but realize our lawyers will undoubtedly feel a need to ask a few questions."

Molly frowned. "I don't see why. The subpoena is quite clear as to our requests. Please remind the lawyers by the nature of the subpoena signed by a Superior Court Judge, Phoenix PD will expect prompt action. Lives could depend on it."

The gentleman's brow shot to his hairline. "Of course. We want to be of help and will do our best. Your list of demands is lengthy."

"Not demands. Requests. Nothing unusual." Molly smiled solicitously. "That's all we ask." She offered her him her hand. "Thank you for your time."

Molly walked out of the bank into the cool autumn air with a sense of relief. Meeting with the first banker had gone well enough. Even though she had several more banks to call upon to deliver the subpoenas, she was confident her results would be equally as good. If she were lucky, the banks would respond promptly. But we all know with luck and five dollars we can buy a Frappuccino.

- 55 -

Days later, the detectives gathered around a table in the conference room at police headquarters. Molly began the discussion. "We received the Medical Examiner's Final Report. It isn't as helpful as we hoped. The cause of death is still inconclusive, as is time of death." She looked from face to face. "Better news is we've received the information we asked for from each of the banks involved. I compiled an evaluation based on the dates each suspect received deposits and made withdrawals.

"Julia Spelling's accounts show typical business activity from the boutique. Nothing of concern there. Her personal checking activity was interesting, but of no value to us. Her recent bank statements showed nothing incriminating. She is still a suspect in the theft of Doris Harmon's ring."

"How about Dr. Spelling?" Schmidt asked.

Molly smiled. "Now, that's where it gets interesting. His checking account statements showed some high-dollar deposits. Sporadically, he transferred varying high dollar amounts from his checking to savings account. He also transferred large sums from savings to checking. All in the thousands, from five thousand to seven thousand, to a couple of ten-thousand-dollar transfers. None of the amounts I've mentioned relate to his ranch salary. If we look at both accounts, we see several corresponding withdrawals in the amounts first deposited in his checking account.

"Not very long ago he bought a rather expensive new car. Wrote a check for sixty-seven thousand dollars for a new Cadillac Escalade. He probably traded something in on it."

"What do you make of it?" Schmidt asked.

"His ranch income is easy to recognize. It's the other income we can't explain, and which raises questions as to its origin. The payor is paying Spelling for something, and that's what we want to know. What is he selling?"

Schmidt scratched his head. "What about Brigg's accounts?"

Molly trailed a finger down the printout. "It looks much the same. The only difference is what he did with the money after he deposited it into checking. Each month, he sent checks varying from five thousand dollars to over ten thousand to a National brokerage firm in Scottsdale. Sometimes, it was bi-monthly. Also, once a month he sent a check to Elaine Briggs in the amount of six thousand dollars." Molly grinned. "I'm guessing they're alimony payments."

"Yes," Schmidt said. "The ex-Mrs. Briggs must have had a talented attorney."

Molly leaned on her elbow. "Beyond that, the rest of the money he spent, according to his records, went for the normal stuff—mortgage payments, utilities, and credit cards."

Pilson rubbed his hands together. "This is getting good. Let's hear about Cindy. What did you come up with there? Can't imagine a secretary's records amount to much, but I'm still curious."

"Cindy may have had something going on the side. She certainly wasn't living paycheck to paycheck. Her savings showed four, three-thousand-dollar deposits. Including the last deposit, that account totals right around thirteen-thousand dollars to date. All her deposits into savings, before the first three-thousand-dollar deposits, were in much smaller amounts—less than one hundred dollars. According to her records, the smaller deposits are more in sync with the salary she receives as a secretary—not very large." Molly pointed at the ceiling. "Remember, we only went back six months with our subpoenas, so whatever was going on before then we can only surmise."

Schmidt asked, "Did we subpoena the deceased's accounts?"

"Yes, we did," Molly said. "Jerrod didn't have significant numbers, except for one. He had a deposit of fifteen thousand dollars. Also, there were three notable deposits in different amounts. My guess is Jerrod received money from Enrique Martinez, the guy whose home we surveilled using our PPD vans. All were around five hundred dollars."

"What do you think that was about?" Pilson asked.

Molly glanced at her notes. "Once again, just a guess, the money was probably for expenses incurred for maintenance of the marijuana field. It makes me think Jerrod was only the owner of record, a front for Martinez who could have put up the money behind the land purchase. If the money he continued to disperse was for the field's expenses, it suggests he assumed the position of ownership and was covering all ensuing expenses for the marijuana. It appears Jerrod used the money for that purpose because he made withdrawals in amounts similar to each amount deposited in his account. There are outgoing checks recorded for amounts paid to the various utility companies serving the Strawberry area."

Schmidt said, "Except for the one large deposit, it sounds like Jerrod's records have little connection to what we found in the other suspects' accounts."

"My thoughts exactly," Molly said.

"What do you think all this means, Molly?" Pilson asked.

"So far, I think it confirms our suspicions of fraudulent sales activities surrounding the theft of stallion semen. The vets may have been paying finder's fees to employees who sent purchasers their way. I suspect Jerrod was paid the two thousand dollars for having found a buyer for the stolen semen. I believe both veterinarians are directly involved as well as Cindy. Also, if you recall, we had our forensic accountant investigate, and in his report, he paid particular attention to the semen buyers in the Middle East." She raised her palms. "But I have another thought.

"Judge Carry suggested money laundering early in the conversation. The land purchases and/or marijuana fields may be the way the mob laundered its drug money. It reminds me of that crazy call I got from the nameless guy at Mesa's airport talking about shipments of cash. That money may have gone out of the country in the final analysis."

"Where do you think those Middle East guys fit in?" Schmidt asked.

"I don't know," Molly answered then hesitated. "If you recall, Briggs entertained several men from the Middle East at Whistler's restaurant. Not sure it will make a difference, but it could, I suppose, especially if the Feds get involved. Arabian horses are esteemed in the Middle East."

"Getting back to Cindy. Why would she be involved?" Schmidt asked.

"Like Jerrod, Cindy may have received finder's fees, or cooperated in other ways... like a middleman... or she could be more deeply involved," Molly answered. Part of her job as ranch secretary is to maintain a breeding journal on each stallion standing for stud service at Harmony Farm. Each time a mare is bred to a stallion, either by AI or natural service, Cindy records in that stallion's journal, the mare's name, her Arabian Horse Registry of America's registration number, and the mare owner's name and address. Prior to year's end, Cindy prepares the ranch's Official Stallion Report and sends it to the AHRA. Cindy shouldn't enter a breeding into the report until payment in full has been received by the ranch, or an arrangement has been agreed upon at the stallion owner's discretion."

"Doris Harmon is the ranch's treasurer. She tells Cindy when the breeding fee has been paid in full or installment payments are received regularly. Semen shipped for breeding purposes would be paid according to their contract... unless the vets black-market it."

Pilson frowned. "Wait a minute. What happens when the resulting foal's owner tries to register it and hasn't paid off the stud fee?"

Molly nodded. "There's the rub. When the foal is born, the mare owner records the birth with the horse registry. If there is no mention of the breeding by the stallion's owner on their filed Stallion Report, the foal is not eligible for registration. So as long as the Stallion Report supports the mare owner's request for registration, everybody's happy. Case closed.

"Assuming everything is done properly, the information provided by all US breeders each year is compiled by the registry. We can go online and find it. I tried it. I was surprised how much a person can learn by tracing back the pedigree of any registered horse. At one time, the registry used to compile the year's breedings into an annual bound book. My grandparents purchased a copy every year."

"No shit," Pilson muttered as if dismayed. "And you know all this because of your ranch life when you were a kid?"

"Yep, my grandmother was the one who took care of getting our foals properly registered. She did the bookwork, and my grandfather worked in the barn. My grandparents never stood a breeding stallion. They worried it could be dangerous for me, but Grandmother had experience making out the stallion report for the big ranch where she worked in

Wyoming, before they came to Arizona. Because of the expensive breeding fees, we only had a few foals born when I lived on the ranch." Molly smiled. "Nothing more exciting than to watch a foal come into the world."

Molly clasped her hands beneath her chin. "Grandmother always asked me to draw the areas of white hair on each foal's diagram—like on the face and pasterns. Grandma would go to the barn and check my sketches to be certain there were no mistakes." Molly laughed. "I felt so important."

Schmidt studied Molly for a moment. 'You loved the horse life, didn't you? I can see it in your eyes, hear it in your voice."

Molly chuckled. "I did. Still do." She glanced at her paperwork. "Thanks for letting me reminisce a bit."

"Not a problem, Skipper." Schmidt paused. "What's next?"

Molly grinned. "On Thursday, Kenneth intends to deliver the newly made emerald earrings to the person he dealt with. I think we should be there to arrest person "X" for the theft of Mrs. Harmon's diamond and emerald ring.

"It's going to feel good to make this capture, but I'm not prepared to make the arrests for the other crimes. When we apprehend for the theft of the ring, we should be prepared to pick up the other suspects for their crimes. Otherwise, I'm afraid they'll be alerted we're coming for them, and they'll head for the hills—literally.

"Last week I worried we had missed something specific in our searches. I'm even more concerned now. It's just a nagging feel, but I can't ignore it. Between now and Thursday I'll spend my time going over everything we've done, along with the results. It may take some legwork, and I made need your help, so please stand by."

"Like what, Molly?"

"I'm talking about loose ends. We don't have a strong enough case regarding Mrs. H's ring. Our murder case is weak in the knees; it's too convenient to believe the gang is behind it.

Maybe it wasn't the mob at all." She paused and studied her partners. "Other than the arrest for Jill Bronson's attack, I don't feel good about where we are with any of this, and I sure as hell don't want to end up with egg on our faces." She stood and sighed. "Hang loose in case I have to call you. We've got until Thursday midday to be ready to make all our arrests by late Thursday afternoon."

- 56 -

By the end of the day, Molly had a search warrant signed by Judge Carry, and had arranged with patrol to meet at nine-thirty the next morning at the Spelling home.

When she arrived at Spelling's house, Molly was pleased to see patrol was already there, but surprised to see a Nickerson Brothers' plumbing truck parked at the curb. As before, patrol officers accompanied her to the front door. She rang the bell, and the patrol sergeant made the recorded knock and announce.

A fellow dressed in navy blue shirt and trousers opened the door. The embroidered Nickerson Brothers' Plumbing badge on his shirt indicated his name was Howard. At first, he appeared curious then his expression turned to panic. "Officers?" His eyes grew wide and he stepped back. "Is everything okay?"

Molly showed the man her badge while introducing herself and the patrol officers. As she walked past him into the house, she said, "We have a warrant to search this house." She glanced around "Is anybody else here with you?"

"No, Detective. I'm working alone. Dr. Spelling called our company early this morning. Had a leak under the kitchen sink. I've just finished."

"How'd you get in?" Molly asked.

"Spelling hides a key outside. He told me where to find it."

How long will you be?" Molly asked.

"I just need to gather my tools. The leak is fixed."

"Alright, one officer will stay with you while you finish.

Molly gloved up and quickly circled the large living room, spotting nothing unusual. In the dining room, she opened the doors of the breakfront and glanced inside then moved on to the drawers below and inspected each one. She hadn't expected to find anything suspicious there, but she was determined to turn every stone.

Finished in the dining room, she headed to Spelling's office and searched the big display cabinet, trying not to disturb any of the scrimshaw pieces. She looked under his desk pad, searched the desk drawers and those in the credenza behind his desk. Satisfied she hadn't overlooked anything, she moved on to the bedroom wing.

In Spelling's room she used the flashlight on her phone to search under his bed and the two bedside commodes. She pulled out each of the drawers and searched through the contents then ran her hand around the underside of each drawer. She did the same with the dresser and highboy. The slipper chair was piled higher with clothes than the last time she was here. Molly approached the chair, paused, and sighed. Nobody warned her at the Academy she'd have to handle men's dirty clothing.

Molly picked up a dress shirt then a couple of tee-shirts, rotating each one back and forth and dropping them onto the floor beside the chair. Beneath the shirts, thrown over the back of the chair, was a pair of chino trousers. A belt was threaded through the belt loops and dangled down toward the chair's seat. The belt buckle rested face down on the remaining pile of clothes. When she picked up the trousers and felt the weight of the buckle swaying at the end of the leather strap, she turned the buckle over in her hand. An ivory rectangle with an elaborate scrimshaw carving was mounted to the brass plate that comprised the buckle. *Billy isn't the only one with a scrimshaw buckle.*

The drawing appeared to be that of a whale's tail, but if you placed your thumb over the base of the tail, some might think it resembled a tree, just like Billy's. Molly's heartrate increased at the sight of it. She laid it out on Spelling's bed and took a picture of it.

She folded the trousers, without removing the belt, and placed them in a large evidence bag then put it into her evidence grip. She went back to sorting the clothes, doubting she'd find anything else as important as the trousers and buckle. Still, she continued, but nothing else materialized. She moved on to the closet but found nothing of interest.

Molly turned around and scanned the room, one last time, doing a mental checklist, crossing off each completed task. She decided she was finished in Spelling's bedroom and moved on to Julia's.

Julia Spelling's room, by contrast to her dad's, was designer perfect. Molly's reaction to Julia's quarters was *neat freak*. She glanced around then placed her case on the floor. She couldn't bring herself to place the heavy grip on Julia's beautiful bedspread. Using her flashlight, Molly searched beneath the bed and each of the furniture pieces in the room. She methodically went through all the drawers and came up empty. Despair crept into her mind. After finding what she believed to be solid evidence in Spelling's room, her hopes for additional discoveries had intensified. She was about to leave Julia's bedroom when a nagging voice in her mind warned her to slow down.

She picked up her case, scanned the room, and turned to go, but looked again at the door to the attached bathroom. Remembering her vow to be thorough, she set her evidence case on the floor, opened the door, and stepped into the small space. The state of Julia's bathroom was as perfect as her bedroom... every fresh, color-coordinated towel folded perfectly.

Molly knelt and opened the cabinet door beneath the sink. She aimed her light inside and studied the contents. The fragrance of the designer soaps wafted toward her. A neat stack of color matched towels came as no surprise. With all the orderly perfection, Molly wondered if Julia had served in the military or was OCD compromised. When she shifted her flashlight to her other hand, the light flashed across a clear plastic bag nearly hidden behind the drainpipe. Molly reached in and plucked it from its place. She recognized the contents before she slid open the zip lock. She held her breath as she slipped her hand inside the bag and felt the silky hair of a blonde wig. *BINGO!*

Molly felt like jumping up and dancing in a circle, but controlled the urge as she mentally screamed, *At last!*

Hurrying, Molly dropped her find into her evidence case and headed for the kitchen. There she left a list of the items she had taken for evidence, added her name and badge number then signed it. She placed the note on top of the warrant. Before leaving the kitchen, she opened one of two tall, closed doors. Obviously, it was the kitchen's pantry. The second door opened into the three-car garage. Molly flushed, mortified. In her haste, she hadn't gone over the garage the first time she searched Spelling's house.

Molly stepped down the two steps to the concrete floor and her eyes roamed the space. She guessed the two empty bays were occupied at night by Spelling's truck and Julia's car. She left her evidence case by the door and circled the gleaming

Cadillac SUV. She approached the back wall and mentally inventoried the items stored there. Garden tools were grouped together and hung neatly on the wall. Next to the various shovels at the far end was a large wheelbarrow, and beyond it, piled high were five, heavily-treaded snow tires, mounted on rims matching the Escalade's.

Beyond the wheels, a half dozen pairs of skis hung in a wall mounted rack. That explained the snow tires for Dr. Spelling's SUV. Apparently skiing was a family hobby.

Molly worked slowly. She examined and evaluated everything she saw. In the corner, a couple of lidded trash cans sat behind twin piles of bagged all-purpose fertilizer, soil amendments, and potting mix. She suspected the cans were seldom used given their unhandy location. Molly knelt on the fertilizer bags, steadying herself with one hand and with the other lifted the lid off the nearest can. She was disappointed to find what appeared to be terrycloth rags. She assumed the rags were used for cleaning Spelling's vehicles. She nearly missed the small piece of white denim that barely poked above and between the rags.

Molly tugged on the fabric, but it didn't give way. Assuming it was large and too deeply embedded in the rags below, she grabbed handfuls of dust cloths and dropped them on the floor behind her. After emptying half of the can, she was finally was able to dislodge the white denim veterinary coverall. She tucked it under her arm and carefully dismounted from the fertilizer pile.

Standing squarely on both feet, she held the wrinkled coverall by its shoulders and shook it out. She surveyed it from the shoulders downward to the hems of the pantlegs. Near the end of the sleeves, and twelve or more inches above the hemstitching at the bottom of the trouser legs, faded red spots stained the white fabric. *Blood spatter? Jerrod's blood spatter?*

Molly gnawed at her lower lip. She had a sudden urge to get to the police lab. She quickly folded the coverall and headed for the door. There, she placed her discovery in a large plastic evidence bag and stowed it in her case. She re-entered the kitchen, added the coveralls to the search warrant's evidence sheet, and hurried to the front door, locking it on her way out.

She thanked each of the patrol officers as they headed to their cars. The officer who walked beside her said, "You look happy, Detective. Did you find something?"

"I sure did." She looked at the officers. "Thank you all for your assistance. It was a successful and worthwhile trip."

Next stop, the police lab for analysis.

- 57 -

Molly raced into the Medical Examiner's office and asked to see Dr. Kendrick, the examiner she spoke with when she picked up the preliminary report. She was directed to his office where she handed him the coveralls, and Julia's wig, and quickly explained the urgency of her visit.

"I understand, Detective. As long as you submit these items with the appropriate paperwork signed by your Lieutenant, I can do a test to determine blood deposits right away, but you'll need a DNA analysis to prove the blood is that of the deceased. That'll take more time than you seem to have. Are you in the same hurry for the wig?"

Molly grimaced. "Can you put a rush on the DNA testing of the blood spots? Testing the wig for DNA is equally important. The fact we have it in evidence is not enough."

"Get the documentation that's required, and I will put a rush on the DNA. Even so, it will require a minimum of two weeks or more."

"I'll get to work on it now and get it back to you ASAP." Molly thanked him and hurried to her car. Her day wasn't done.

Seated behind the wheel, she grabbed her phone and dialed Larry Pilson's number. Feeling frantic, she tapped her fingernails on the steering wheel. Patience was never Molly's long suit.

Pilson answered. "Hey, Mol, what's up?"

"Larry, will you get in touch with Sergeant Hilliard and ask him to meet with us as soon as I can get there. Grab Schmidt, too. In the meantime, start the paperwork to rush blood and DNA testing."

"Arnie's here with me now. How far out are you?"

Molly took a calming breath. "I'm coming from the lab. I'll be right there. Put on a fresh pot of coffee. We're going to be awhile."

"You got it."

The three detectives sat around the table in the conference room with Sergeant Hilliard, discussing the success of her search at Dr. Spelling's home. As Molly finished her explanation, Pilson showed her the completed paperwork ordering a rush evaluation by the Medical Examiner based on the evidence she left at his office earlier. It appeared Hilliard had heard enough. He reached for the document and signed off.

He smiled from person to person. "Excellent work, detectives." He turned to Molly. "Before you arrived, Larry and Arnie explained why you needed a rush by the ME's office. I agree timing is everything to maintain control of the number of perpetrators once you make the first arrest."

He turned to Larry Pilson, pushing the paperwork toward him. "How about you hustle the signed forms over there right now."

Larry stood. "Sure thing, Sarge." He picked up the paperwork and hurried out of the room.

"Thank you, Sergeant," Molly said. "I hope we get the cooperation from the ME's office we'll need."

"Don't worry about it, Molly. If you don't hear from them pronto, let me know and I'll apply the necessary pressure."

"Thank you, Sergeant." Molly smiled.

Hilliard shook hands with Molly and Arnie then headed out the door.

Schmidt waited for Hilliard to close the door behind him before saying, "Okay, Mol, you tore outta here this morning like you were shot from a circus cannon. How'd you do?"

"I did great. At least, I think so." Molly described the time she spent re-searching Spelling's house. Sprinkled through her descriptions were brief bursts of chuckling and a few laughs of pure delight, born of relief.

Molly rubbed her forehead. "When I was driving to Spelling's, I was hoping to find something—anything. But I never dreamed I'd come away with Spelling's belt buckle that's a close match to Billy's. The artistry on the buckle is of a whale's tail, but it could be construed to be a tree—like Jerrod's scratches in the dirt. That's strike one against Spelling when it comes to Jerrod's murder. Finding the blood-spattered coveralls is strike two—if DNA confirms it's Jerrod's blood. Of course, finding the blonde wig is my strike three."

She smiled at her partner. "Pretty good for one day's work, right?" She grinned and punched Schmidt's shoulder. "That, my friend, is called a Sagittarian Miracle!"

Schmidt laughed. "Yeah, but it's not strike four."

Molly chuckled. "There's no strike four in baseball."

Arnie rested his hands on the table as if he was about to stand. "What if we had a strike four?"

Molly's head whipped around. "What are you talking about?"

Schmidt gave her a wide smile. "We were busy too, Mol." He tipped his head to the side and stared at Molly. "It's like this. Larry and I got to talking and we recalled that comment in the ME's report about blunt forced trauma. Remember? No weapon was associated with it?"

Molly's cheeks warmed. "Yeah, yeah, go on. . ."

"Larry and I took a little drive out to the ranch. It was a beautiful day; the ranch was serene; and you weren't peering over our shoulders," he said smugly.

Molly leaned forward in her chair. "What the hell do you mean? Peering over your shoulders?"

Arnie chuckled. "You know that thing you do. . ."

Molly frowned. "I don't do a thing—I don't have a thing. Get to the point."

Schmidt cleared his throat. "All right. All right." He chuckled.

"Larry and I drove out to the ranch and took a good long look at the murder scene. He remembered how Jerrod's hand had lain in direct relationship to the rocks that lined the flowerbed. From there, we guessed about the exact location of Jerrod's parked truck. We turned over every rock at the base of the flowerbed. Examined them closely. By golly, Larry turned over a rock that appeared to have blood on it." He demonstrated with his hands. "The rock was about the size of a small cantaloupe and somewhat jagged. It could be the murder weapon. The bloody spots on the rock are somewhat dotted with dirt, but it is possible the lab guys can find enough clean blood to test."

Arnie grinned. "Like you, we hustled it down to the lab. They said they'd call us if they found enough to test."

Molly felt like hugging him, but of course, she didn't. Instead, she raised her hand and high-fived her partner.

Schmidt laughed. "We're one hell of a team." He beamed.

Molly smiled at him. "Yes, we are.

"And I don't peer over your shoulders..."

- 58 -

The sun had dipped behind the city's buildings when Pilson burst into the conference room. "I hoped to catch you guys still here. Got 'er done. The ME took a look at Hilliard's signature and nodded. Said he do his best." He looked from Molly to Schmidt. "I think we'll get the cooperation we need from the ME. I just got a feeling."

"As long as Larry's back, let's stay and lay out Thursday. As you know our jeweler friend, Kenneth plans to deliver the newly created earrings to their owner, or whomever comes to get them, around five o'clock."

"What's your concern?" Schmidt asked.

"If you agree, I want to arrest whoever comes for the earrings. If we do that, it won't take long for word to spread through the ranch employees. As we previously discussed, it may scare a few people and they might run for cover. We sure as hell don't want to let that happen." She glanced from face to face. "Jill Bronson's attacker has been picked up and is being held. I think we have enough evidence now to arrest the other suspects, whether it's for murder or theft or fraudulent sale of horse semen."

The men blankly stared at her as if thinking it through. "Are you going to arrest Spelling for murder? Are you certain Billy isn't involved?" Schmidt asked.

"I think we have grounds to hold Spelling until the lab's DNA results come back then charge him for Jerrod's murder if we have a match. I'm relying on Billy to come for the earrings. If so, he'll already be held in jail. We easily have Briggs on the stolen semen crime."

"What about Cindy?"

"Her, too," Molly said. "The financial records are enough proof for us to haul them in for questioning. I think we'll get a confession or two once they are interrogated."

"Have you talked to Sergeant Hilliard about it?" Pilson asked.

"Yep. I talked to him on the phone a couple days ago. Although at that time it was wishful thinking on my part, I wanted him to be aware. He's on board. We know now, he shares my concern that some of the suspects will flee if we delay. With the evidence we have, we can hold them long enough for interrogations. I'm optimistic we'll get confessions or admissions, and with help from the ME's office, we should have solid forensics. We also have witness testimony. I believe the prosecutors will accept our case and make the charges."

"Okay Molly, how do you want to handle the arrests?" Schmidt asked.

"I'll call Judge Carry and request the arrest warrants before day's end. I visualize the three of us, plus a team of two officers backing up each of us."

Schmidt gave a slight nod. "So, that's nine arresting officers and six cars?"

"Yep," Molly said. "Plus two officers, each with a car to haul in Billy Fenton, or whomever comes for the emerald earrings, and Julia. When we go to the ranch to make our arrests, I want to flood the place with police and enough cars to bring in every suspect."

"How do you want to arrange it?" Pilson asked.

"We need a staging area," Molly said. "The parking areas at Desert Ridge Mall should work perfectly. There are enough shops with plenty of parking to enable us to spread out our cars so they'll be inconspicuous. We'll stay in touch by radio."

Schmidt nodded. "I agree. That entire commercial district is large enough so the number of cop cars well-spaced will hardly be noticed. Once the arrests are made at the boutique, we can group together, preparing to head for the ranch." He glanced at Molly. "Will you arrive early at Julia's boutique to be on scene when the pickup person comes into the shop?"

"Yes," Molly answered. "Four o'clock ought to be about right. I'll arrange for two officers. One will join me in the shop and the other will wait in his car. If the officers come with partners, all the better. As soon as Julia and the pickup person are placed in separate cars, and are on their way to our downtown headquarters, the rest of us will head for the ranch."

"The ranch covers a lot of acres, Pilson said. "How will we handle the arrests there? I'm afraid when the patrol cars arrive, we may send suspects scattering in all directions."

"Tomorrow I'm going to call Jim Harmon and have him invite the entire staff to the manager's office for a small celebration and a surprise announcement." Molly grinned. "I'll even have him pick up a cake! When I explain to Jim what we intend... knowing him as I do... he'll be happy to lend us a hand."

Schmidt and Pilson grinned. Pilson said, "You've thought it through perfectly, Molly."

She nodded. "I've had plenty of time to think about it. Tomorrow I'll touch base with each of the various commanders who are supplying our assisting officers and walk them through the plan. If they want me to meet with their people, I'll have time to do that. We can't go to Julia's boutique before four o'clock in the afternoon."

"Do you plan to arrest her for before the pickup is made?" Schmidt asked.

"Exactly. It's best if she's not there when we arrest the pickup person. If Billy, or whomever, walks in to pick up the earrings, I don't want a scene. I want it quiet and easy. I'll make the arrest, the assisting officer will cuff him or her, and they'll be out of the shop like nothing's happened. Kenneth is used to closing the shop, so we've no problems with that."

Pilson heaved a pensive sigh. "Making this many arrests is a big deal. Organization will be everything. Can we go over it again tomorrow? Don't get me wrong, Molly, I have every faith in you. Nobody crosses tees or dots i's better than you, but we're coordinating a lot of bodies."

"I hear what you're saying, Larry. That's why I've kept tomorrow open. If any of the commanders want us to get together with their people, you guys can help me with that."

"Of course," Schmidt said.

Pilson nodded. "Definitely."

Molly smiled at the men. "Let's meet for breakfast tomorrow at "Eggmania" at Desert Ridge Mall before coming to the precinct. Seven o'clock? There'll be very few people there at that hour. We can get a fresh lay of the land.

- 59 -

On Thursday morning, following breakfast with Pilson and Schmidt at Eggmania, Molly headed into headquarters. She called each of the commanders who were supplying her team with the officers needed to make the multiple apprehensions, scheduled for the next afternoon. She provided them with the location and time to meet. She asked if they would like to meet in person with her, but Molly was assured it would not be necessary.

Her next call was to Jim Harmon. She explained the situation and asked for his cooperation. "Will that work for you and your parents?"

"Of course. Mom and Dad will be relieved to have this over and done with."

"Realize, we're only making the arrests. Whoever we bring in will be kept in our custody until they are charged with the crimes they've committed."

"I get it. It still feels like a heavy weight is about to be lifted. It's been stressful to work with people we trusted, knowing the harm they've caused us. I'd like to face the rotten bastards and tell them what I think of them. Mom, on the other hand, will probably be so pleased, she'll offer to bake the cake."

"Believe me, my partners and I understand the heartaches you've been through these last few months."

"We're in your debt, Molly. You've helped us through a very difficult time, kept us updated and answered all our questions." He paused. "When will you and your officers arrive at the ranch?"

"We expect to arrive between four forty-five and five o'clock this afternoon. We'll come from Desert Ridge Mall in six cars and park them in front of Gene's office. The Arrest Warrants are being created right now."

"Desert Ridge?" he asked. "I assume Julia will already have been arrested." He hesitated. "I can't believe she's involved."

Molly cleared her throat. "I hear you. I don't know her motive as yet. But greed is powerful. Based on our investigation, she is the prime suspect in the theft of your mom's ring. Obviously, there are others involved.

"I would suggest you invite the staff to congregate at Gene Belmont's office at four-thirty, and after you invite them to join your family for the celebration, don't work with them today. Do something else... go to the driving range... or an afternoon movie... same with your parents. Show up just prior to the time of the gathering. That way you won't be pressed with questions while trying to work."

"Makes sense. I'll speak to Mom and Dad right now. They're both still at the house. The news will make them happy and as disappointed as it has me. But once they have a little time to think about it, I can assure you they'll be thrilled to do whatever you say. I'll call you back after I've spoken to them and invited the crew."

"Perfect. I'll speak to you later."

A few minutes past four o'clock, Molly walked into Julia's Boutique. She and Kenneth made eye contact. She didn't see Julia. Kenneth pointed beyond the changing rooms to the curtain that closed off the back room. Molly nodded and walked directly to the doorway, pushed the curtain aside and called Julia's name.

Julia was bent over her worktable attaching price tags to newly arrived Calvin jeans. She turned at the sound of her name. "Oh, Molly, how nice. Can I help you with something?"

"Not at this time." As Molly spoke, Officer Janson walked into the workroom.

Julia's jaw dropped. Her voice quavered. "What's this about?"

Molly said, "Julia Spelling, you are under arrest for the theft of Doris Harmon's diamond ring." She motioned to the officer to take over. He strode across the room to Julia, handcuffed her, and led her outside to his waiting car. Molly followed them as far as the door then walked over to Kenneth's workstation. She smiled at him. "That went smoothly. Let's hope the next arrest goes as well."

A few minutes later, Officer Williams, with the body dimensions of a football tight end, walked into the boutique, glancing around the shop as he approached Molly. "This is a nice store." His voice seemed to come from deep in his chest. He pointed to the door. "Janson just left with the prisoner. She was cooperative. Everything went well outside."

Molly looked up at him. "Fingers crossed for the next one."

Williams grinned. "It will be fine. I never have much of a problem."

Kenneth gave a nervous laugh.

"I can see why," Molly said. "Let's wait in the backroom for the man, or woman, who's coming to pick up the stolen property."

Williams spotted the curtained doorway and pointed. "Right through there?"

"Yes," Molly said. There are chairs and a small refrigerator with soft drinks. Would you like one?"

"Sounds good." Williams followed Molly through the doorway.

Over her shoulder, Molly called to Kenneth. "Can I bring you something to drink?"

"I don't think so, but thanks."

For the next fifteen minutes, Molly and Williams killed time, speaking about their careers with the Phoenix Police Department while they sipped their beverages. Molly lowered her bottle and asked, "I heard you chose not to sit for the Sergeant's exam."

A voice broke the silence in the front of the store. "Hey, Kenneth. Are my earrings ready to go?"

"Sure are, Franklin. How're ya doing?" Kenneth responded. "Got 'em right here." Kenneth opened the small envelope and spilled the earrings onto a velvet pad. "What do ya think?"

"They look good to me," Franklin said. As he paid Kenneth for his work, Molly walked from the back room and approached Kenneth's workstation. The man's back was to her. As she neared him, she said, "Hello, Billy, what are you doing here?"

Billy spun around.

Kenneth slipped the studs into the envelope and placed it into his lockbox.

Billy turned back and glared at Kenneth then at Molly, his eyes wide with fearful surprise. "Ah... just picking up a gift." Footsteps behind Molly caused Billy to look past her at Williams then into Molly's eyes. "What's going on?" His voice shook.

Molly studied Billy for a moment. "Billy Fenton, you're under arrest for the theft of Mrs. Doris Harmon's diamond ring."

"I never done that," he shouted angrily. "It wasn't me."

"You can tell me all about it next time I see you," Molly said as she stepped out of Officer Williams' way.

Williams spun Billy around, reached for his wrists, cuffed him then nudged Billy toward the door.

Kenneth waited for them to be out of sight before facing Molly. His brow rose. "Damn! Now I've seen it all." He chuckled. "They say it's never actually like how we see it on TV, but that sure looked the same to me."

Molly grinned. "Two nice arrests. It seldom goes that smoothly, especially with a male, but Williams' size is intimidating. I'm sure he meant it when he said he rarely has a problem." She gave Kenneth a warm smile. "You did a good job; played your role very well. That's one reason why it went smoothly. So thank you."

Kenneth handed Molly the small envelope containing the emerald earrings he'd made. She stored the emeralds in her evidence case, thanked him once again, and asked him to lock the store when he left. "I have no idea what might happen to the shop, but I'm sure you'll hear from somebody—a lawyer probably, with instructions."

Molly left the shop and headed directly to her car. She locked her evidence bag in the trunk and slid into the driver's seat. Using her radio, she spoke to her crew indicating the first step had gone well.

Schmidt's voice came in clear as he gave the command for all cars to fall in behind him at the mall's Tatum exit and caravan to Harmony Farm.

- 60 -

The motorcade drove into the ranch quietly, no sirens, no flashing lights. Their approach had been discussed and decided upon by Molly and each of the commanders.

The six cars created a half circle in front of the porch of Gene Belmont's office. Molly's car, in third position, was parked in line with the porch steps. The police officers exited their cars in unison and swarmed the office with Molly in the lead. Pilson and Schmidt followed behind her.

Two officers jogged around the building to the end of the stallion barn. There, they quietly entered the stable and walked past three occupied horse stalls on either side of the center aisle, stopping at the back door of the office. Two officers remained on the front porch to prevent anyone from leaving through that door. Four police officers entered the Gene's office with Molly. Gene Belmont took his position next to the front door behind the cadre of police.

Molly addressed the Harmon family. "We'd like you to return to the main house. Detective Schmidt will walk with you." Schmidt led the family out the front door and escorted them to their home. Molly faced the ranch employees and explained why the police were there.

Two patrolmen stepped forward to stand on either side of Molly who addressed the Senior Vet in a stern voice. "Dr. Briggs, you're under arrest for the fraudulent sale of stallion semen. Please go with these officers." Whispering could be heard as Briggs was handcuffed and led from the room.

"Cindy Harper, please step forward."

Cindy's hand flew to her mouth, and she gasped. She glanced behind herself then glared at Molly. "Why? I've done nothing wrong," she shouted." Molly held back a smile.

Once again, two patrol officers moved to Molly's side. "Cindy Harper, you are under arrest for aiding and abetting the theft of Mrs. Harmon's diamond ring and the fraudulent sale of stallion semen."

Cindy appeared unable to control her temper as she glared angrily at Molly. As the officers approached her, she accepted the inevitable and followed instructions. The officers quietly took Cindy into custody. The surrounding murmuring grew louder.

Schmidt, who had returned, and Pilson moved next to Molly. Their eyes settled on Spelling.

"Dr. Spelling," Molly said. "You are under arrest for the murder of Jerrod Branson and for the fraudulent sale of stallion semen."

"You'll never prove that!" Spelling yelled. "I would never..." The two officers who had returned stepped forward and handcuffed Spelling. They led him out to a waiting police car. The ranch hands who remained now chattered loudly.

Big Bev's voice wailed above the others. "Oh, my God! This is terrible. I thought they were good guys."

Alphonso groaned "Dios mio! This is not good."

Little Bev scoffed. "Well! I knew those two were sonsabitches."

"Yeah, me, too," another junior groom barked.

"Are we all going to lose our jobs?" Little Bev asked whoever might be listening. "I don't want to leave the ranch," she cried.

Gene, who still stood beside the front door, remained quiet.

Molly raised her voice above the prattling crew. "People, people, it's over. You are free to go. I suspect Mr. Harmon will address everyone in the morning." She glanced from person to person. "Don't let the horses suffer. Please finish feeding them before you leave and be back on time in the morning to start your day as always. The horses will want their breakfasts." She smiled broadly at the ranch hands.

Before leaving, Gene said to Molly, "Thanks for reminding them they must still come to work." Molly nodded.

Little Bev, on her way out, approached Molly again. Fear evidently made Little Bev grimace, and her concern was obvious in her quavering voice. "Do you think our jobs are safe?"

Molly was slow to answer. She pursed her lips. "I see no reason why they wouldn't be. You've done nothing wrong. As far as the veterinarians are concerned, I understand the ranch has an ongoing working arrangement with outside vets, so Gene and Jim Harmon will quickly have that under control. All the training staff, except for Billy are still here. Talk to Jim or Big Bev, they'll have reliable information to share over the coming days.

"You've already started grooming the show horses for the Scottsdale All Arabian show. Don't stop." Molly smiled at the girl. "Don't worry so much. It'll be fine."

A tear trickled down Little Bev's cheek. She swished it away with her hand. "Thank you. I hope you're right. I love working here—on this beautiful ranch. Mr. and Mrs. Harmon treat us right." She caught up with Big Bev, slipped an arm around her waist, and they walked out the door together.

- 61 -

When Molly left Gene's office, she thanked him and Jim Harmon who had returned from the house, for their assistance in arranging the gathering of ranch employees. She smiled at each man. "I'll keep you informed."

She turned to Jim, "Expect to get hit with a gazillion questions in the morning. Your crew will need reassurances their jobs are safe. Little Bev is quite upset."

"Thanks for letting me know. I'll make it a point to talk to her. She's such a sweet kid. Are you going to stop by the house on your way out?"

"No, I've gotta get to headquarters. My team and I will undoubtedly work late... lots of interviews and paperwork with all the apprehensions we made this afternoon." She smiled. "Please thank your parents for me. The party plan worked perfectly. I didn't get a chance to sample your mom's cake, but it looked great." She studied Jim. "You must be feeling a sense of relief knowing the thieves who harmed you and your parents have been arrested, along with Spelling's arrest for Jerrod's murder."

He raised his brow. "You're exactly right. Our thanks go to you Molly, for the professional you are. There's a lot to think about with all the fraudulent activity, let alone Jerrod's murder. It'll take us a while to get over it, I'm afraid. Especially Mom. We'll start working immediately to replace those who've been arrested. Briggs and Spelling were excellent vets. What they've done has hurt the ranch, but we'll recover. I doubt I can say the same for their reputations. No doubt replacing them will be the first thing Dad addresses in the morning. He has excellent contacts in the veterinary world... here in the Phoenix Valley and across the US. He already mentioned an equine vet in Colorado he intends to contact. So we'll see.

"It's hard to accept both of them were stealing and selling semen. I know I should be mad as hell, but right now I'm more heartsick, disillusioned, I guess. Tomorrow I'll be angry. I'm worried about Mom. She'll be slow to recover from the shock of it all. She's always looked for the good in people."

He reached for Molly's hand. "You wouldn't like a change in careers, by any chance? With your background in the horse industry, we could use you around here."

Molly grinned. "I don't think so. It's at a time like this I feel pretty good about the work I do. But I'll be around. We still have loose ends to tie up." She turned and saw Larry Pilson and Arnie Schmidt waiting for her. "I have to go, Jim. I'll see you soon."

Her partners sat in their respective vehicles, motors running. When Molly walked toward her car, both detectives turned their cars around and headed out. Molly steered her car into line behind Larry Pilson.

It was six o'clock in the evening when Molly and her partners returned to headquarters and settled each suspect in an interview room with a detective. They spent hours questioning suspects and were satisfied with the results.

When Molly and Arnie Schmidt interrogated Dr. Briggs, he placed the blame on Dr. Spelling. After two hours of questioning, Briggs became confused, frustrated that the detectives didn't believe him. He admitted he was a participant in the scheme to steal from his employer, but insisted it wasn't his idea.

Cindy broke down almost immediately when Larry Pilson began his interrogation. She admitted she had participated in the scheme to black market stallion semen, but insisted she'd been forced to by Briggs, who threatened he'd have her fired. She was terrified of losing her job, admitting it would financially ruin her.

She denied her part in the theft of Mrs. Harmon's ring. While in another room, Billy confessed to Sergeant Hilliard he was given the ring by Cindy, who had stolen it when the cleaning girls were in the house. Jerrod, who was in love with Julia, bought the ring from Billy and gave it to Julia.

During his interrogation, Billy claimed everyone on the ranch would recognize Mrs. Harmon's ring and wouldn't forget what it looked like. He believed Julia would have been familiar with it when Jerrod gave it to her. Billy accused Julia of removing the emeralds and asking him to take them to Kenneth, the jeweler in her boutique, to be made into stud earrings.

When Billy was asked why he thought Julia accepted the ring, he explained she was offended when she discovered the earrings Jim had given her were man made. She was heard to say at one of the parties she would never be seen wearing fake jewelry. It was beneath her. Her word: *Preposterous!*

Molly and Pilson followed their interrogation of Dr. Briggs with their first session with Dr. Spelling. After an hour of pounding Spelling with questions, they turned him over to Schmidt.

At first, Spelling insisted to Schmidt that he had not harmed Jerrod Branson, but an hour later, with Schmidt bearing down hard, Spelling tripped over his lies. In desperation, he whined it was because of Julia. He couldn't allow Julia to be associated with a bum like Jerrod.

Spelling glared at Schmidt as if he should understand and shouted, "When she announced she intended to marry him, it was the last straw." He struck the table. "He was an ex-con! For God's sake, my daughter was too good for that scum." Tears slipped down his face. "Julia's too good for any man. I raised her to be perfect. And she is."

Schmidt hammered Spelling with questions until, a half hour later, Spelling broke down. He admitted he called Jerrod and asked for his help, telling him to come to the AI facility. When Jerrod arrived, Spelling grabbed a scrimshaw letter opener from his display, before heading for Jerrod's truck where they argued over Julia.

Spelling held out a little longer, still insisting he hadn't touched Jerrod. But ultimately he lost his resolve and admitted, in a fit of strong agitation, he'd stabbed Jerrod several times with the letter opener. When Jerrod still fought with him, Spelling smashed Jerrod's head with one of the rocks from the flowerbed.

Around midnight, the suspects were transferred to county jail where they were booked for the crimes they'd committed.

By then, the night shift Detectives had arrived, willing to assist with processing if needed. It appeared everyone in the homicide division had heard about the multiple arrests. Also, their fellow officers from the various units who had been assigned the job of helping with the coordinated apprehensions arrived and offered their assistance. Phoenix PD officers and detectives stopped by to congratulate Molly and her team when they returned to headquarters.

Pilson and Schmidt smiled proudly as colleagues acknowledged the arrests and specifically the style in which they were made. One patrol officer asked, "Has anybody ever made an arrest of five suspects in a matter of hours?" Nobody responded. "It's gotta be some kinda record."

Pilson laughed. "Not in Chicago these days!"

Molly smiled at Pilson's quip, but at the same time she felt somewhat overwhelmed by the attention she received. While thanking her colleagues for their compliments, she heard her name mentioned many times throughout the room as her partners deferred the accolades to her and her excellent work.

Watching her partners enjoying the moment, receiving praise and congratulations then diverting the praises to her, caused Molly to fully value again, and appreciate once more, the teamwork that had solidified the partnership between Pilson, Schmidt, and herself. Her team. The men had been great to work with. But crime never sleeps. Molly hoped they'd work many more cases together in the future.

Her thoughts turned introspective as she thought of the Harmon family. She felt sadly for the sorrow inflicted upon them. But knowing she'd served them well, as she'd been trained to do, made her eyes mist with happy tears. Her colleagues' praise added to her happiness. These moments were few.

She recalled, early in her career, Lar, who was her partner at the time, telling her to fully enjoy the wins and ecstatic moments whenever they happened, because they wouldn't come along very often. How right he'd been. All these years later, she relived that moment. Lar was so right. She smiled to herself. Lar had been an excellent teacher and guide. For only a moment she wished he hadn't broken her heart. Instantly, she dismissed the thought and forgave him.

After all the hands were shaken and compliments paid, the team settled down to complete the paperwork.

As Molly reached for the next form on the pile of documents, her cell phone rang. Her boss's name appeared in the ID window. Molly answered, "Good morning, Sarge. What are you doing up at this ungodly hour?"

"Same as you, Molly, same as you. I've been studying the recordings and the videos of the interviews you conducted. Very good job, Detective."

- 62 -

It was four-thirty the next morning when Molly and her partners walked out of PPD's headquarters. Arnie Schmidt pressed the button to call the elevator. "How about some breakfast, Mol? Lenny's, up the street, is open. How about one of their Wednesday Early-Bird Specials? Last week, the Desk Sergeant told me Lenny's has Dutch Babies on their menu now. Ever hear of it? It's a cross between a big old pancake and a crepe, baked in a hot oven, with blackberries dumped in the middle and covered in whipped cream... and it's a plateful. I took my kids there last weekend, and my son ate all of his plus half of his sister's."

Molly stared at him. "You're kidding right?"

"No way. I wouldn't kid about something like that. One bite and you'll be declaring it another Sagittarian Miracle."

Molly smiled and glanced from man to man. "No thanks. I recognize BS when I hear it. I'm going home and sleep until noon." She hesitated, afraid her emotions might run away with her. But emotions be damned. "I want you both to know how proud of you I am. Your work was excellent from beginning to end."

"What do you mean *end*?" Larry Pilson teased. "I'm not going anywhere." He leaned around to look Schmidt in the face. "How about you, pard? You going somewhere?"

"Oh, hell no. I still have way too much to teach Mol. One of these days.

I'm sure, she'll admit astrology is a bunch of crap."

"What?" Molly raised her voice. "You've got a lot of nerve after all the clues I shared with you thanks to my astrological skills."

Schmidt dropped his voice. "Yeah, you're right. C'mon, I'll treat us all to breakfast. You'll sleep better, Mol, with food in your stomach."

"Okay, okay. We'll go to breakfast, and I'll do my best to run up the bill."

Molly crawled into bed at quarter to six that morning. In minutes, she slid into a deep sleep. She was in the middle of a nightmare, lost in a thick haboob, a dense Arizona dust storm, when a warning bell rang in the distance. She ran toward it as the clanging became louder and louder, but she couldn't locate its source. Finally, she opened her eyes and realized her cell phone was ringing.

Light streamed around the bedroom's blackout shade, and she spotted her phone near her knees. She sat up, grabbed it, and barked *hello*.

"Detective Raines? This is Dr. Dressner from the ME's office. I'm calling to let you know we have gotten back a few results. Thought you'd want to be informed."

"Yes, thank you. I'm anxious to hear what you have."

"The blood traces on the rock your partners brought in are that of the deceased. We were lucky to get those results back so fast. I'm sorry to tell you we do not have the DNA results on the stains on the coveralls nor the DNA on the wig. However, we did more investigating on the puncture wounds that showed dark stains and discovered the stains were caused by a mixture of very old ink once used to highlight the scrimshaw carvings from long ago. Apparently, it tends to break down when it comes into contact with human sweat."

"Wow!" Molly chuckled. "Who'd a thought? Kudos for the great research. Thank you for calling. And thank your team for me. I truly appreciate all your work. I'll update my paperwork ASAP."

Molly lay back against her pillow, pondering the news of the scrimshaw coloring agent. She rolled onto her side, hoping to sleep for at least another hour, but in less than ten minutes her cell phone sounded again.

"Molly? Did I wake you? It's Jim Harmon."

She checked her bedside clock. Ten-forty-five. "No, it's okay. I slept in—making up for a long night. Is everything okay?"

"Everything is just fine. Everybody is working... and smiling. An hour ago Dad did a great job soothing everyone's fears about their jobs. He answered all the questions like a pro."

Molly yawned. "Oh, that's good. Is there something I can do for you?"

"Can you say case closed?"

"I sure can—well, mostly."

"Are you ready to have some fun?"

"I sure am."

"Now can I ask you out—like for a date?"

"Sure can."

"Have you ever seen the Christmas lights at Tlaquepaque, just outside Sedona? They're opening next week—a little earlier this year."

"No, but I've always wanted to."

"Then let's go."

Molly hesitated. "Can we go up and back in a day? I may have some follow up work to do even though we consider the case closed."

Jim chuckled. "No problem, assuming we don't have trouble with snow and ice. We shouldn't. My rig has four-wheel drive, so I think we'll be fine."

"Sounds like you've thought of everything."

Jim chuckled. "Didn't I always think first of your needs?"

"Well you used to. Can't say much for the present."

"If the show ring was Act One for us, let's call this Act Two and see how it goes."

Molly laughed. "Sounds good."

"Perfect. Now, would you like to have dinner with me this Saturday?"

"Real date?"

"Yep."

"I'll be holding my breath."

"You're my kinda girl."

"Damn straight."

Acknowledgements

No matter what the endeavor, success of our efforts is never gained without help.

My thanks go to Susan Budavari and Alicia Federici who provided excellent feedback for this story. Thanks to the beta readers who searched out small (and not so small) errors, inconsistencies, and omissions while at the same time following each plot point. Thanks, also, to the beta readers who provided honest opinions and well-thought-out suggestions.

It is with heartfelt pleasure I thank Tim Moore, Phoenix Homicide Police Detective, Retired, for his help with police procedures and interactions in this story. Tim has helped many Phoenix-based writers, providing information both technical and practical. I am indebted for his generosity of counsel.

My thanks go to the members of the Sisters in Crime Grand Canyon Writers for their encouragement and support.

And finally, thanks to my family, especially Don for his willingness to act as "fresh eyes" in reading my manuscript once I determine it is polished enough (every writer knows what I'm talking about), and to Traci, Tim, Julie and Kei for their continuing support.

About the Author

MERLE McCANN is known for her National literature award-winning Longjohners Mystery Series for middle grade readers. She has published many short stories featuring Arizona, Mississippi, and Washington locations. McCann's work won best in all categories and genres in the Dixie Kane Memorial as well as Arizona Authors Association annual National literature contest. Born in the Yukon, raised in Seattle, she has traveled the United States and Europe with her husband, pursuing their Arabian horse business. She has also worked as a paralegal, event planner, and scenic photographer, and lives with her husband in Scottsdale, Arizona.

Made in the USA
Las Vegas, NV
03 July 2023